Puck the Holidays

A Vipers' Sin Bin Novel

K.D. Miller

K. D. Miller
P.O. Box 14330
New Bern, NC 28561
www.kdmillerbooks.com

Publisher's Note: This is a work of fiction. Names, characters, places, and incidents are a product of the author's imagination. Locales and public names are sometimes used for atmospheric purposes. Any resemblance to actual people, living or dead, or to businesses, companies, events, institutions, or locales is completely coincidental.

Book Layout ©2017 BookDesignTemplates.com

Puck the Holidays/ K.D. Miller
ISBN: 979-8-9887609-1-7

To Kayleigh.
Your love of hockey and hockey romances made me want to
write this. So, by the laws of friends who turn into muses,
Connor is officially yours.
...SMASH

A note to the readers:

Puck the Holidays is 90% sweet, fun, spicy, feel-good holiday love story—and 10% keep-you-on-the-edge-of-your-seat suspense involving an unhinged ex. For that bit, please be aware that there is mention of stalking behavior, with physical, emotional, and verbal abuse involved. If these things are triggering to you, please proceed with caution.

I pucking love you all.

-K.D. Miller

"I'm trying to get in the holiday spirit...but the damn bottle won't open."

-Hattie McNamara, probably

Contents

Chapter One

HATTIE

❄ · ·❄· ·❄· · ·❄· · ·❄· · ·❄

Christmas is the worst.

Don't come at me, I have my reasons. But I stand by my statement: Christmas. Is. The. Worst.

Ok, so to be fair, it isn't exactly Christmas itself that I hate. Or, well, it didn't start out that way at least, but what is the happiest time of year for most people, is the worst time of year for me. It's been that way for practically my entire life. Almost every single year without fail, crappy things always happen to me, *all* within a week or so of C-Day. So, after a while, everything about Christmas just turned sour and it became one giant bad omen for me. Guilty by association, I guess. *Sorry, Santa.*

I am neither holly nor jolly. I deck no halls and trim no trees. I mean I don't yell "bah humbug!" at people or spit on bell-ringing Santas in the street or anything. I'm fully aware that my issues with Christmas are my own and don't begrudge anyone else who enjoys the season, but I still avoid most things if I can help it. I've been called Scrooge and Grinch and Oscar the Grouch and every other name you can think of around the holidays, but I've learned to deal with it.

Even so, the fact that Christmas seems to have crept further and further back in the year, encroaching on all of the other months, drives me freaking crazy and doesn't help my lack of love for the entire thing. I narrow my eyes at the dancing Santa figurine on the counter of the coffee shop. It's *September* for fuck's sake, but half of the places I've gone today are already full of Christmas decorations, some of them even playing Christmas music! Right beside the pumpkins and skeletons are elves and reindeer. What in the hell is *that* about? It seems illegal to me.

I grab my peppermint mocha—one of the things I admittedly love about this time of year, even if it comes early: peppermint *everything*—and head out into the cold. I've only been in Seattle for a few weeks, and I'm already missing my southern beaches like a severed limb. But this job offer was huge for my career, sounded like something I would absolutely love, and it had the added bonus of getting me as far away from my ex, Josh, as possible.

We'd broken up almost a year ago—or, well, more accurately I had left him when I'd finally gotten tired of being in a relationship with a narcissistic, alcoholic asshole who was prone to fits of rage at the drop of a hat—but he was having trouble understanding what the words *it's over* and *restraining order* meant.

At first it had been relatively harmless: angry, drunk texts and voicemails, apology flowers at work the next day, the same kind of stuff he'd done throughout our two-year relationship and what I kind of chocked up to normal break up behavior (at least for him). But over the past few months it had gotten steadily worse. He would show up at my house with no warning or invitation, be waiting for me outside my office when I got off work, started calling and texting me nonstop to the point where I had to get a new number—*twice.*

When I'd gotten the restraining order, he'd gotten less obvious about it, but he was still there. I can't explain how, but I could just *feel* him. I would come out of a coffee shop and swear I saw his car pulling away from the curb, or be shopping and see a familiar Longhorns hat in the crowd, though of course I could never prove it was him. We lived in Texas for cryin' out loud—you couldn't spit without hitting ten people wearing Longhorns gear.

It started to get scarier when I came home from drinks with a few coworkers one night and I *knew* he'd been in my house. I could smell his cologne, could tell that he'd rummaged in my drawers. He'd even turned on the shower to leave a note in the fog on the mirror that I found later: a heart. Simple. Non-threatening. At least on the surface, but combined with everything else, it was scary as hell.

I went to the police, but of course, there was no actual proof—the lock hadn't been jimmied, no broken windows, nothing amiss or out of place really. Even the heart on the mirror could just be waived away as something that had been there forever, something from back when we were dating since I admittedly rarely clean that mirror. He was escalating, but he was also slicker than pig snot on a radiator and knew *exactly* how to toe the line—and talk his way out of it if he did ever happen to cross it. He'd been that way his entire life from what I'd pieced together hearing drunken stories from his friends. He was that guy that everyone loved, that just made you want to trust him with a few words and an easy smile, and could get away with murder while standing over the body with a bloody knife in his hand.

Even if he did slip up and I managed to find some real proof, I was pretty sure Josh's father's lawyers would get it thrown out and he'd be back on the street stalking me within a few hours—

and I was honestly a little afraid of what he might do if I put him through all of that hassle. I'd heard from a friend that he'd lost his ever lovin' mind when he'd gotten notice of the restraining order, punched a hole in the wall of the apartment and everything. Josh might be charismatic and just has a way of making everyone love him, but he has one hell of a temper that he hides beneath the pretty face and designer clothes.

I was starting to get really, *really* freaked out, and that's when the call came in from the Seattle Vipers. I'd accepted immediately. I loved it in Galveston and had been really happy there for the most part, but I needed to get away. I honestly didn't think that Josh would keep things up if I wasn't in the same city anymore. If I wasn't there, within easy reach, he'd finally move on and I could just put the whole thing behind me, start over clean.

So, I gave my notice at work, packed up what would fit in a trailer (which was mostly just my clothes, books, and bed), sold the rest, and moved my happy little beach bum ass clear across the country into the land of cold and wet and gloom. They had "beaches" here, everyone was quick to point out, but it wasn't even close to the same. Even still, I'd found a cute place right on the Sound, and being so close to the water did make me happy. I've always had a thing for water: beaches, lakes, bayous—it all called to me. So, with Seattle being surrounded by water, I guess it wasn't *too* terrible of a place to end up, all things considered.

I sigh when I pull into the parking garage attached to the arena: the maintenance crews are already hard at work turning every light pole into a candy cane and hanging wreaths above the concrete entrances and exits.

"Et tu, Brute?" I groan as I park my SUV—which I'd had to put snow tires on for the first time in my life. What is *that* about?—and grab my stuff. I head through the *Employee's Only* entrance and up the elevators to the third floor where the majority of the offices are. Marketing and Media Relations share a wing with Finance, Human Resources, and a handful of other departments; the big wigs—CEO, CFO, owner, head coach—they all have their own wing on the other side of the arena, the full expanse of the rink and stadium seats separating us. The locker rooms, training facilities, and security offices are on the bottom floor, beneath the ice. I've been given the grand tour, but haven't officially met any of the players yet, though I've seen them from afar during practices and I've read their bios.

I honestly don't really know much about hockey. I've watched *Mighty Ducks* and *Miracle* makes me tear up, but that's about the extent of my knowledge on the subject. But what I *do* know a shit ton about is marketing and PR and that's why I'm here. Attendance has been on a steady decline for the Vipers for the last couple of years despite the team itself doing fairly well in the standings, so they decided it was time to bring in some new blood. It had been the owner's daughter who had suggested bringing in someone a little...younger to help out. Someone who understood how social media worked and what a hashtag was.

Emily, Vipers owner Vern Greenwood's daughter, and I had met by chance at a wedding of a mutual friend a few years back. We'd been seated at the same table and ended up chatting most of the evening and exchanging contact info. I post a lot about work on my social media accounts—or I used to. I've been fairly quiet on them lately because of Josh—and I guess that's how my name ended up in the running for the position of Assistant Director of Marketing and Media. I owe her more than she could possibly realize. Despite the timing being uncomfortably close to my

Dreaded December, I figure the job offer is the universe's way of making up for all of the terrible things it's given me over my lifetime. It still owes me big time, but I'm trying to take this as a good start. Hell, maybe this December won't actually suck.

Fat chance.

"Morning, Hattie."

"Mornin', Bobby. How are ya?" I ask as I sit my coffee down on my desk and take off my coat. I'd had to get a *real* coat this year, one that would actually keep you from freezing when the temps dipped below zero. The fact that I actually live in a place where negative temperatures are a real possibility is just batshit crazy to me, but I'm trying my best to keep an open mind. I mean, snow is pretty in all those Hallmark channel movies, so maybe it won't be so bad.

Bobby leans a shoulder against the doorway, pushing his thick glasses up his nose. He's in Marketing and Media with me, but on the data analysis side of things. He runs all the numbers, sees where things are working and where they aren't, gives us statistical predictions for the future based on the current trends. Basically, he's a genius and makes my brain hurt.

"Not too bad. Are you ready for the player shoots today?"

I'm excited but nervous. This is my first project in my new role and I think it's a pretty good one. One thing that the Vipers sorely lack is a real social media presence—hardly anyone actually knows any of the players, couldn't pick them out of a lineup if you asked them to. Literally. We had a lineup and asked people around Seattle if they could point out any of the Vipers. The results were less than ideal. Die hard fans of the sport of course know them and they're all mini-celebrities in the hockey community, but I want *everyone* to know their names, to want to come out and watch the games and feel that home-town team pride whether they grew up on hockey or don't know diddly squat about it.

So, they lack the social media imprint that we need in this day and age, but what they don't lack? Good looking men. Like, *obscenely* good looking. To the point where I was concerned I'd walked into one of those spoof teams, the ones that act a fool and entertain the crowd and are usually stacked with hot dudes.

And, as shallow as it sounds, good looking athletes are total money on social media these days, so I've been brainstorming ideas to capitalize on that piece of it, but also ways to bring in the real fans of the sport and the team. I want to cater to all demographics, do anything and everything possible to help get the team where it needs to be. We have a few weeks before the season officially begins, and I think I can really get things started off on the right foot before game one. Well, that's the goal anyway.

So, not *only* for the eye candy aspect, but also to let fans get to know each player and feel like they can connect with them, I'd pitched a "Meet the Vipers" series. Everyone had loved the idea, and my boss had given me complete freedom to run with it. Rumor has it that Al is ready to retire and the goal is to have me primed to take over by the time he's ready to call it quits. Of course, it all depends on how well I manage to turn things around, so these first few months are crucial for me, because I desperately want that job. Despite it being cold and rainy and completely different than anywhere I've ever lived, I already like it here, and I already love the Vipers organization.

The people all seem great. Hardworking, but laid-back, which suits me perfectly. I'm motivated as all hell and I work my ass off at everything I do, but I can't function in a place that's too stuffy and rigid. I'd had a job at an uppity law firm once where the women were required to wear hose. *Hose* for fuck's sake. I lasted about three weeks before I had to say goodbye to that highfalutin' crowd. Thanks, but no thanks.

But here, everything is more relaxed and far more welcoming. The owner of the team had even come to personally meet me on my first day, which was completely shocking on the one hand—I mean, he was a billionaire with more important things to do than meet one of hundreds of employees in his organization—but on the other hand, with the way Emily was, I wasn't shocked at all that her father would be just as kind and genuine as she was.

And I'd heard nothing but good things about Vern since day one. Everyone seems to absolutely love him, which is one reason that they're all really hoping that I can do what I was hired to do. If I can't, he might have to sell the team and they'll be moved to New Jersey.

So, no pressure or anything.

"I think so. I've got my basic questions...somewhere," I say, glancing around my office. Bobby grins, golden eyes roaming over my admittedly messy desk. "It's chaos, but it's organized chaos, I promise...Oh, there they are!" I pull a folder out from under a stack of articles I'd printed on the newest social media trends and some sports-specific marketing books I'd found online. I wave the folder at him in triumph and he chuckles lightly.

I like Bobby. He's friendly and welcoming without being overbearing and hasn't tried to dig too much into my personal life like some people have. *Looking at you, Kelly.* She's Al's personal assistant and though she seems nice enough, she is constantly spilling tea on the entire organization, from players to custodial staff and everyone in between. She somehow seems to know everything about everyone, so I've been tight-lipped about myself. I *have* heard some juicy stories about some of the players though, so that's been...enlightening. What I've gathered so far? Hockey players are on the whole, well, *players.* I can't blame them, I guess. They have fans obsessing over them, girls practically throwing themselves at them, and most of the guys are exceedingly hot. Why shouldn't they enjoy that little perk of their chosen career?

It automatically rules out the idea of me ever dating one of them, though. I've been there done that with the whole casual sex thing, or dating a fuckboy who cheats on me with everything with a pulse thing. I'm over it. Besides, after Josh, I don't think I can be trusted to make good decisions when it comes to relationships.

Things had started out so great with him. I'd fallen hard and fast. Josh was so funny and charismatic, the life of the party and I'd desperately wanted to be a part of it with him. I got completely wrapped up in all of it, and by the time I found my way out of the haze, his true self was coming out more and more, but I felt stuck. Looking back, I can see that he was the CEO of Six Flags and every last one of them was red, but it's hard seeing that when you're in the thick of it. Or maybe you do see it, but you don't want to, so you make excuses or tell yourself you're overreacting or imagining things, somehow make it your fault and make yourself colorblind.

So, yeah, it's better that I put dating on the back burner and just focus on work and, I don't know, get a few cats or something.

"Do you have the fan questions?"

"Right here," he says, handing over a list of questions submitted by fans on the various Vipers' social media platforms. They are working on hiring an assistant to help me with all this stuff, but Bobby graciously offered to help out for the time being.

"Did we get some good ones?" I ask, scanning the list.

"Oooh yeah. Apparently, many fans want to know how big Rizzo's...uh...*stick* is." A faint blush darkens Bobby's light brown cheeks and I bark out a laugh.

"Lord Almighty, the internet is a wild place."

"That it is. But I mean...how big do you think it is?" He wiggles his eyebrows and I shake my head, tossing a balled-up piece of paper at him. He bats it away, leaning backwards out of my door to look down the hall before turning back to me. "Looks like the film crew is here. You ready?"

I take a deep breath. I've done stuff like this plenty of times in the past. Granted, it's never been for something as big as a Professional Hockey League team, but I know I can do it. I shove the nerves away and put on my game face, so to speak. I nod and head out to meet the crew.

Chapter Two

CONNOR

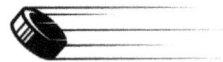

"So, what exactly is going on today?" I ask Rizzo while I lace up my skates. I admittedly hadn't been paying much attention when word had passed about something happening today. Something for marketing? A commercial or promo or something maybe?

Rizzo is checking himself out in the mirror, turning his shirtless torso this way and that, looking like a complete tool. Anthony Rizzo is one of the best centers in the league and one of the best puck handlers I've ever seen. He might also be the world's biggest playboy, but I can't really blame him.

"They're filming like mini Q-and-A segments for social media. Something about letting fans get to know us or whatever." He turns and smiles at me. "As if the fans don't know *me*," he scoffs. Rizzo has quite the fan base in the hockey world, but thanks to his personal social media posts that usually involve doing stupid shit shirtless, he has an entirely different type of fan group thirsting for him twenty-four-seven. Turning back to the mirror, he runs a hand over his chest and asks, "Anyway, do you think I should get a tattoo?"

I roll my eyes. "You've asked me this at least once a week for the past year, dude. Shit or get off the pot already." Rizzo would be described as the clean-cut, preppy boy. You know, the *All-American quarterback from the small town that dates the head cheerleader* type of vibe. Blonde hair, blue eyes, chiseled jaw, melts panties. You know the type.

He's one of the few on the team that doesn't have a single tattoo. I, on the other hand, look more like I belong in a biker gang than in front of a net, with piercings and tats for days. One full sleeve, another half, chest, back—you get the idea.

Apparently both looks are very popular with the female fanbase though—and a portion of the male one. I can't tell you how many times someone has told me point blank that they want to suck me and fuck me right then and there, no matter where the then and there happens to be. Bar, airport, stadium bathroom, coffee shop—you name it. And Rizzo gets even more invitations than I do. I don't know if it's just the allure of fucking someone somewhat "famous" or what, but there is no shortage of opportunities almost everywhere we go. Rizzo calls them Puck Bunnies, which is awful, but the term has kind of stuck despite my better judgment.

But that's just part of the gig and we all love it, regardless of if we take anyone up on the invites or not. All of us have mini-God complexes I'm sure, at least to some extent. How could you not? Hearing your name chanted by thousands of people, feeling the ground shake from the force of the cheers and screams. All for doing something that you love more than almost anything. All for playing a fucking game, like we're all still just kids fucking around on the ice. It's wild and can definitely go to your head.

"Listen, you have to think hard before you deface a perfect canvas like this," Rizzo quips, gesturing to his body. I toss a shirt at him, unable to keep myself from laughing. Rizzo is one of those guys who would absolutely be a fuckboy, except that he's too nice. He's cocky and gets more tail than should be humanly possible, but he's never a dick about any of it. Off the ice anyway. On the ice, he's an absolute fucker, but then again, most of us are.

"Just get dressed already. I'll see you out there."

When I emerge from the tunnel that leads from the locker room up to the ice, I see a small group milling about in the stands by the edge of the wall on the other side of the rink. One of the guys has one of those big fuzzy things on a stick. What's it called? A boom mic I think? Then I spot the tripod. So, this must be the film crew.

I think the whole meet the players thing is a great idea. Not only is it nice to do stuff for the fans, but maybe (hopefully) it'll bring attendance numbers up a bit. We do pretty well, have ended the season in the top five for the last few years, but even so, the stands seem to get emptier and emptier. There's even been talk about offers to purchase the team and move it to Jersey. I *really* don't want that to happen. If it does...well, it may just be the end of my career. I love hockey more than almost anything on the planet, but there's one thing that I love even more that requires me to stay in Seattle. My life can't work anywhere else. So, I'm willing to do just about anything to help get the numbers up. I'll pull a Rizzo and play shirtless if I have to. *Anything.*

"Alright, they're going to do these interviews with each of you one at a time," Coach Ulrich says, his Icelandic accent thick. "Some of you should do yourselves a favor and practice while you wait," he looks pointedly at Tyson and Mickels, who grin and give him *oh come on* looks, "but do what you want until it is your turn. Full practice will begin in two hours."

I know there will be no shortage of people willing to whack pucks at me while we wait, so I start stretching.

"We betting today?" Howey asks, skating around me backwards.

"Oh you know it, asshole."

He rubs his hands together like he can't wait to set the terms. "I get three in, I get to borrow your bike this weekend."

It's supposed to be unseasonably warm this weekend, and I'd planned on riding too. He could just come with me...Then I narrow my eyes at him as realization dawns.

" *Which* bike?"

His brown eyes glitter with mischief. "The blue Indian."

You fucker. I grit my teeth. That's my favorite fucking bike. If he so much as scratches the paint on her...but then I stop myself and give him a cocky smile. He won't be getting shit past me.

"You're on."

He lets out a loud *whoop* like he's already won. I just smile. Justin Howe—who we of course call Howey because if it's one thing athletes love, it's a good nickname—is good, our lead scorer actually, but I'm better. I'm not being cocky, or maybe I am a bit, but it's also the truth.

"And when I win, I get your cabin for New Years."

He snorts. "You can have it even if—*when*—you lose. We're spending it with Trinity's family down in Miami this year, so the cabin is all yours. Just like your bike is gonna be all mine." I laugh, shoving him in the shoulder. He puts his hands up, preparing to fight, but before we can start messing around, one of our assistants yells at me from across the ice.

"Shep! You're up!"

Howey straightens and reaches out to muss my hair and then brushes invisible dirt from my shirt. "You look great, dear."

I shove his hand away, laughing, and skate to the other side of the rink. As I approach, I see the guy with a camera, the one with the mic, someone with a headset and a tablet, and—*wow*. A woman is there talking to Coach Lantz, and she is...*wow*. Seriously, she deserves a double wow. Tall and slender, though not a twig, with brownish-red hair set in those loose, wavy-curls that I love, brushing just past her shoulders.

She smiles warmly at Coach, and—*Fuck me*. Dimples. She's got *dimples*. Dimples are like my kryptonite. Don't ask me to explain it. She's in a black dress that hugs her in all the right places, and I just stop myself from rubbing a hand over my mouth. *Get a grip, Shep*. Granted, it's been a while since I've been with anyone, but still, you'd think I'd never been laid with the way I'm lusting after this girl.

I slid to a stop near the edge of the wall and she looks over. Her eyes are a deep, ocean blue, her black liner winging out at the corners in an alluring way. I always love when girls do that cat-eye thing. They widen slightly as she takes me in and I grin. I'm usually *a lot* for people at first glance.

"Hattie, this is Connor Shepherd. Shep, this is Hattie McNamara, our new Assistant Director of Marketing and Media."

"Nice to meet you," I say, extending my hand.

"You too," she says as she places her hand in mine. I don't know if I imagine the soft inhalation before she quickly withdraws her hand and tucks a curl behind her ear. Probably. "So, uh, we're doin' a *Meet the Vipers* series so the fans can get to know y'all a bit. We've got some standard questions and some fan-submissions too. It won't take too long."

She's got a sweet southern accent. Not over the top, but a nice little drawl that will have most of the guys desperate to get in her pants. I'm not sure where she's from, but it's definitely not Seattle. I wonder how long she's been here. Where is she from? Did she move for the job? *Why am I suddenly so God damn interested in this random stranger?*

"I'm all yours," I say, giving her a smile that's *just* this side of flirty. She gives me a tight smile back and I worry that I've made her uncomfortable, but then I get the idea that she's just trying to keep things professional. Totally understandable.

"Alright, here we go. Oh, and remember to keep it PG rated if you can."

I laugh. "Ah, you already interviewed Roman, didn't you?" She scrunches her nose and her tight smile turns into an easy one. Roman has no filter whatsoever and reporters had learned fairly quickly to either be ready with the *bleep* sound, or to just not ask him any questions at all. I chuckle, shaking my head. He's a good guy, just doesn't seem to know how to utter one sentence without at least five expletives in it.

"I'll be on my best behavior. Promise."

She nods at the camera guy and then turns back to me. "Ok, here we go. We'll start easy: What's your name and what position do you play?"

"I'm Connor Shepherd and I'm the goalie for the Vipers—everyone calls me Shep."

"And how long have you been with the Vipers."

"This is my—" I raise my eyes upward, doing the quick math in my head "—seventh season." *Fuck, seven already?* Feels like just yesterday I got the call that the Vipers wanted me, and I'd left the Kodiaks. Rizzo and I *both* left them, actually, and now there's definitely bad blood when we play each other. Rizzo and I have been nearly inseparable since freshman year in college, and I always joke that he couldn't survive without me so he had to follow me all the way to Seattle. He of course claims that I would be nothing without him and so he took pity on me and came with. Honestly, I can't imagine playing without him on the ice with me, so whether I dragged him along or he followed or however the fuck it happened, I couldn't be more thankful.

We do a handful more typical get-to-know-you type questions:

Where am I from? *Outside of Bangor, Maine originally.*

Where did you go to college? *Cornell* (which gets a surprised, but I think impressed, arch of her brows).

When did I first start playing hockey? *Got my first skates when I was five.*

Just as she starts on the fan questions, the guy in the headset cuts in.

"Sorry, we're having an issue with the audio. Give us just a second."

He and the sound guy turn away to have a chat, which leaves Hattie and I standing alone together in a bit of an awkward silence.

"So, uh, how long have you been in Seattle?" She gives me a questioning look. "The accent," I say by way of explanation.

"Only a couple of weeks, actually," she admits. "I moved for the job." She doesn't offer more, so we lapse into another bout of silence. She seems a bit...stiff. Not standoffish or rude, exactly, but like she's just reluctant to do the whole small talk thing.

Again, totally understandable. Ninety percent of the time, small talk is the worst.

While we're waiting, the facilities guys drive a giant crane onto the middle of the ice and start hoisting a huge wreath up onto the jumbotron hanging in the center of the arena. She huffs out an annoyed breath, staring daggers at the decoration.

I huff out a laugh. "Are you against wreaths, or just decorating early?"

"Christmas in general," she responds.

"What?!" I ask incredulously. She gives me a challenging look and my brows draw down. "Is it like a religious thing?"

"Nope. I just hate Christmas."

"How can you hate Christmas?"

"Red and green aren't my colors," she says with a wry smirk, the word coming out like *cuh-lers* and I don't know why it's so attractive, but fuck me, it really is.

"I find it hard to believe that any colors aren't your colors," I say honestly, not even trying to flirt. Ok, maybe a little. "But seriously, how can you hate it? It's the best." She stares at me, looking like she's trying to decide if I'm yanking her chain. "Seriously, I fucking love it. Oh, sorry," I wince, then shrug. "Well, we aren't filming right now, so I get a pass." Her lips curl upward, one dimple peeking out. *Damn her.* "I love Christmas. The lights and the music and the food. Ah, God, is there anything better than a Christmas cookie fresh out of the oven?"

"You know you can make those cookies anytime, right? They aren't regulated to Christmas time only."

I shake my head. "Nope, they don't taste the same any other time of year. It's science." She laughs lightly, seemingly despite herself. "So, you seriously hate Christmas?"

"Christmas and I...have bad blood," she hedges and though I'm keenly interested in whatever the hell that could possibly mean, I don't push. That seems like something you share with someone you've known for more than five minutes.

"Well, I love it," I say again. I really do, always have. Christmas was a huge thing for our family and I have the absolute best memories of spending time together around the tree every year, skating, sledding, decorating cookies. All of it. It kind of makes me sad that Hattie doesn't share my love for the holiday, that maybe she doesn't have the cherished memories of it that I do. She studies me.

"What?"

"You just don't seem like the Christmas-lovin' type, I guess."

"And what type do I seem like?" I ask, leaning my forearms on the top of the wall.

"A playboy-hockey star-biker?" she says with a hike of one shoulder.

I huff out a laugh. "Well, I do ride, and I am admittedly a star," I say with a wink. For some reason, I feel the need to add, "But I'm not a playboy." I'm not sure why I want her to know that. It's what most people assume about all of us, and it usually doesn't bother me. It's just kind of how it is. Plus, I used to be almost as big of one as Rizzo, but I've changed over the past few years. The random hook ups, the one-night stands on the road, all of that isn't really my deal anymore.

And I want her to know it. Not that it matters, really. I'm not trying to get in her pants or anything right now, but, I don't know, maybe we could be friends. She's new in town. Maybe she's lonely without her friends or family around—though of course she could have a significant other that moved here with her for all

I know. But maybe she could still use someone to show her around. Maybe I should offer? Would that be too much? I mean we are kind of co-workers in a round about way, so that wouldn't be too weird of a thing to offer, would it? Or maybe that's precisely why it *would* be weird.

Fuck, my head is starting to hurt. I don't think I've over thought anything like this in...well, basically ever. And it's not even a real thing. It's a hypothetical situation. *Get a fucking grip, Shep.*

She gives me a dry look. "I've heard quite the opposite, actually."

"I *used* to be, but I'm reformed," I tell her with a grin, and her lips curl again. Our gazes lock and I get one of those instant connection feelings. Not love at first sight or anything like that, I'm not an idiot, but just when you know you mesh with someone on some weird cosmic level. Like you know in an instant you're going to be friends. I had it when I first met Rizzo almost twenty years ago, and a handful of other times in my life. I'm just about to ask if I can show her around town, but headset guy cuts back in.

"Ok, sorry about that. We're all good."

Hattie gives that tight smile again and shifts back into her more rigid persona from before. Is that her work face? I totally get that. Off the ice, I'm mostly easy going and a teddy bear—only in one real area does that *not* apply—but on the ice? I'm a completely different person. Ruthless. Laser-focused. Rabid. I've threatened to rip someone's head off with my bare hands, and wouldn't have thought twice about actually going through with it. So, I get having a different personality when it comes to the job, especially in a new one when you're trying to prove yourself and make an impression and all that.

We finish up a few fan questions and then she has me pose for a few still shots. She furrows her brow as she watches, running the small diamond pendant along the chain around her throat, and I can practically see her wheels turning as she thinks hard about...something. She tilts her head to the side and then she straightens like the idea sent a jolt through her, eyes lighting up.

"You own a suit, right? I mean, y'all are like football players where you arrive to games all dressed up usually?"

"Um, yes..." I say slowly, not quite understanding her thought process.

As if reading my thoughts, she does a spinning motion with her finger near her temple. "I promise there was a connection up there somewhere that got me from one place to the other." I grin at that, really digging this girl. "But I just got a great idea for another promo." She sounds giddy. "Ok, anyway, you're all done. It was nice meetin' you."

"Nice meeting you, too." Should I ask? Might as well. "Hey, if you need any help, I'm around."

"Help?"

"I mean, with your place or finding things around town or anything."

"Oh. Uh, thanks, I appreciate it." She sounds a little surprised, but not entirely offended, so that's good. I nod and skate off. If she wants to take me up on the offer, she has access to all my contact info. I stare up at the wreath as I skirt around the edge of the crane and shake my head. I cannot believe she hates Christmas.

Once I'm closer to the benches, I open my arms wide and yell, "Howey! We doing this shit or what!?"

Chapter Three

HATTIE

❄ · ·❄· ·❄· ·❄· ·❄· ·❄

The *Meet the Vipers* series has been going really great. The videos have gotten tons of views and we've used them as promos to drive up attendance at the season opener in a week. Despite the Christmas décor already going up all around me, I've planned a Puck-or-Treat event for Halloween at the end of the month and am working on some more fall-themed promotions and things too. *Christmas can back the fuck off, please.*

I've done a handful of things with the players over the last two weeks and meeting them has been...interesting. Most of them seem like decent guys, but there are a few that definitely seem to live up to the rumors from Kelly. Anthony Rizzo told me to call him, and I quote, "for a good time, beautiful," with a wink before skating off backwards that first day. I would be lying if I hadn't been a little flattered and maybe even flushed a bit—he's absolutely gorgeous, it would be impossible *not* to be affected by him flirting—but I would *not* be calling him. Ever. He was the worst out of all of them, and though gorgeous and seemingly not *actually* an arrogant jerk, he had a different girl—or sometimes *girls,*

plural—with him every other night if the stories were to be be-
lieved.

My mind admittedly keeps seeming to circle back to Connor.
Or Shep, I guess. I know that's what everyone calls him—apparently hockey is big on the nicknames thing—but I wonder if
that's what he actually *likes* to be called. I haven't asked him outright, though we've chatted a bit here and there over the last two
weeks when I've been doing promotional stuff or when we run
into each other going to or from the gym. Mostly superficial
stuff—*this weather, huh? How's work? How's practice? Do you
still hate Christmas?*—but it's been nice. It's only one of those
rare instances where I vibed with him immediately, that weird
connection clicking into place as soon as he'd skated up for his
interview and grinned at me. A *friendly* connection, I mean, but
it's definitely there. We laugh at stupid shit at the same time, or
someone will say or do something and we both somehow catch
each other's gazes at the same time, rolling our eyes or making a
stupid face. We haven't hung out or anything outside of work, but
who knows. Maybe I'll take him up on his offer one of these days
to show me around town. Right now, I'm too busy, but...maybe
soon.

I'm not gonna lie, I'm ridiculously excited for the video today.
The idea had come to me when we'd been taking shots of Connor
for the *Meet the Vipers*, and I saw how much the camera fucking
loved him. And it should. He's gorgeous by all accounts, though
in a completely different way than I'm used to. He's tall and built,
with broad shoulders and thick, muscled arms that seem to strain
the material of every shirt he wears. He's a bit brawnier than some
of the other players, but I guess that would be advantageous in a
goalie, and it only adds to the attraction. He looks like the type of

guy who could pick you up, toss you over his shoulder, and take you to bed without breaking his stride. The type that could hold you up against the wall...I flush inwardly.

Not that I've ever had that happen or thought about it happening or wanted it to happen or anything...not *much* anyway. Josh had always been way more, um, tame in the bedroom. Not that there's anything wrong with that, but it had never quite quenched my thirst, if you know what I mean. Things were fine and I had a rabbit if I needed it, but I'd always craved more than just *fine.*

Connor's hair is a bit on the longer side, a dark blonde, with matching scruff across his chin and lip, a bit too long to be called stubble, but maybe not enough to be called a full beard either. It looks damn good on him though, whatever it is. His eyes are a deep green with a starburst of gold around the middle and he's got one hell of a smile. I can easily see why girls throw themselves at him. He's just got a rugged sexiness to him that I can't explain. I can see him riding a Harley, but just as easily chopping wood out at a cabin in the woods. Each scenario is equally enticing.

One arm is fully covered in tattoos, the other one inked to his elbow, and I've seen the edges of more peeking out from beneath his collar, so I know he has more on his chest. I wonder where else he might have them. His back? His torso?

Seeing the photos of him when we'd been doing the *Meet the Vipers* interviews, I'd suddenly wanted to see him in a suit, knowing he would look drop-dead sexy in it, the rugged and the chic coming together. I loved the idea of the juxtaposition between dirty hockey gear and dressing to the nines, so, I'd gotten the idea for a little transition magic video for Clipper, the new trending social media platform.

Now, I wait in the long corridor outside the locker rooms for the team to get here. We've already done the part with them in their gear, now it's time for the suits. They'd been given strict instructions to come looking their best, and thankfully heard very little grumbling from them. They really are a good bunch of guys. They start arriving and I'm so not disappointed—they look amazing and I can already see in my head how awesome the video is going to turn out.

"Wow. Y'all clean up nice," I say, smiling as they shuffle into the hallway.

One of the star wings, Tanner Juliard—or Jules, of course—puts his hand over his heart. In his thick Boston accent, he pleads, "Ah God, please say that again. *That accent*!" He reaches over and grips another player's shoulder, squeezing hard and shaking him. "Am I right?" I laugh and shake my head. They've all seemed to thoroughly enjoy my accent. There's one guy, Nelson, from Virginia, but that's about as southern as anyone on the team gets, so I'm a bit of a novelty apparently.

Now, I ham up the accent a bit and quirk a brow at him when I say, "Behave, Jules. Don't make me call your momma."

"Ah, *God*," he says again, biting his fist dramatically. I try and fail not to laugh. They're actually really fun to be around and none of them have really outright hit on me. The few that have, it's really been mostly harmless flirting, or done in a way that doesn't make me want to puke—actual invitations to dinner or drinks, or going to see a movie. I'd had half a mind to accept a few, but decided against it. Not only had I decided dating a hockey player wasn't for me, I don't think dating anyone right now is a good idea. I need to focus on work and figuring out my life. I still don't even have furniture in my house for crying out loud. So, a kitchen table first, then dates.

But overall, being around the guys has been great. I already kind of feel a bit of a little-sister-with-twenty-older-brothers kind of vibes, and honestly, it feels nice.

"Ok, go ahead and pull up the other video so we can get them in the right spots," I say to Natalie—Nat— my very own assistant. She just started and she's a freaking rock star. I honestly don't know why she even wanted to be my assistant with the resume she has, but she seems content and I'm lucky to have her. Between the two of us, I have zero doubts we can flip the Vipers media plan and outreach on its head and really get their shit on point.

I look at the screen and then start arranging the guys so that the transition will be smooth as butter.

"Annnnd, let's see, ok, Rizzo needs to go here. Is he here yet?" I glance around, but I honestly can't see much other than the chests of the guys closest to me. I'm not all that tall to begin with, but I swear each and every one of these dudes is at least six feet tall, some well over.

"No need to panic, I have arrived!" Rizzo calls in a smooth voice from behind me. I turn to find him gliding down the hallway towards us, arms outstretched and smiling a million-dollar smile. I study him appreciatively. He looks like he stepped off of a red carpet somewhere in a sharp navy suit, but then I catch Connor behind him and my mouth goes dry. *Holy. Shit.*

He's wearing the absolute hell out of that suit. It's a slate gray, and the crisp white shirt beneath makes his skin look even tanner, the dark lines of the tattoo snaking up from his chest visible just beneath the collar looking stark against the white. It's obviously expensive and tailored to fit his large frame, hugging him perfectly. He looks like an ad for a cologne that you know is gonna smell like heaven. His hair is slicked back, his scruff trimmed nicely, and when he catches my eye, his lips curl into a crooked, sexy smile. *I'm staring. Am I staring? Stop staring. I can't. Jesus, Mary, and Joseph, send help.*

"Dear God, I love this job," Nat says, low in my ear.

"It, uh, has its perks," I say, with a shaky laugh, smoothing my hands down the front of my sweater absently.

"How do you want me?" Rizzo asks with a salacious grin, making it abundantly clear that he's *not* talking about for the video. Nat makes a tiny squeaking sound, like a mouse, and I pull my lips in to hide my smile. Rizzo arches a brow in interest, shifting his smile to her and extending a hand.

"Anthony Rizzo, at your service." Nat takes his hand and her cheeks flush.

"Uh, Natalie." She shakes her head. "No. Nat. I'm Nat."

"Why don't you get Rizzo in the right spot, Nat?" I say, amusement in my tone and she cuts her eyes at me, giving me a narrowed look. I arch a brow back.

She recovers, her confident demeanor settling back in place. "Sure, come with me."

"Oh, *gladly*..." Rizzo says, trailing off as Nat leads him away, her shoulders tight. *Oh, she may be in trouble with that one.*

I cough to cover my laugh.

"So...?" Connor asks, extending his arms and looking at me expectantly.

"It'll do," I say, noncommittally, though I have to force myself not to stare. I almost say that I wouldn't kick him out of my bed, but I figure that'll definitely be taken as flirting. I always flirt to an extent, it's just how I am, maybe just part of being from the south honestly, but that comment may be overtly flirting, and I don't need to be flirting with any of them, least of all Connor Shepherd. In this particular moment, the reason I don't need to flirt escapes me, but I'm sure it's a good one. Probably.

"It'll do?" He snorts, but then studies me, tilting his head to the side. "You're shorter."

"Huh?" I blurt eloquently. His lips quirk upward on one side.

"The last time I saw you, you were much taller," he clarifies.

"Oh, heels," I say with a shrug. Without my six-inchers on today, I only come up to just below his chest. Most everyone else here wears jeans and sneakers to work, so I'd decided after those first couple of weeks of wearing dresses and heels, that I could relax my own wardrobe too. I like dressing up every now and then, but I'm far more comfortable in leggings and a t-shirt, so I was relieved to be able to dress a bit more casually at work.

"So, I'm not gonna lie, I don't *quite* understand how this little video is going to work," Connor says, eyeing the line of all of his teammates while Nat shifts them around.

"It'll make sense once it's done, I promise." I hope. If I can make it work the way it looks in my head, it'll be awesome. "Ok, so you're over there by...I honestly can't keep all the names straight yet. Mustache and Sideburns. Go stand between them."

Connor chuckles quietly. "Mustache is Jonah Parrish—Rish. Sideburns is Henrik Glanowski—Nowski."

"Right. Got it." I don't got it, but I will soon. I'd made flashcards with each player's picture, name, nickname, position, and stats last night so I could start studying. It's my job to know all these guys and use my knowledge of them to help get fans' asses in the seats, and I take my job seriously. Connor gets into position and after a few tweaks, I think we've got it.

"Alright y'all," I say loudly enough for them all to stop their low conversations and look my way.

"Say that again!" Jules calls and most of the other guys laugh. I smile, but ignore him.

"On the count of three, I'm gonna have you all jump straight into the air. When you land, feel free to lean into the vibe a bit. Straighten your tie, keep eye contact with the camera, tilt your sunglasses down—that kind of thing. Play up the sexy," I add, and a few whoops rise up among the players. I chuckle. "We'll do it a few times and combine all the shots into what I'm hoping will be a video that will go viral."

"I had something viral once," Rizzo says and everyone either laughs or groans or both. Connor reaches around Mustache— Rish—and shoves Rizzo in the shoulder. I just shake my head. *They're children, the bunch of them.*

Based on the research I'd been doing on Clipper, this type of thing would absolutely get attention. The app tracks the content that you watch and uses an algorithm to send you more videos that are similar. So, my entire video feed is pretty much nothing but hot athletes in various states of undress right now. Not that I'm complaining or anything, but...my job is super weird sometimes.

We go through the process a handful of times, making a few tweaks here and there when I compare it to the previous footage, I've gotta admit, they all rock it. Some of them too well. The way Rizzo stares into the camera and runs his thumb across his lower lip is going to get someone pregnant through the screen somehow. Don't ask me to explain the physics, but it's going to happen.

I tell myself not to watch Connor but of course I don't listen. There's something about him that continually pulls my gaze his way. He's more understated. Instead of eye-fucking the camera like Rizzo, he looks slightly away, smiling this secretive, sexy smile, and rubbing a tattooed hand across the back of his neck before lifting his eyes upward slowly....

Fuck.

I have to look away, heat flooding my cheeks and a slow shiver working its way down my spine. This was a terrible idea. A brilliant one actually, but terrible all the same. I make sure that I have myself under control before I yell out to them.

"Alright, I think we got it! Thanks guys!" They all mill around a bit, small groups breaking out into conversation. Nat and I look over the footage, pointing out shots we definitely want to use.

"Are you coming to the game tonight?"

I look up from the tablet screen to find that Connor has made his way over to me, away from the rest of the group. He absently unbuttons the top buttons of his shirt, pulling the collar open. I swallow hard before yanking my eyes back up to his face. I don't know what is wrong with me. He's just a guy. An extremely attractive guy, but still—just a guy. A guy that I think I could be really great friends with actually, so I need to get my hormones in check ASAP.

"Oh, yeah, I am. Gonna do some work in the crowd tonight, get a feel for how the games usually go and get ideas on what we can improve, how we can drive up attendance." The season doesn't officially start for another week, so this is more like a preseason game. But, it'll give me a good baseline for where things stand and get a feel for everything before we really get started.

"Do you ever take time off?" he asks, not critically or full of spite, the way Josh used to, but with humor and even a bit of admiration in his tone.

"Not when I'm in a new job trying to prove myself," I say, matter-of-factly.

He nods as if understanding. "Well, try to enjoy some of the game too if you can." He walks backwards, and starts smiling, straight, white teeth gleaming against his tanned skin. *He must spend a lot of time outside when he isn't on the ice,* I think. "I'll be the one standing in front of the goal with the Vipers jersey on." I roll my eyes, but smile, and he winks before turning and catching up to some of the other guys.

I stare after him as he playfully fights with Rizzo. He might look like he would fit in with a dangerous motorcycle gang, but I get the feeling Connor is kind of a teddy bear. Goofy. Fun. Easygoing. There's something about him that just draws me to him, makes me like him, and I don't mean physically, though obviously there's *definitely* that aspect. I just feel like I could hang out with him, eat pizza or binge watch movies, bitch about work or play beer pong. So, yeah, I think I'm going to take him up on his offer sooner rather than later.

"I'm pretty excited to see how we're going to edit this all together to make something awesome out of it," Nat says, pulling my attention away from the guys' retreating forms and yanking me out of my own head.

I grin at her. "Well, let's go play around then."

❄ · · ❄ · · ❄

The video came out amazing, even better than I'd planned. It started with all the guys looking like sweaty messes in their practice uniforms. They jumped up and when they landed, they were all magically transformed into handsome devils in their sharp suits. I posted it an hour ago and it already has over four hundred thousand views, with the numbers climbing every second.

"Oh my God, you're a genius," Nat says, high-fiving me.

"I think you might break the internet," Bobby adds, eyeing the video over my shoulder.

"That's the plan," I grin. "Now, let's go see what this whole hockey fuss is all about."

I'm pretty pumped to check it all out, actually. I am going to be working, like I told Connor, but I do plan to try to relax and enjoy the game some too. Maybe in the second half. Or...wait, I don't think that's right for hockey.

"Is it halves?" I ask as the three of us make our way up to the private box reserved for staff. The game is already underway and I can feel the dull reverberation from the crowd and loudspeaker beneath my feet. A thrum of excitement goes through me. I've always loved going to big sporting events, namely football games, and I miss Death Valley like an old friend. When I'd been a student at LSU, I never missed a single home game. Even when I broke my leg tailgating, I was back in the stadium with a cast and crutches before kickoff, loopy as all get out on pain medicine, but cheering on my Tigers like my life depended on it. After graduation, I tried to make it to at least a handful of games a season. "Like football? Oh! Is there a halftime show?" I ask excitedly. I'd always loved watching the band during halftime.

Bobby chuckles. "No. Hockey has periods. Three of them, with fifteen-minute intermissions in between."

"Oh. Interesting." I really do need to step my knowledge of the actual game, but I've been so busy with everything else, I haven't had time to dive into that piece of it yet. Maybe I could ask one of the guys to help me. Maybe Connor? Er, Shep. *Ugh, whatever.*

"Ok, let's grab some food and then mingle a bit and get some shots for the social media pages and whatnot."

Though the crowd is a bit thin, it isn't as bad as I'd been expecting. *I can so fix this*, I think with absolute certainty. *I can do this.* As we walk around, I can see the excitement and joy in the faces all around me. Everyone truly seems to love being here, and there are obviously some die-hard fans, so I can definitely work with that. I get a lot of good insight and already have some good thoughts on how we can improve things. We make a few videos to use for social media posts and upcoming promotions, talk to some fans about things they'd like to see, and give away some swag which makes us very popular.

After a while, I decide to turn work brain off—or well, let it run in the background anyway, it never completely goes off—and just enjoy the game. Our staff badges get us past security and into some reserved seats right along the glass not far from our goal. There's a time out or something happening, so Connor pulls his helmet off just as I'm taking the last step to my seat. He runs an arm over his sweat-soaked face before shoving his wet hair back. He looks even more massive than usual with all the pads on, and I frown for a minute. Does he really need all of those? I mean, I know people are hitting pucks at him, but...can they actually hurt him? Like *really* hurt him? Even football players don't wear that much padding and they get bulldozed by three-hundred-pound tanks on the reg. *Maybe goalies are just big babies*, I think with a wry grin, imagining saying just that to Connor and seeing his reaction.

He scans the crowd, smiling and waving to a few kids, which makes me smile. I'm glad he's one of *those* types of players, the kind who seem to understand that they wouldn't even have a job if it weren't for fans, that he's basically just a glorified kid himself getting way too much money to play a game. Too many athletes get too big for their britches with that shit if you ask me, act above it all, hardly even acknowledging their fans. It pisses me off and it's one reason why I've always loved college sports far more than professional ones. The college kids seemed to be there for the love of the game, and a lot of the professionals seemed to only care about the money and the fame. No thanks.

Then he turns and our gazes meet. His grin widens and I give him an awkward little wave as I sit down hastily. Some kind of signal that I don't hear or see must alert Connor that break time is over because he pulls his helmet back on and somehow...transforms. I can't even really explain it, but it's like every muscle in his body goes rigid, like he's on high alert. I can't see his eyes, but I somehow know that they're scanning the ice, picking up on minute details that I can't possibly see or understand. Even crouched before the net, nearly immobile, he looks intimidating and almost dangerous. Lethal. Intense. There's a contained power in his stillness that's fascinating and beautiful and impressive, like one of those big jungle cats getting ready to pounce.

A whistle blows, and commotion breaks out in the middle of the ice. It's utter insanity, and I can't even see where the puck is. Everything is too fast, moving at fucking warp speed, and I have zero hope of tracking anything at all. The guys all move so fast it's like they're flying over the ice, not even actually touching it. It's impressive as hell, but just plain crazy. I don't even realize the puck is anywhere near the other goal when the crowd erupts in cheers. Apparently we scored. *What? How??*

"What the fuck is this game??" I yell over the crowd. Nat laughs as she settles down beside me, expertly holding three full beers between her fingers. Bobby and I each take one and the three of us cheers. After I take a long sip, I say, "How do y'all even see what's happening? I can barely tell where the puck is and as soon as I find it, it's somewhere else."

Nat laughs. "Once you watch a bit more, it'll get easier."

"Oh my god!" I gasp when one of our guys slams one of theirs into the wall with such force, I can't understand how bones don't shatter. "Is that *allowed?*" Next thing I know, a fight breaks out. An honest to God fist fight. I know hockey is known for fighting, but come on! Throwing punches? Seriously? "Ok, that *definitely* can't be allowed."

Bobby laughs. "It's always fun watching a game with a newbie."

Rizzo handles the puck like it's part of him, like the stick and the puck are both just extensions of his arm. He skates faster than almost anyone else out there. At one point, he drops to his knees and slides on the ice, but pops back to his skates a heartbeat later, the movement so fluid and graceful and quick, I honestly wonder if I imagine it for a second.

Some of the guys from the other team make their way closer to our goal, skating like bats out of hell right at Connor. If I were him and saw that coming at me, I'd be shittin' bricks. But he looks so at ease, so ready. A loud smack splits the air and before I can even comprehend what's happened, Connor has the puck in his glove. The crowd goes crazy and my mouth gapes. How could he even see that, let alone catch it? His reflexes are insane, faster than I thought humanly possible. And now I understand the pads. I can only imagine how fast that puck is going, it's like a bullet hurdling at his chest. Over and over, shots are fired at him, and over and over he deflects them in the blink of an eye. He's *really* freaking good. I mean, I have no real frame of reference, but, to my completely untrained eye he looks freaking fantastic.

Fights break out here and there, guys are put in the penalty box, and pucks fly into the freaking crowd like foul balls at a baseball game.

"This sport is fucking crazy," I say after a particularly brutal collision happens against the glass right in front of us, making me yelp and duck my head as if they're going to come through and land on top of us. Nat laughs loudly at my reaction, and Jules actually grins and winks at me before skating off.

"It is, but it's amazing, isn't it?" Bobby says, eyes filled with excitement. "I freaking love it. I used to play when I was a kid. My dad was my coach, it was kind of our thing," he explains. "I was never all that good, truth be told, but I still love it."

"That's really sweet," I say, before breaking off into another yelp when the puck bounces off the glass in front of my face. He snorts into his beer and I flip him off, but laugh. He and Nat both try to explain some bits about the game, but I'm not quite following most of it yet. I will eventually, but trying to listen to their explanations while trying to also keep track of the puck—*where the hell is it now?*—and not flinch or scream every time it, or a person for that matter, hits the glass is nearly impossible.

But, despite all the crazy, I'm enjoying the hell out of it. Once I really understand the game, I know I'm going to love it and may just become a bona fide hockey fan. I cheer and scream and boo along with the rest of the crowd in our section, though to be fair, I don't know *why* we're booing. We drink and laugh, and I end up have the best night I've had in quite a while.

When it's all over, we take the win four-to-nothing, and it's exhilarating. Connor catches my eye and I give him a thumbs up with one hand and take a giant bite of the cotton candy I'm hold-ing in the other. He grins and chuckles, his shoulders shaking a bit, and looking way too good even with his hair drenched in sweat. He skates over and tosses a puck over the top of the glass. I fumble it for a second trying to catch it with one hand, but man-age to grab it eventually—without dropping my cotton candy, thank you very much. I do a little mock-curtsey when I finally have it under control and he laughs.

"Figured you needed a souvenir of the night you lost your hockey V-card." He winks and I laugh while Nat and Bobby raise their mostly-empty cups in cheers.

Connor winks and skates off to the join the rest of the guys filing off the ice and heading to the locker room I assume. I turn the puck over in my hand, a smile creeping across my face.

I think hockey may be my new favorite sport.

Chapter Four

"Can I have your autograph?" a sweet voice says from just behind me in line at the coffee shop. I turn, expecting to find a fan, but instead see Hattie grinning at me. She looks just as beautiful as she always does—hell, maybe even more beautiful in her tight jeans and zip-up hoodie, her hair in two loose braids beneath an LSU ball cap. Casual and sexy all mixed up together in a way that honestly isn't really fair—but she seems more relaxed today, a bit of the heaviness gone from her shoulders. I know that the things she's done so far on our social media channels has worked great, and Rish heard it from someone that our seasoner opener is actually almost sold out, which hasn't happened in a while. Apparently the uniforms-to-suits video had gone massively viral—whatever that means exactly. I'm honestly not really up on social media all that much, though I guess I should be. I do know that viral means good, though, so I'm happy that it turned out to be a win.

"It'll cost you," I tell her with a wry smile.

"Oh really? I didn't know that you charged for that sorta thing. I'm a little disappointed."

"The opposite actually: you have to let me buy you a cup of coffee."

Her smile widens. "I will never turn down coffee. Ever. If I do, you know that I've been replaced by a robot or an alien."

I chuckle a bit. "Good to know."

"So, you seemed to enjoy the game last night. Or the cotton candy at the very least," I say with a smile, remembering her giving me a thumbs up and chomping on a giant puff of blue.

"The cotton candy was on point, but the game wasn't too bad either," she says with a grin. "No, it was great actually. Work wise, it was really helpful to see everything in person and I've already got tons of stuff cookin'." She winkles her nose a bit before adding, "Some of which is Christmas related." I would seriously love to understand her hatred of the holiday. "But aside from the work side of things, it was really cool. I mean, the game itself is total batshit insanity that I don't actually understand whatsoever, other than the obvious puck-in-net-equals-points part, but I liked it. It was a bit more brutal than I realized," she admitted, "I mean, hockey and fighting are pretty synonymous, but seeing it in person was somethin' else. Really fun, though."

We order and a father and son come up asking for autographs and pictures while we wait for our coffees. Hattie whips out her own phone and asks if they're ok with her sharing some pictures on the Vipers official website and social media accounts, and they eagerly agree. She takes their contact information and lets them know that there will be VIP tickets waiting for them at the box office for the first game. The kid's eyes light up like it's the best day of his life and it makes my chest feel all warm inside. I don't give a flying fuck if that's lame or whatever. I remember being that kid, remember that feeling of excitement and joy of going to a real game with my dad. I love how easily Hattie just created what will be a cherished memory for them like it was nothing. I know that she didn't have to do that by any means, but she wanted to.

"Do you, uh, want to sit?" Hattie asks once we have our drinks, sounding a bit nervous and gesturing toward a small table in the back corner near the fireplace. We head out for one last set of preseason games this afternoon, and while I'm always excited to play, to feel the rush of the adrenaline that shoots through me as soon as I step foot on the ice, the trips are always hard on me these days. So, I'd planned to grab my coffee and head home to get ready to leave, but I can't pass up this invitation. I'd be lying if I said I hadn't been thinking of Hattie way more than I should be since meeting her.

I don't really get nervous before games anymore, haven't in decades really. An electric kind of excitement, sure, but not nervous. But when I'd seen her watching the game last night, a flitter of actual *nerves* ran through my stomach. I'd admittedly shown off a bit more than usual, knowing she was watching, hoping she would be impressed.

So, yeah, I'm definitely not going to say no to having coffee with her. I nod and we settle into the mis-matched chairs, which is one of my favorite things about the place. Seattle is known for a very popular coffee chain that shall remain nameless, and don't get me wrong, I don't mind their stuff at all, but I like the hole in the walls, the hidden gems.

"So, hockey's not popular where you're from I'm assuming?"

She blows lightly over her steaming cup, and the scent of peppermint fills my nose. God, I love that smell. I have a weird obsession with candy canes and have honestly stopped buying them around the holidays because I'll eat an entire box within a few hours. It's an addiction. But damn if I don't lean forward as the steam from Hattie's cup wafts towards me.

"Correct," she says with a half grin.

"And where would that be?" I ask, taking a sip of my own drink and kind of wishing I'd gotten whatever peppermint concoction she had.

"South Louisiana originally," she says, pointing to her hat with a smile, "but I've been living in Texas for the last few years."

"Ah, I was going to guess Texas."

She shrugs. "The accent always gives me away. So, yeah, I was born and raised in the church of the pigskin. *That* game I understand. Hockey? Not so much."

"Well, I don't know if you realize this or not," I say, leaning back casually in my chair, "but I *might* know a thing or two about the game...if you had questions, I mean." She gives me a dry look and I can't help but laugh.

She holds her hand out and curls her fingers inward. "Well come on then, Hot Shot. Gimme the run down."

So, I do. I try to explain the game in a way that I hope is easy to understand without seeming like I'm talking down to her. She listens intently, nodding in understanding and asking questions when she doesn't. After a while, she sits back and crosses her arms over her chest.

"So, it's just cold soccer," she says matter-of-factly.

I snort into my coffee, nearly choking. "I guess that's one way to look at it, yeah. The biggest difference is that you probably *shouldn't* try to use your head on a hockey puck."

"Har har," she says, rolling her eyes but smiling. We chat a bit more about this and that, nothing too deep or personal, but it's nice. Easy.

"Are you settling in ok so far?"

"It's...an adjustment, that's for sure. I miss the warm and the beach," she says, sadness leaking into her voice. She gets a faraway look, and I'm sure she's imagining everything she left behind, everything she's missing, but the look of wistful longing suddenly transforms into something else. A flash of fear? *Odd.* She shakes herself and continues on. "But it was time for a change, so I'm happy I moved. I'm still learning my way around though. I pretty much know how to get to and from work, the grocery store, Target, and this coffee shop, but not much else. My house is still only half furnished too. Well, not even really half, but I haven't had time to really go shopping, or even find places to go shopping." She sighs.

"Moving sucks balls," I say honestly. She glances up and her lips quirk.

"Yes. Yes, it really does, but this move is totally worth it." That strange look of fear or discomfort crosses her face again, but she quickly pushes it away, grinning. "But now I'm regretting selling all my furniture."

I smile back, and though I don't want to, I know I need to go.

"Hey, I gotta run and get some things taken care of before we fly out this afternoon, but this was nice."

"It was," she agrees as we both put on our coats and head outside.

"Hey, so when we get back from these games, we have a few days off. I could help you find what you need for your place if you want, show you some of my favorite spots and hidden gems?" She chews her lip, looking like she's debating. I wonder if she's worried because she thinks I'll expect something, and, given my past reputation, I don't blame her, so I add, "No expectations or strings attached. Strictly platonic."

And, to my surprise, I mean it. I mean, of course I'd be happy to take Hattie to bed—I'd have to have serious brain damage not to want her like that—but I'm happy to just be friends. Coffee and chatting with her today was so damn refreshing. I didn't feel any kind of pressure to be anyone but myself, no stress to be charming or flirty, or to make sure I *wasn't* charming or flirty that she didn't get the wrong idea. I was just...me.

And it was fucking fantastic.

I haven't had that in a long time honestly, so, hell yeah, I'm down to just be friends with Hattie. She eyes me, trying to take my measure and decide if I'm bullshitting her, probably. I lean back against the front of my truck and cross my arms over my chest.

"Scout's honor. Friends only. I wouldn't let you kiss me even if you wanted to—which, of course, you will." I grin at her and wink.

She laughs out loud at that, her dimples peeking out making me regret promising no kissing for a half a heartbeat. But she seems to relax and the tension goes out of her shoulders.

"That sounds really great, actually."

"Kissing me? Of course it sounds great. I'm a fantastic kisser." She shoves me playfully in the shoulder and we both laugh. "So, not to sound like I'm hitting on you, but can I get your number?"

"Actually just give me yours," she says, pulling her phone out of her back pocket. "I don't even remember this new number yet honestly, it's like my third new one in the past few months." Why the change so many times? I give her my number and she types it in, my phone buzzing in my pocket a second later. Now I have hers too.

"Let me know when you're back in town."

I've gotten thousands of numbers in my lifetime probably, but for some reason, getting this one has my pulse racing. Fucking stupid, I know. I mean, I literally *just* promised her that this was just a friends thing thirty seconds ago, that I wouldn't try or expect more. But still, here I am damn near giddy at the idea of having her number, like I'm fifteen fucking years old again and Jessica Thompson agreed to go to the movies with me.

"I will," I promise, wondering if I'll be able to restrain myself from texting her from the plane today, or the hotel room tonight. Probably not, but it will be alright. Friends text, after all.

"But just a warning: I'm going to make you do all the touristy stuff too. Ferry boats and the Space Needle and the giant troll statue under the bridge. Oh! Is the hospital from Grey's Anatomy real? It's probably not real, is it?" She looks thoughtful but shrugs. "I think I'll even wear an *I heart Seattle* sweatshirt while we're at it."

I laugh again, loving this girl—in a friendly way. I love that she doesn't take herself too seriously, and I know that she's completely not kidding about playing tourist. She's excited about it, not saying any of it in a mocking way.

"I'll buy you one myself with a matching hat."

She smiles and nods. "Deal. Uh, stop all the pucks?" she says, scrunching her nose and grinning at her terrible attempt at a good luck. "That was bad," she chuckles.

"It was," I agree.

"Don't suck, buttercup—how about that?" She sticks her tongue out and I laugh.

"Much better." We both seem reluctant to leave, but I really do have to go. "I'll see you in a couple of days."

"See ya," she says. "Have a safe trip."

I hop in my truck and she ducks into her SUV. I honk and wave out the window as I pull away.

Best cup of coffee I've had in years.

Chapter Five

HATTIE

I'd actually almost turned around and walked out of the coffee shop when I saw Connor there, having a completely ridiculous knee-jerk reaction of revulsion: he was following me, just like Josh. Then I realized how stupid I was being seeing as how *he* was there first. I would technically have been the one following him. I don't know why my mind takes things in weird contexts now after Josh's behavior. It's like he poisoned it somehow, like now instead of an innocent girl ringing my door bell trying to sell candy bars for a cheerleading fundraiser (that I very much *do* want to buy), my very first thought is "he's here" and a cold fear skitters up my spine.

He never actually *did* anything to me technically, so my reactions aren't completely logical, but...I can't explain it. I just know he was getting close to snapping, that sooner rather than later, he was going to show up at my door—and not just to chat. There was just something in his eyes, something lurking just beneath the surface that honestly scared the hell out of me. Hence moving across the country to avoid that exact scenario.

Having coffee with Connor had turned out to be nice actually. *Really* nice. He was surprisingly easy to talk to, very laid back with a good sense of humor. It was almost easy to forget how incredibly attractive he was. *Almost.* But the way he'd been with the fans, especially the kid, had kind of melted my heart a little.

I'd told him to text me when he got back, but I've already gone to the gym, gotten a ton of ideas worked up for upcoming events at the arena, scheduled a week's worth of social media content, and binge-watched *Criminal Minds* for a few hours. I'm bored and restless and I can't get Connor out of my head. The way he'd smiled and laughed, a low, husky rumble that emanates from his chest. A chest that stretched his green henley tight in all the right ways. The green of the material made his eyes seem deeper, like the color of the moss on the trees after it rains. They were gorgeous and I could imagine if he looked at you the right way, they would promise all kinds of dark and sensual things.

I'd gotten the feeling that he's a teddy bear before, but now I'm convinced that he's a teddy bear in all aspects except for two: the ice and the bedroom. In those, I'm fairly sure he was very similar: intense; aggressive; unwavering; way too skilled. I shiver, letting that particular train of thought run right off the fucking rails, my eyes sliding shut as I imagine...

My eyes snap open.

"Get a fucking grip, McNamara," I mutter to myself. I've established that I won't be dating any hockey players, and that if and when Connor and I do hangout, it will be as friends. That's what I need right now. A friend. A *real* friend. After I'd gotten away from Josh, I'd realized how many of my friends were actually *his* friends. I'd tried to talk to some of them after the breakup, but even after I'd told them all the things he'd been doing, the things he'd threatened in his drunken rants, none of them seemed to care all that much—or would turn around and tell him everything I was saying, which only led to even more drunken rants from him about me "spreading rumors" about him.

It all made me realize that they were never really my friends to begin with, and it wasn't until I got out of Texas that it really hit me how Josh had slowly found ways to cut my friends from college and back home out of my life. It got to the point where I just accepted not talking to someone instead of having to get in fights with him about it constantly. It's so fucked up now, looking back, and I feel like a completely shitty person because of it. I make a mental note to try to reach back out to friends, try to mend fences and hopefully rekindle some old relationships.

So, yeah, a friend would be awesome right about now, and I *could* be friends with Connor, easily. He'd laughed and cut up with me during coffee, we had a good amount in common, and I just had that connection with him that isn't really quantifiable. Plus, he has really big muscles, so if I find some new furniture for my place, I'm sure I can talk him into hauling it around for me.

So, here I am, about to text him. It wouldn't be weird to go ahead and text him, would it? Friends text each other all the time. Though, we technically aren't officially friends yet, are we? Work acquaintances I suppose. More than that. Work friends? I mean, he definitely made it seem like he wanted to hang out, so I don't think he would think anything of it if I texted him...

"Oh my God, shut up," I tell myself, shaking my head. I'm being annoying as hell.

I quickly type out a text and hit send before I can start this stupid round-about in my head all over again.

Hattie: Hey.

That's the result of all of my worrying and overthinking? *Hey?* I roll my eyes and throw the phone into the couch pillow, getting up to throw another log on the fire. Other than the location, my two favorite things about this house are the built-in bookshelves in the living room, and the fireplace. It's gorgeous dark gray stone, soaring up two stories, and burns real wood. The living room, kitchen, and dining area are all open with a balcony from the top floor overlooking the entire space. There's a spare bedroom and an office upstairs, the master downstairs—with a second fireplace. It isn't a large house, but it's gorgeous and I'd immediately gotten that homey feeling.

I'd gotten extremely lucky that I found it when I did and that the owners were very motivated to sell. They were a lovely older couple who wanted to move to be closer to their grandbabies. The husband had built the house himself and there were so many beautiful custom touches that I instantly fell in love with it. Thankfully we closed extremely quickly—a perk of paying for it outright with all cash. My mom had left me a sizeable inheritance when she passed (and sizeable was really just being modest and tactful—it was a huge fortune to be quite honest) and I'd been smart with my money over the years. So, I had more than enough saved up to buy this place and still have plenty in savings.

My phone dings as I hold my hands out to the flames and I freeze. I force myself to walk calmly back over to it.

Connor: Hey, Mac.

My lips curl upward.

Hattie: Hockey players and your dang nicknames...

Not a second later, a facetime call is coming in. My heart thuds for a minute and I curse myself for barely even looking in the mirror since showering and deciding I was going to veg out the rest of the day, but then I remind myself that we're just friends—or working towards that anyway—so it really doesn't matter what I look like.

"What's wrong with nicknames?" he asks as soon as the call connects. I laugh a bit.

"Nothin', but speaking of: do you like being called Shep?" I ask, finally voicing the question that's been bugging me for weeks.

"Sure I do," he shrugs.

"I mean off the ice. Is that what your friends call you?" I realize then that most of his friends are probably other hockey players, so maybe it's not really a fair question. "I mean, is that what you want *me* to call you?" I ask, finally getting around to my real question.

He considers that for a long minute, before saying, "Sure. It's what most of my friends do call me, on or off the ice, so you're welcome to use it too."

I nod. That takes care of that. "So, uh, good flight?"

"It was terrible, actually. Turbulence like fucking crazy and Howey puked on Rolo's shoes. It was a mess."

I can't help but laugh. "I'm sorry, that sounds disgusting."

"Oh it was. Howey likes to eat beef jerky on flights."

I make an exaggerated gagging sound. "Ewww, can you not?"

He just grins and we end up talking for almost two hours while he lounges in his hotel room. Not about anything in particular, just random bullshit. I'd forgotten how nice it is to do this, to just talk and laugh and be stupid without worrying or having to pick my words carefully so that nothing gets taken the wrong way, starting a fight.

"Then Rizzo waltzed right out of the locker room, like it was nothing," Connor says, finishing a ridiculous story about the time

Connor had taken Rizzo's lucky underwear and hidden them, "saying that if he didn't have his lucky underwear, he wouldn't be wearing anything at all."

I laugh so hard my stomach hurts. "So he was just walking around nekkid as a jaybird?!" Connor makes a sound that is somewhere between a snort and choking.

"What in the fuck did you just say?"

I grin and realize that I've barely *stopped* grinning the entire time we've on the phone, my cheeks actually starting to hurt. I say slowly, pronouncing every word, "nek-kid as a jay-bird."

Connor laughs again. "Ok, I think I'm with Jules on this whole accent thing. What else ya got?"

So, we start a whole new conversation on what Connor dubs my "Southernisms,"[1] and I swear I almost pee my pants by the end of it when he starts just making up completely ridiculous things and claiming they could be southern sayings.

"You're as jimbly bimbly as a biscuit's nutsack." When I bark out a choked laugh, barely getting out the word "*what!?*" he adds, "Hey, I think that's a good one actually."

"I can't breathe," I wheeze, wiping tears out of my eyes.

"The south is a crazy damn place, that's all I've determined after this conversation. These crazy sayings and the fact that you eat those creepy little lobster things..." He shudders dramatically.

"Crawfish are delicious, thank you very much. But you *gotta* suck the head..." His eyes go wide and I bite my lip, scrunching my nose. "Oh my God, that really didn't come out right." We both burst out into another fit of laughter and I'd nearly forgotten what this was like: having someone I could just be me with, no

---

[1] A compilation of *Southernisms* can be found at the back of this book.

expectations, no pressures, just being stupid and talking and God, it's nice.

A knock sounds in the background on Connor's end of the line. "Oh crap, hey I gotta run. I forgot I was supposed to have dinner with some of the guys."

"Have fun. I'll talk to ya later."

"Maybe I'll see if they have crawfish," he teases. "Bye."

With that, we finally hang up—two and a half hours later. *Holy shit.* When was the last time I talked on the phone that long on purpose? I smile as I poke around in the fridge for something to eat, laughing lightly as random bits of our conversation spring to mind. After that phone call, I'm definitely feeling much better about the idea of being friends with Con—er, *Shep.* It's going to take some getting used to. He's been Connor in my head for the last few weeks, and I have a feeling he's going to remain that way, though I'll do my best to call him Shep to his face, as requested.

And now I'm apparently Mac. I already know it's going to spread and the entire team will be calling me that by the time they get back from this trip.

The thought actually makes me smile. It's like I'm officially part of the Vipers now, like I really do belong here.

❄· ·❄· ·❄

"Are you sure you're lifting??" Connor grunts out as we attempt to maneuver a plush, oversized chair through my front door. It weighs a freaking ton, but as soon as I'd seen it, I needed it in my life. I immediately pictured lounging in it by the fireplace, reading or napping, and I had to have it. We'd loaded it up in Connor's truck fairly easily, but now Connor's bulging muscles—

which I have *not* been ogling—and the chair are having an all out battle of wills.

"Of course I am!" I huff out. I'm admittedly not much help in the grand scheme of things, really, but I *am* trying. "Set it down for a sec."

It thuds to the ground and we stare at each other over the chair between us, wedged in my doorway. He narrows his eyes at me, sweat dripping lazily down his temple. He takes his hat off, wipes the sweat away and then pulls the cap back on backwards. *Damn him.* There is just something about a man in a backwards hat...*Focus, Hattie.*

"What?" I demand.

"I don't think you're lifting at all."

"Am so! It's not my fault that the great Connor Shepherd is a weakling." His eyes go wide. "Oh, I said it. All those muscles," I gesture to all of him, "are only for show apparently." I arch a brow in challenge and his mouth pops open in astonishment before he snaps it shut, eyes glittering with something between incredulity, irritation, and amusement.

"Move," he says in a stern voice. I eye him warily but do as he says. He takes a few deep breaths, bends down, and hoists the damn chair through the doorway himself. I yelp and leap forward to try to help before hastily backing out of the way as he shifts his grip and lifts the entire fucking thing.

"Shep!" I cry, worried he's going to hurt himself. If I'm responsible for the Vipers' star goalie getting hurt because I was being a turd, I'll never hear the end of it.

"Where?" he grunts.

"By the fireplace," I blurt. He man handles the beast of a chair across the room and sets it down with a heavy thud on the edge of the shaggy rug we'd picked up yesterday. We've been quite the busy beavers running around Seattle and honestly, it's been amazing. I'm starting to feel more like myself than I have in years, and I think it's because I can just truly *be* myself with Connor. I don't have to be "on," when we hang out. I can just be goofy or crabby or quiet or rowdy or whatever I want to be in the moment. I don't have to worry about if my hair and makeup and outfit are perfect (something Josh was constantly complaining about on my "slouchy" days. He absolutely hated when I wanted to run around in leggings and a ballcap), I don't have to worry about getting a stern look if I order a second beer (which was rich coming from a certified alcoholic), I can yell at the TV in the bar during a football game or heaven forbid burp without being told to "behave." It really is shocking and, to be totally honest, fucking *embarrassing* to see how I'd been with Josh. I *shouldn't* feel embarrassed, I know that, but I can't deny that there is a degree of shame there, that I let him do that, that I let him chip away at who I was a little at a time.

But not anymore. Never again.

Connor straightens, breathing hard and rolling his neck and shoulders. I'm about to call him a moron when I'm struck mute: he lifts the hem of his shirt to wipe his face and dear God almighty. My mouth goes dry. Other areas do the opposite.

Holy. Shit.

His stomach is flat and tight, corded with muscles that bunch and flex as he moves. The dark lines of his tattoos dance across his tanned skin like living things. What looks like a dragon wrapped around a Celtic cross covers most of his left side, the bottom of the cross splitting through the indecent indention beside his hip, dipping below the top of his jeans. I can see the bottom of something that covers his left peck, but I'm not sure what it is.

He's sexy in a way that I can't even fully comprehend, in a way that I've never experienced before. I've dated attractive men in the past, but no one like Connor. It isn't just the physicality of him, though that is impressive and mouth-watering, there's something more. Like you know exactly what promises his body is making, the things he can do with it, the things he can make you feel. There's a strange, quiet ferocity in that small glimpse of him shirtless that I know I'll be thinking about long after the sight is gone.

He'd taken me for a ride on his bike yesterday and as I'd wrapped my arms around him, holding tight while he gunned it down a scenic highway, making me whoop with excitement, I'd known he had an amazing body, could feel the hard planes of his stomach, the dips and ridges of his abs. But *seeing* them is a whole different experience. I squeeze my thighs together as a big ole wave of lust rushes through me, both from the memory of being so close to him on the back of that bike, breathing him in as I leaned against his back, splaying my hands across his front, and from the way his stomach flexes now as he moves.

Yes, we are just friends, but there is no rule that says you can't have lusty thoughts about your friends. Where do you think the entire notion of friends-with-benefits came from? Not that there will be any benefits with Connor, but I'm not going to pretend he isn't sexy as all get out. I'm not naïve or delusional or blind.

He drops his shirt and I quickly yank my eyes upward. He thankfully doesn't seem to notice as he flops into the chair and points an accusatory finger at me.

"One: I am not a weakling. Two: you should know better than to issue a challenge to someone like me. And three: you owe me a fucking drink or twelve."

I blink several times and clear my throat lightly.

"Someone like you?"

"Someone whose job it is to be professionally competitive. I don't back down from a challenge, Mac. *Ever.* It goes against every fiber of my DNA. Whether it's hockey, quarters, or Pictionary, I'm in it to win it."

"So, what I'm hearin' is that game night will be *really* fun?" He huffs out a laugh and looks around the relatively sparse living room, slightly better now with the big chair to complement the old couch that the former owners had offered to leave behind.

"So, you like to read I take it?" He jerks his chin towards the shelves, filled to the brim with books.

"Just a bit." A lot. I read a book a week usually, sometimes more. I think half of the trailer on the way up here was book boxes. He runs the fingers of his left hand absently over the knuckles of his right, over the thick, dark metal rings he wears on his index and middle fingers. I don't know why, but everything about it is attractive: the tattoos, the rings, the gesture itself. I think I have a problem.

"I used to read all the time, but don't have much time to anymore." At my surprised look he says, "Yes, hockey players can read." I toss a throw pillow at him and he catches it easily, wrapping his arms around it and hugging it to his chest.

"What kind of stuff do you like?"

"Mostly fantasy, with a good crime thriller thrown in the mix every now and then."

"Really?" I say, brows rising in surprise. "I wouldn't have pegged you as a fantasy guy."

"Psh. Magic and dragons and vampires? Hell yeah." His lips curl upward into an amused grin. "Would it also surprise you to know that I was very big into D&D? Like... *very* big."

I grin. "You're just a big ole nerd, aren't you, Connor Shepherd?"

"Huge. And you think that's extremely sexy, don't you?"

I throw another pillow and he lets this one smack him in the face. "Shut up and come on then. I owe you a drink or twelve, remember? And I'm starving and there's football on. I'll show you what a *real* sport looks like." He narrows his eyes at me and I give him the sweetest smile I can muster.

"Come on, smart ass," he says, hoisting himself off the chair and tossing the pillows back at me in quick succession, "I know just the place."

Chapter Six

CONNOR

Being friends with Hattie is...interesting. It's great, don't get me wrong, but it's becoming harder than I thought it would to *only* want to be friends. We've hung out a few times and we text a good bit, though we still haven't shared anything super deep. I get the feeling that she's got something in her past that she's hiding. Or not hiding, exactly, but that she doesn't want to share just yet, like maybe she's ashamed of it or something. I'm not going to push. I haven't exactly shared all of my personal shit with her either, though I am starting to feel a little guilty about that, like I'm hiding something or keeping secrets. It isn't that, exactly, but some parts of my life I keep very, very private. But I know we'll get to the point of *really* sharing soon enough. It's all very new, but that connection is undeniable. She's already one of the first people I want to talk to every day or if I see a stupid meme, she's one of the first people I want to send it to.

I seriously love being around her. I feel like I don't have to try hard to be anyone but myself when I'm with her, like I can just be me, whoever that is. Sometimes I feel like I lose track of *me* with all the many hats I'm wearing these days, but I find it again when

I'm with Hattie, even just talking to her or texting each other stupid memes. It's easy and carefree.

And I think that *she* doesn't feel like she has to be on for me either, like she's just herself when we're together. Sometimes, it feels like women are being who they think I *want* them to be, or whoever they need to be for me to take them to bed, and that can get old pretty quick.

We opened the season a week ago to a completely packed house. I don't think anyone can deny that at least a part of that has to be due to Hattie. She's been working her ass off to turn everything with the organization around. Events, fan outreach, social media—everything you can think of. Almost every day she's set up outside the locker room with Nat and a camera and some kind of question for all of us to answer: what super power would we like to have; if we weren't hockey players, what would we want to be; who were our childhood crushes. Sometimes she throws in riddles or brain teasers just to make us sweat I think. It's made coming to practice even more fun and we all look forward to the *Mac Question of the Day*. The videos she posts of the answers all clipped together are great—and usually hilarious—and even I've made a point to get on social media to check them out.

We've had three more home games since the opener and Hattie's been at every one of them, always finding her way down to the glass instead of hanging out in one of the boxes up top, which always makes me smile. All of the guys absolutely love her and she's quickly become an unofficial part of the team, like a little sister or something almost.

One night after practice, me, Hattie, Nat, Rizz, Jules, and a handful of other guys go to a sports bar around the corner from the arena.

"Offsides is when the player crosses the blue line before the puck" Hattie says, a little haughtily, answering Rizzo's question. We've been quizzing her on the rules to help her really learn all the ins and outs of the game.

Rizz throws his hands up in triumph. "She can be taught!" Hattie tosses a fry at him but he merely picks it up and sticks it in his mouth, grinning at her.

"High-sticking," Jules says, chiming in.

"When one of y'all hauls off and whacks another one above the Mason-Dixon line like a heathen." We all laugh at that and she takes a little bow.

"Ok, ok, let's try a real test," I say over the rim of my glass, giving her a challenging look. She arches her brow, giving me one right back. "Rapid fire hockey slang."

Jules laughs. "Oh, this'll be fun."

"Psh, bring it on. I hear all y'all talking your ridiculous nonsense all the time. I got this."

"Says the girl who said something was *cattywompus* not five minutes ago." I give a pointed look. She rolls her eyes. "For every wrong answer, you take a drink," I say, upping the stakes.

"Bring it on, Shep."

"Alright. Sin Bin"

"Psh, that's easy. Penalty Box. Where most of y'all belong at all times, both on and off the ice, might I add."

Rizz raises his glass. "To the Vipers Sin Bin! May it ever be full of our depraved, sinning selves." His gaze lingers on Nat as he says it, eyes sparkling with obvious flirtation and invitation. He knows better than to go there, but he can't help flirting with anything with a pulse. We all raise our glasses and cheers, "hear hears!" ringing out around the table.

"I think we should get shirts made. Make it an official club," Hattie says, grinning. Another round of cheers to that idea, and I guess now our little group has now *officially* become the Vipers Sin Bin.

"Ok, ok: biscuit."

"Oh, the puck, right?" I nod and she grins.

"Barn."

"The rink." She gives a cocky waggle of her shoulders and I narrow my eyes, bumping Jules with my shoulder, telling him we need to up the ante here. "I thought this was supposed to be hard?"

"Alright, hot shot: Gongshow," Jules offers, crossing his hands over his chest.

"Uhhh...shit." She takes a drink and we all boo. She tells us to fuck off and then waves on for the next one.

"Chicklets."

She scrunches her nose. "Gum?" She ducks her head and takes another drink. "Oh wait no! It's teeth right?! That doesn't count! I got that one!" We all laugh and keep up the game.

"Facewash!"

"Yard sale!"

"Beaver Tap!"

Hattie sets her beer down after her third drink. "Alright, ain't no way these are all real hockey terms. Y'all are makin' shit up." Her accent gets a little thicker the more she drinks and I'm not the only one who notices.

"Ain't no way, huh? Dart tootin'!" Bobby says mockingly and Hattie shoves him playfully in the shoulder. I've never really talked to Bobby before tonight, but I like him a lot. He's down to earth and seems like a really good dude.

"You hush your mouth, Bobby Hastings."

"Puck Bunny," I say, continuing the game.

"Oh that's easy: the things Rizzo likes to stick his dick in!"

We all bust out laughing at that and declare it a correct answer. Rizzo looks mildly offended for half a second but then shrugs, knowing it's damn well true. His eyes cut to Nat for the briefest of moments but he quickly yanks his gaze back to Hattie, raising his glass her way.

"Touche," he says, inclining his head.

"Ok, but seriously, I'm gonna need a list of all these or something,[2]" Hattie says, downing the rest of her drink.

One afternoon a few days later, she and Nat come down to run through some upcoming events with us, getting volunteers and whatnot. There's a Halloween trick-or-treating thing this weekend and a few other fall-type things, and though it's still over a month away, a handful of the things she's asking about are Christmas related. Which reminds me of her strange hatred of the holiday.

"Are you going to this thing tomorrow?" she asks, waving the flyer for a Halloween party at one of the bars downtown that Rizz and a bunch of the guys are going to.

"Nah, how about you?"

She hikes a shoulder. "Maybe. If Nat or Bobby are going, I might tag along. I'll have to figure out a costume quick, fast, and in a hurry though."

---

[2] A glossary of hockey slang can be found in the back of this book

"You can never go wrong with a naughty school girl. Just throwing it out there," I say with a grin and she smirks.

"Well, good thing I already have the plaid skirt and crop top then." I clench my jaw at the picture of Hattie channeling her inner Britney Spears and quickly shove the image away. I lean my forearms on the edge of the wall and she does the same from the other side.

"So, are we officially ask-deep-personal-questions-friends status yet?"

She watches as some of the guys fuck around on the ice, just being stupid. "I'll never understand how y'all do that," she says, shaking her head.

"Do what?"

"Skate like that. Or in general I guess."

My eyes fly wide. "You've never skated before? Like *ever?*"

"Oh, right, act *soooo* surprised that a girl from southern Louisiana hasn't strapped knives to her feet and yee-hawed around on fuckin' *ice*," she says dryly, giving me one of those looks of hers that says *bless your heart* (which she's explained is southern for *you're an idiot*).

I chuckle but don't let her derail my thoughts completely. "Ok, so we're coming back to this skating topic later, but answer the other question."

"Oh sorry. Umm, yeah I guess so...Why?" She eyes me warily.

"Well, if we're that kind of friends now, I was going to ask you to explain your hatred of my favorite holiday."

She lets out a long breath, as if she's relieved, like she was dreading me asking something else. I wonder what she doesn't want me to dig into.

"It's not really the holiday that I hate, but it's gotten wrapped up in my annoyance with this time of year, so now Christmas as a whole equals shit for me." I furrow my brow. She studies me for a long moment, absently twirling a lock of hair around her finger, as if deliberating if she's going to explain. Finally, she decides to share.

"For almost my entire life, bad things always happen to me in December. More accurately, within a week or so of Christmas."

I narrow my eyes at her. "Seriously?"

"Seriously," she says with a hard nod.

"But...surely not *that* much could have all gone wrong in that one particular week. Not enough to make you hate the entire thing."

She leans forward to lean her own arms on the wall beside mine, a spark of challenge in her blue eyes that's admittedly...sexy. I like challenge. I like games and competition. I like being pushed and pushing back, especially in certain areas that involve very little clothing...I shake myself inwardly, not letting my mind wander in that direction.

"When I was four, our house caught fire two days before Christmas. The next year, our dog died on Christmas day. When I was seven, we were in a car wreck. The next year, my dad walked out on us—literally went out for "milk for Santa" on Christmas Eve and never came back. What a fucking cliché right?" She shakes her head and rolls her eyes flippantly, but I can see the flash of pain there even after all these years. "Flat tires, missed flights, break ups, stitches twice, food poisoning once. I was even mugged by a guy dressed as Santa." Before I can protest that she has got to be kidding on that one, she raises her right palm. "Hand on the Bible, Jolly Old St. Nick stole my purse."

My jaw hangs open in shock. How could one person have such impossibly bad luck? She smirks a little, like she just won this little game.

"See. Christmas and I are not on speaking terms. I don't have a problem with anyone *else* enjoying the holiday—though when people decorate before Thanksgiving, that does overcook my grits a bit—but over the years the entire thing just got too wrapped up in all my bad memories and now, I just want to get through December in once piece and pretend Christmas doesn't exist."

"That...I honestly don't even know what to say to all of that. I've never met anyone who truly hated Christmas before. Even the Grinch comes around at the end!" She laughs lightly.

"Why do you love it so much?"

"Well," I say, thinking about it seriously, "I suppose for the opposite reasons you hate it. Take all of your bad memories, and replace them with amazing ones. That's my experience with Christmas. It's always been...magical for me. I know that sounds stupid and cliché and whatever else, but it's true. Our family always made a huge deal out of it. It was the only time of year we got to see my grandparents because they lived in Italy—grandpa was a teacher there and grandma's family owned a vineyard—but they *always* made the trip for Christmas, so the entire family came together from all across the country at my uncle's cabin up in the mountains in Colorado. The pond out back is where I learned to skate, we would all go sledding and have epic snowball fights, we'd make cookies, my mom would constantly be singing Christmas carols under her breath while she was doing damn near anything, like she didn't even realize she was doing it..." I trail off when I catch her look. She's staring at me with an odd expression that I can't quite decipher. "And I'm going to shut up now," I finish, rubbing a hand over the back of my neck, a little embarrassed.

"No, that all sounds...it sounds really nice." She sounds sincere, but also so wistful, like she wants those memories to be her own so badly she nearly aches. It tugs at something in my chest uncomfortably. I make a decision, quick and fast, like most of my decisions. I'm known for being a bit impulsive. Not reckless, exactly, but I don't take a long time to deliberate on things. I see the options in front of me and make a choice, simple as that.

And then I follow through on that choice, no matter what.

"Well, that's that then. I've officially made it my mission to make this Christmas your first good one."

She snorts. "Good luck with that."

"I'm serious. I'm going to fill this holiday season with so many great memories, you and Santa will be besties by New Year's Eve."

"You seem very sure of yourself," she says, a hint of a smile on her lips.

"Oh I am. Haven't you heard? All hockey players are cocky assholes." She huffs out a laugh and then eyes me in that way that tells me she's studying me, her wheels turning and burning in that head of hers.

"Alright, my turn for a personal question then."

"I suppose that's fair."

"You said you were a reformed playboy." I nod. "So, why the change? I've seen the women at the games and the ones who a lot of the guys end up leaving with. I've seen some of the comments on social media posts." She doesn't sound bitter or jealous the way some girls would, just matter of fact and maybe even a little amused. "So, why did you decide to stop...indulging?"

Before I can answer, Coach calls my name, beckoning with a raised hand.

"I gotta go. I'll tell you more about it later, but the main gist is that that life just wasn't for me anymore."

She looks a little skeptical, but nods and waves as I skate away. I wonder what she thinks about it. Is she asking just out of curiosity or because she's interested in something more than friendship and wants to be sure I'm not really that guy anymore? I'm not going to push anything with Hattie, I'm going to let her take the lead here and I'll be good with whatever she wants because I'm already loving having her in my life as a friend. If it stays that way, I'll be alright, though a part of me will always wonder.

I'd be lying if I didn't want her physically. *Dear God* do I want her physically. I think about it way more often than I should, think about all the different ways I could take her, the different things I could do to make her squirm and moan and scream. I let myself daydream about what she might like, what might drive her wild. I have my ideas, and it's rare that someone surprises me in that regard, but I feel like if anyone could do it, it would be Hattie McNamara.

But until she decides otherwise, we'll remain just friends.

Chapter Seven

HATTIE

One of the best perks about working for the Vipers, other than getting paid to hang around with and film a bunch of ridiculously attractive hockey players, of course, is the gym. It's as big as an entire Fitness World, but nicer than any gym I've ever been to in my life. Every machine is top of the line and in pristine condition, the convenience of it being in the same building as my office is aces, and somehow, despite a bunch of hockey players using it every day, it doesn't smell like Eau De Sweaty Dude. So, bottom line: it's awesome.

There are times when it's reserved for the team, but any others, it's open for any staff member of the organization to use. I head down late in the afternoon for my daily workout, waving to the handful of players that are here. They have their own time, but a few always end up coming in again for a second workout of the day. I guess when you're literally paid to be in good shape, you take it pretty seriously. I'm slightly hung-over still from the Halloween party the night before, but I'm still going to force myself to run. Or maybe jog. Or possibly just walk.

The party had been pretty fun actually and I'm glad I went, though I admittedly wish that Connor had been there. I drunk texted him a few times, but thankfully nothing too crazy. Mostly talking about the costumes and giving him a play-by-play on all of the girls competing for Rizzo's attentions throughout the night. He'd left with three of them in tow—a slutty nurse, a slutty pirate, and a slutty Tootsie Roll (which, why is that even a thing??)—and I'd be lying if I wasn't insanely curious as to how that particular configuration worked once they got wherever they were going.

I make my way towards the treadmills sitting in front of the floor-to-ceiling screens. The sections in front of each treadmill can be changed to a different scene, so you get the feeling that you're actually outside running on the beach or through the woods or up a mountain or whatever you want. It's pretty freaking cool. Though I prefer running outside, my lungs do *not* love running in the cold, so for now, this will do. Plus, I can pretend I'm back running the beaches along the Gulf.

I slow my steps as I get closer and see a little girl sitting on a bench nearby, reading a book. It's refreshing to see a kid actually reading and not just playing on a tablet, but I'm a little confused on why she's sitting in here alone. I'm sure she's somebody's daughter and they're just in the bathroom or something, but I've always loved kids and want to be sure she's ok, so I approach her.

"Hi," I say, giving her a warm smile.

She looks up from her book, big golden-brown eyes meeting mine, and smiles back. Her light brown hair is in two French braids that I'm honestly a bit jealous of: mine never come out that straight and smooth—with a cat-ears headband. She's wearing a NASA t-shirt with a glittery tutu skirt over bright purple leggings, and pink Converse All Stars. Basically, she's the cutest kid I've ever seen in my life.

"Hi," she says back, voice high and sweet. "I'm Ollie."

"That's a pretty name. I'm Hattie."

"I have a doll named Hattie!" she says excitedly, grinning widely and showing off a missing tooth. "Or, well, I used to. I kind of played mud fight with her and, uh, I think she got buried out there." She looks thoughtful for a minute and then shrugs. I think she must be seven or eight and is utterly adorable. "My *real* name is Olivia, but everyone calls me Ollie."

"Well, it's nice to meet you, Ollie. Whatcha readin'?" She turns the book towards me so I can see the cover and I grin. "That's one of my favorite books!" I tell her, a vivid memory of my mom reading *Matilda* to me in the hammock by the pond slamming into me like a sledgehammer. It's a good memory, but it makes me suddenly miss my mom so much it makes my chest ache. My nose burns as tears threaten, but I push them away. It's like that sometimes, even though she's been gone for almost six years now. I'll be fine and a memory will rear up and nearly drop me to my knees. People always say that time heals all wounds, but I don't think that's true. I think time just gives you the opportunity to learn how to live with them, to learn to survive around the pain.

"I was actually Matilda for book character day at school three years in a row when I was a kid," I tell her.

"I was the mouse who eats the cookies last year. I got to wear overalls. But this year, I'm definitely going to be Matilda!"

I grin at her and glance around. No one is paying us much attention or acting like she's theirs, so I still don't know who she is.

"Who do you belong to? Is your mom or dad here with you?"

"Oh, I'm just waiting for my uncle." She glances past me and grins widely. "There he is! Uncle Con! She knows Matilda!"

I turn to find Connor striding over, hair damp and leaving wet spots on the shoulders of his gray shirt. He smiles at her as he approaches us and it's a new smile, one I've never seen before. His entire face lights up, eyes sparkling with deep and unbending emotion. He obviously loves this kid more than just about anything on the planet.

"Is that right?" he asks, looking at me as Ollie stands up on the bench, poised to leap. Connor doesn't take his eyes off of me as she jumps and he catches her easily, swooping her up and settling her on his shoulders in one practiced, fluid movement that they've obviously done a thousand times.

"Yep!" Ollie says before giggling. "Your hair is dripping on me." Connor winks at me and then shakes his head like a dog, flinging water on all three of us. I yelp and Ollie giggles even more, that great peeling laughter that kids have.

He maneuvers her off of his shoulders and leans down to stage whisper, "I think I saw Uncle Rizzo heading this way with donuts." Ollie lets out a squeal of excitement and bolts from the gym. I get the feeling that she's quite at home here and knows her way around, and she apparently knows Rizzo enough to call him *Uncle* too. Connor must babysit her a lot or something. He hasn't mentioned having family in Seattle, and, I realize now, I haven't ever asked. Now I kind of feel like a bad friend.

"So, she's as cute as a bug's ear." He arches a blonde brow and I laugh. "She's about the cutest thing in the universe," I clarify.

"That she is," he agrees easily. He's still staring towards the door, but finally turns to meet my gaze. "You asked me why I stopped with the random hook ups and partying and being a playboy and all of that? She's why." I frown, not quite understanding. "She lives with me. I—" He cuts off as he turns to see Ollie sprinting back into the room, face covered in the remains of a chocolate donut, Rizzo trailing behind her. My eyes are wide in surprise. She *lives* with him? Like, full time? Does his sister or brother live with him too, then? Is this a temporary situation? Are they ok? I have so many questions.

"Need a spotter, Mac?" Rizzo asks with a waggle of his brows as he saunters up to us.

"Can we get pizza for dinner?" Ollie asks and Connor laughs, that half-indulgent, half-exasperated laugh that parents do. I'm still so confused, and it must be plain on my face.

"Uh, would you like to have pizza with us tonight?" Connor asks, telling me without words that he'll explain everything over dinner. "What do you think, Olls? Can my friend Mac here come to dinner?"

"Yes! Please, Hattie? We can finish *Matilda*!" Her tiny brow furrows. "Wait, why do they keep calling you Mac?"

I laugh. "Because hockey players are silly and think everyone needs a nickname." She considers that for a second, her little face serious as she contemplates my statement, weighs it over.

"They are silly," she agrees. "But I like Mac. It's like mac-and-cheese, which is my second favorite food. No wait—*third*. First is pizza, then dino nuggets, *then* mac-and-cheese. Anyway, will you come have pizza with us? I only like cheese, but we can get pepperoni if you want."

"Uh..." I glance up at Connor, trying to read him, but I'm too curious to pass up the invitation. "Sure, I'd love to."

"Sounds good. Our place around 7? I'll text you the address." He plucks Ollie's headband off and puts it on his head, and she giggles like a hyena as she jumps up trying to get it back. I can't help but laugh. Connor winks. "Enjoy your workout. See ya, Riz."

Ollie says her goodbyes and the two of them leave the gym, Ollie skipping and hopping like a little puppy, gesturing wildly with her hands as she tells Connor something.

"Talk about being wrapped around a little finger," Rizzo says after they're gone. I turn to him, questions ready to fly off my tongue, but, in a rare moment of seriousness, he holds up a hand. "It's not my story to tell, but he'll fill you in at dinner I'm sure. He's pretty private about that side of his life. I mean, all the guys know Ollie, of course, but not many others. You should feel honored that he's letting you into that part of his world." He studies me for a long second, seeming like he's going to say something more, but then changes his mind, his customary rakish grin back in place and the levity back in his tone. "So, about that spotter..."

·.··.·*

Connor's house is a gorgeous farmhouse-style nestled back among a thick forest right on the lake. It's large, but not obscenely so like you might expect a professional athlete's house to be, and sits on what must be at least a few acres. The long driveway serpentines gracefully through the trees, a stone bridge arching over a small creek, before opening up to a wide front parking area. A four-car detached garage sits off to the right and I spy at least three motorcycles and a jacked-up jeep inside through the open doors. The country girl in me instantly wants to take that beast muddin'.

A wide lawn stretches to the left of the house, the trees surrounding the edges protectively, with a giant playset in the middle along with a trampoline. The door opens just as I put the car in park and Ollie sprints across the wide front porch and down the stairs.

"Hi Mac-and-Cheese!" she says, grinning, her tongue stained purple from a popsicle or lollipop.

"Ollie! Your coat!" Connor shouts as he walks out onto the porch, holding up a purple jacket. I wave and smile.

"Come on, I'll show you my room!" Ollie says, tugging me forward by the hand. She doesn't slow, and I give Connor a quick *hey* before I'm yanked through the door. I'm immediately enveloped in warmth as we step foot inside. A roaring fire crackles in the over-sized fireplace, giving the whole house that amazing real burning wood smell that I've quickly become obsessed with since moving here. I think it reminds me a bit of the big bonfires we used to have back home growing up and just makes me feel safe and happy.

The living room is open to the kitchen, a large island dominating the space, and dark, exposed beams run along the high, steepled ceiling. An open stairway leads up to a loft-type space that overlooks the living area. The back wall of the living room is all windows, and over-sized glass doors open onto a wide wooden deck. A few hundred yards of manicured lawn sit between the deck and the lake, snow-capped mountains in the distance. It's idyllic, like something out of a magazine or movie.

The living room is clean, but not spotless, which I like. There are toys and coloring books here and there, a stuffed dragon sitting on the coffee table, and a zip-up hoodie thrown over the back of the couch. It's homey and gorgeous and I immediately feel comfortable. It's masculine, with lots of dark wood and leather furniture, but not overly so. The perfect mix of rustic and chic, and I wonder if Connor paid someone to come in and decorate, or if this is all him.

Connor trails after us as Ollie leads me down a hallway to the right of the living room.

"Ollie," he says semi-sternly, though his tone is full of affection, "we don't man-handle our guests."

"Oh," she says a little sheepishly. "Sorry." She drops my hand and holds hers behind her back.

"It's ok," I assure her. "Can I still see your room?" Her eyes light up and she nods enthusiastically, skipping down the hall to the open door at the end.

Connor sighs. "Sorry. She gets a little excited around new people, especially new people who love *Matilda*. Can I get you a drink?"

"Yeah, that would be great. Whatever you have is fine."

He nods and takes my coat, heading back down the hallway. Ollie spends the next few minutes showing off her room and small attached playroom, which are admittedly pretty awesome. It's an eclectic mix of princesses and dinosaurs and glitter, and seems to suit her personality to a T. After all the proper *oohs* and *aahs*, we head back into the living room where Connor is waiting. He hands me a beer with an apologetic look, but I shoo him away, letting him know that I'm fine. I love it, actually. In another life, I think I would have wanted to be a kindergarten teacher.

"Hey Olls, how about you color Mac a picture for her office at work?"

"Oooohhh I know just what to draw!"

She shoots off down the hall, emerging a few seconds later with a stack of paper and two tubs full of crayons, markers, and colored pencils. She settles in at the kitchen table and Connor nods towards the living room. I shuck off my boots and tuck my legs beneath me as I sink into the couch. He sits beside me, a little bit of a space between us. He eyes Ollie over the back of the couch for a minute before turning back to me.

"My sister died three years ago," he says, diving right in. My eyes widen in surprise, a small gasp escaping my lips. I reach out, settling a hand on his forearm.

"Oh God, Shep, I'm so sorry."

He nods his head in that way that everyone does after they've lost someone. The nod that says *thanks* and *it's alright*, even if it isn't, but what else can you do or say? I did the nod too many times to count after I'd lost my mom.

"She was sick—cancer—but it went really fast. So, she had enough time to plan, but not nearly enough to help any of us get used to the idea of being without her. Ollie's dad died overseas when she was just a baby. Hannah and I had always been close—Irish Twins," he adds with a smile, "almost exactly twelve months apart, and I've been lost for Ollie from the second I saw her in the hospital the night she was born, so I didn't think twice about agreeing to take her after...after Hannah was gone." He takes a deep breath before continuing and I remain quiet, letting him take all the time he needs. My heart hurts for him, but I'm so glad he's sharing this with me. According to Rizzo, he doesn't do it often.

"Ollie was barely four when Hannah passed. I don't think she remembers much, not really, but we talk about Hannah a lot and I show her pictures and videos to help keep her mom here with us as much as possible, ya know?" I nod. "I officially adopted her about a year ago. Her aunt and grandparents on her dad's side live here in Seattle. They're still very much in her life and help me out with her so much with my schedule. Anytime we have away games, she stays with them, and they watch her while I'm at practice or whatever. They're great people and very much part of my family, regardless of the lack of blood between us. I'm *really* lucky."

I glance over the back of the couch to where Ollie has her head bent over the paper, tongue sticking out to one side in concentration as she draws. Looking back to Connor, I tell him honestly, "So is she."

He lets out a long sigh and runs a hand through his hair. "Thanks. It's not easy, I won't lie about that, but she's the absolute best kid. I know every parent says that about their kid, but she really, really is. She's smart and sweet and funny. She's already been through way more than any kid should ever have to go through, but she's so strong. She's goofy as all hell, has energy for days that I need to find a way to bottle for myself or sell online, but she's the best thing that's ever happened to me." The smile on his face makes my heart clench. It's an absent-minded smile, the kind that shows up when you talk about something you love without even realizing it.

He pulls his gaze back to me again. "So, yeah. You asked what stopped me from...*indulging* in the perks," he says with a crooked grin, "Ollie happened. I couldn't be living that life anymore, not with a four-year-old to take care of. When it all first happened, I was kind of just drowning. Everything was kind of like one crazy, chaotic fever dream. I buried my sister—my *best friend*—and became a dad all at once, and though I'd been around as the fun uncle for her whole life, being a full-time dad was completely different. I had no idea what I was doing. At first, I kept up my same old shit, but I remember the exact moment when I knew I had to change. I was lying in bed next to some girl at a hotel in Denver and it hit me: I was a *father* now. Maybe not by blood, but Ollie would be my daughter in all the ways that mattered for the rest of my life. I knew she deserved better than that, knew that I needed to be a better man if I was going to be a real dad to this kid, the kind of dad mine was for us. And so I became one," he says with a hike of his shoulder.

I know I'm staring at him, but I can't help it. *Dear God, Connor Shepherd really is one of the good ones.* Hearing him talk about Ollie, seeing his obvious love for her, hearing him talk about needing to be a better man so he could be a good father to her? Well, my ovaries practically explode. As someone who has always loved kids, who desperately wants a family of my own someday...and who's ex-boyfriend's response to my miscarriage was *thank fucking God*—yeah, it's impossible not to fall a little bit in love with Connor today.

Our gazes hold for a long minute and something starts to build between us, something forceful and heady and dangerous. His eyes seem to darken as I watch, the gold standing out brightly against the green like a flame in the forest. They dart downward, staring at my lips as they part on a soft inhale. My pulse races and my chest feels heavy and hot. I need him to stop staring at my lips. I need him to stop looking at me like he wants to shift forward and press his own to mine. I need him to stop looking so good and smelling so good and being practically perfect. *I need to say fuck it and just grab the front of his shirt and yank him to me, make him show me if he can live up to all of my fantasies.*

My fingers actually flex in my lap in anticipation, but just before I can do anything stupid, the doorbell rings. I actually jump in surprise, barely stifling a yelp. I take a shuddering breath and a slow smile curls his lips upward as he lets out a long exhale.

"Pizza!!" Ollie screams, leaping up from her chair and running for the front door. Connor and I both laugh a bit, the strange spell that had been trying to work its magic over us broken. He rises from the couch to get the door, but my hand snakes out and grabs his wrist, halting him. There's something I need to say, that I need him to know.

"You're a good man, Shep." He holds my gaze for an endless moment, but eventually nods, giving me a heart-stopping smile.

"I made you fall in love with me a bit just now, didn't I?"

I release his arm and grab a pillow, whacking him in the chest. "No one likes you."

"Everyone loves me."

"Hurry uppppp," Ollie begs from the front door, apparently knowing she isn't allowed to answer the door herself. Connor chuckles and heads to get the food.

The rest of the night is filled with pizza, ice cream, fort building, and me reading *Matilda* to the rapt audience of Ollie, Connor, and about fifteen stuffed animals. Ollie eventually falls asleep in the make-shift tent, the stuffed dragon—who I'd learned was named Pickles even though he was purple, not green—clutched in her arms.

"Should we try to move her?" I whisper as Connor helps me to my feet after I climb out of the fort.

"Nah, she's ok for now. I'll crash on the couch and move her if she wakes up during the night."

He walks me to the car, and I shiver against the bitter cold. The temperature has been dropping steadily and I wonder if I'll see my first real snow soon. I can't decide if I'm excited or not.

"Hey, do you have plans for Thanksgiving?"

"Oh," I say surprised. I haven't really thought about it honestly. I've been so focused on all of the crazy things coming up for work and the start of my nemesis of a month, that I kind of forgot Thanksgiving was even a thing. It hasn't really been a big deal for me in a while, not since my mom died. Josh didn't really have a family unit either, so his idea of thanksgiving was getting drunk and watching football at the sports bar up the street that always stayed open on the holiday. His mom had left when he was a kid, and his father had been one of those rich dads that just threw nannies and money at his son, hoping that he miraculously became a semi-functioning human at some point. His dad traveled a ton for business—on his private jet, of course—and only saw Josh maybe once a month, at least before he sent him off to boarding school. Then it was maybe two or three times *a year*, at most. So, yeah, Josh had been all too happy to ignore the traditional family holidays with me. I almost snort with a humorless laugh— it had been one of the many reasons I thought he was perfect for me.

"I hadn't really thought about it," I tell him, honestly.

"Well, you're welcome to join us if you'd like." I open my mouth to respond, then close it. Would that be weird? Would it seem too much like a girlfriend thing, not a friend thing? Somehow knowing the exact direction of my thoughts, he adds, "A few guys on the team are coming too. The ones who don't really have family or can't travel home or have no idea what Thanksgiving even really is. We're introducing turkey and pumpkin pie to Roman and Nowski" Seeing the big Russians' reactions to a traditional American thanksgiving feast is just too enticing to pass up.

"I'd love to, yeah. What can I bring?"

"Sedatives for Mowser. He likes to do karaoke when he gets into the wine and he can't carry a tune in a dump truck." I laugh at the image. "You don't need to bring anything." I begin to protest, but he stops me, "But I know that you're not going to accept that." We both smile. He already knows me so well. "So, bring whatever you'd like, whatever your family liked to have. We can never have enough food with these guys around."

I nod and head home. It's still a few weeks away, but I'm excited for my first real Thanksgiving in years, my first Thanksgiving with my new friends who are quickly becoming family.

Chapter Eight

CONNOR

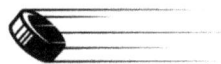

"Come on in!" I yell from the kitchen, though I'm not sure whoever is at the door can hear me over the dance party happening in my living room. Ollie has Hannah Montana blaring from the speakers and four of the guys from the team dancing along with her obediently.

"When she has yellow hair, she is Hannah?" Nowski yells over the music to Mowser. "But she is same person as with brown hair, but has different name? Is she spy? This is children's show?"

Ollie giggles at his accent and jumps on the couch, singing at the top of her lungs in a terrible off-key wail. It's a good thing she's adorable.

"Quite the party," Hattie says, entering the kitchen. I spin and smile, noticing the huge banker's box in her arms. I quickly lay my knife down on the cutting board and rush towards her.

"Here, let me help you with that." I grab the box, quirking a brow in question. "Are you moving in or..."

I set it down and she takes the top off, smacking me in the back of the head with it.

"You said you can never have too much food, so..." She shrugs. I lean over the now open box and inhale deeply, moaning. I can't tell exactly what it is since the dishes inside are all covered, but whatever it is smells *amazing*. When she offered to cook some "real southern food" for us, I didn't envision all of this. "I made biscuits and gravy, dumplins, green bean casserole, and biscuits—all my mamaw's recipes." My mouth waters.

"Marry me. Marry me right now."

She laughs and calls me an idiot, and I grin as I swat her shoulder with a dishrag. Things have been great the last few weeks, and we've gotten really close. It was like once I dropped the Ollie-Bomb, whatever small wall had remained between us disintegrated. We've hung out almost every day, I've shown her the sights—including the tourist attractions, as promised—and we've finally gotten her house completely put together. I dutifully put together four new bookshelves for her office upstairs and they're already almost completely full since I showed her this awesome independent new and used bookstore not far from her place.

The owner literally had to find boxes for us to carry out to the car for everything Hattie bought. *Boxes*. Plural. But my God the way her entire face had lit up as she wandered the shelves, trailing her fingers over the spines, handing me book after book after book to hold—it was amazing. Getting to watch someone love something in a totally unfiltered, uninhibited way is rare and a gift, and I'm grateful that I was able to see it.

"Oh! What if we did a book drive at the arena? For a local school or library?" she'd said, eyes wide with excitement as we'd driven back to her place. "If you bring a new or gently-used book to donate, you get like $10 off admission or something."

"I think that would be amazing," I told her honestly, loving that her mind was always working, always thinking of ways to not only help our organization, but to help the community as well. She'd already gotten tons of charity stuff set up, we'd put on a free hockey camp for underprivileged kids, some of us had helped rebuild a community center, and we'd just got done with a huge free thanksgiving dinner event in the parking lot of the arena yesterday where most of the team handed out meals.

So, she'd run with the idea and next week, we're having the first annual Vipers' Book-A-Thon. She somehow credited me with helping her come up with it, though I literally did nothing, but I wasn't going to complain about the giant hug she gave me in thanks. So, yeah, things have been awesome with us.

I'd honestly been a little nervous that the moment on the couch that night had spooked Hattie. Hell, it spooked me a bit. I'm good with us being friends, know that it's probably the smartest choice given the circumstances, but in that moment, I'd wanted nothing more than to pull her to me and press my lips to hers, to settle her over my lap and run my fingers through her hair, to feel her body against mine.

And it wasn't just the physical need that rode me in that moment, it was the intense connection between us. It was like talking to my oldest friend in the world, I felt so at ease and comfortable and I actually thought *this. This is how it's supposed to be. This is what I've been missing*.

Not that I feel like my life is *lacking*. I'm well aware of just how lucky and blessed I am. I get to play the game I love and make decent money doing it. I have brothers in all of my teammates, brothers I would fight to the ends of the Earth for. I have the best kid in the world and an amazing support system.

But sometimes, I do feel like something's missing, that a piece of the puzzle is still out of place. I'm not lonely exactly, but that's about as close as I can get to describing it. I want someone to share moments with, someone who can be a part of this life with me, be a partner, a *true* partner, having my back and being strong when I can't be. I've broken down alone in my room more than once since the day Hannah died. Sitting on the edge of my bed with my head in my hands, just breaking apart because I wasn't sure if I could do it all, wasn't sure how in the fuck I was supposed to raise a kid and be the star goalie and keep everything together. It's hard. Really fucking hard. Worth it, of course. A thousand percent worth it. I don't regret taking Ollie in for a second, but anyone who thinks that becoming a father overnight is easy is smoking the good shit.

So, yeah, sometimes I think it would be nice to have someone there with me through all this shit. And I can't say I haven't thought about Hattie in that way since we started hanging out, but I don't want to push things. She's quickly become one of my closest friends and one of the most important people in my life, and I would never want to risk that.

"Oh and pie!" she cries. "I made pies. There's another box still out in the car."

"I'll go get that, you relax. Sara!" I call and when she turns, I jerk my head in a beckoning gesture. She heads over, eyes widening ever so slightly as she looks at Hattie. I don't blame her—Hattie looks amazing in dark jeans, a deep orange sweater, and her hair in long, loose curls. She got it colored last week, bringing out the natural red within the brown a bit more. She'd teased me for even noticing until I reminded her that I grew up with a sister who was basically attached to my hip. If I hadn't noticed Hannah's new haircut or color or makeup routine, she would haul off and slug me—and she could fucking *hit*. She grew up on the ice right beside me, playing with the boys. She was tough as nails. So, I learned to pay attention. Plus, my dad taught me to notice things like that, to be a real gentleman—*off* the ice. On the ice, he taught me to be a holy terror and take no prisoners. *Life is all about balance.*

Sara mouths *wow* at me as she approaches and I try to hide my smile. "Sara, this is Hattie. She's the Assistant Director of Marketing and Media for the Vipers. Hattie, this is Sara, Ollie's aunt."

"It's nice to meet you," Hattie says, grinning.

"You too, Connor has been talking about you nonstop." She grins and I roll my eyes. "Assistant Director of whositwhatsit sounds very fancy and important."

Hattie laughs. "No, it's not that big a deal—"

"Yes, it is," I cut in. "Don't let her downplay it. She's the one responsible for getting attendance up at the games and making everyone love us."

"Well, that is quite the feat—they're all a bunch of overgrown idiots, really." Hattie snorts and I flip them both off.

"Sara, will you get Hattie a drink? I'm gonna grab the pies from the car."

Sara's eyes light up. "Pies? Tell me more about these pies..." she says as she loops her arm through Hattie's and the two of them head to the wet bar on the other side of the living room.

I chuckle as I leave them to grab the other box from outside. I'm so glad Hattie decided to come, and when I walk back inside, she's across the room talking to Ollie's grandparents, and everyone is all smiles. I have one of those moments then as I take in the scene. All of it: the dance party, the laughter, the smiles. My heart is so fucking full I can barely stand it. How the hell did I get so lucky to deserve all of this?

I honestly don't know but I thank God for it every damn day.

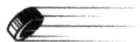

December is officially here, so I am now fully focused on my plan to make Hattie love Christmas. Ok, maybe not *love*. I don't think one great December can erase all of the terrible ones she's experienced before, but I can sure as shit give her some good memories to battle against the bad. And I'm not above using a seven-year-old to do it.

"Mac-and-Cheese!" Ollie cries as we walk through the corridor towards the locker rooms. She drops my hand and sprints towards Hattie, who holds out her arms, waiting for Ollie to leap into them. I grin when Hattie lifts her up, spins her around, and then sets her back down so they can perform their official Super Cool Best Buds Club handshake. Take one guess who named the club.

"Ok, seriously, if you don't ask her out soon, I'm going to," Sara says, watching the two of them cackle as they screw up the handshake over and over. Just like everyone seems to do almost instantly, Sara had fallen completely in love with Hattie at Thanksgiving. Sara just broke up with her long-time girlfriend and has no idea how to be single, so she's only half joking when she talks about asking Hattie out.

"Go for it," I said breezily. "As long as I can watch."

She shoves me playfully. "Pervert." She shifts her gaze back to Hattie, letting her eyes travel down Hattie's lean body and back up again. Hattie's in an emerald green v-neck sweater and skintight jeans that look far too good on her, and I'm not about to lie and say that I don't take an extra second to check out her ass in the damn things. *Mercy.* Sara sighs. "Though we could make a *killing* with a For-the-Fans account..."

I promptly shut out any images *that* particular statement tries to conjure to mind before I have to adjust myself, and we join Ollie and Hattie.

"Mac, you remember Sara."

"Of course I do," she says with a roll of her eyes that only makes Sara smile wider. "How's your momma an' 'em?" Hattie asks. God help me, I love when her southern comes out in full force. It's so incredibly sexy for some reason. Don't ask me to explain. Her *y'alls* and *darlins* and thousands of other little southern idioms have a direct line to my cock. Maybe it goes back to my crush on Daisy Duke as a kid? Who the fuck knows. And I'm not the only one—Sara had made Hattie say "pee-can pie" about a hundred times at Thanksgiving until Hattie couldn't breathe from laughing so hard.

The two of them catch up for a second before I nudge Ollie and give her a meaningful look, reminding her of our plan. Her eyes widen in excitement.

"We're getting our Christmas tree this week!" she announces to Hattie.

"Oh wow, that sounds awesome!" Hattie says, matching Ollie's enthusiasm. "Like a *real* tree? From a lot?"

"Yeah! But not from a lot, from the *forest*! Uncle Con chops it down himself with a big axe, and then we strap it to the car and we drive it home and decorate it with all these really pretty decorations that we bought at the store and some that I made at school and like a *million* lights and we listen to music and make cookies and will you come??"

It takes Hattie a minute to catch up with all the rapid-fire information Ollie just threw at her—all in a single breath, I might add—but then her eyes widen in surprise.

"Pleaseeeeee?" Ollie begs. Literally, hands together at her chest, puppy dog eyes, the whole shebang. Hattie looks at me, giving me a suspicious half-glare, but I merely grin.

"You can't say no to that, come on." I point to Ollie who's still playing the adorable beggar. "I told you I don't take challenges lightly. I'm pulling out all the stops on destroying Dreaded December." She glances back to Ollie and sighs.

"I would love to come."

"Yay!!!!"

"Ok, I think Uncle Con needs to get ready for the game. Come on, I'll get you some cotton candy—get you all sugared up for Aunt Sara," she says with a wink at Sara. I watch as the three of them go, and that feeling of completeness settles in my chest again. *My family*, I think. *That's my family walking away.* Then I shake myself, realize I'm a fucking idiot, and head into the locker room.

"Oh my God, it's huge!" Hattie says in awe, staring up at the tree that Ollie picked. The one I'm about to fell with my axe in one mighty chop. Or well, in a few mighty chops probably.

"That's what she said," I say with a smirk, gesturing for her to step back.

Hattie quirks a brow. "Really? That's not what I hear, darlin'..."

I glance towards Ollie who is happily walking along a fallen log like it's a balance beam, making sure she's out of earshot. Then I turn back to Hattie, holding her gaze.

"What did I tell you about me and challenges, Mac?" I say, voice pitched low. "Are you gonna make me prove it right here and now? Because I'll fucking do it and you know it." Hattie actually gasps softly, and I'll be damned if she doesn't actually look intrigued by the idea for a second before she grins and tosses a handful of snow at my face. *When had the little devil picked that up?* I sputter in surprise, wiping the snow out of my scruff that's somewhere between stubble and an actual beard while she giggles.

"Wouldn't want you to get frostbite, Shep." I give her a look that promises payback but she only laughs harder. "Come on, get to chopping. It's as cold as a witch's titty out here."

I bark out a laugh, but say, "yes ma'am" and take off my coat, shoving it at Hattie. She takes it and Ollie skips over to watch the show. I take the tree down in a few swings, admittedly showing off a bit.

Ollie yells "Timber!" and the tree falls, a cloud of snow puffing up where it collapses. We got a light dusting last night, but it's supposed to really hit in a few days. I've already gotten Hattie's place all stocked up, checked her snow tires, and brought her a truck load of firewood, so she should be all set for her first real snow.

We get the tree in the truck, head home, and start the decorating. I keep watching Hattie from the corner of my eye as she helps Ollie put on lights and ornaments, or as the two of them direct me on where to put the ones near the top where they can't reach. She seems happy, a warm smile on her face the whole time, laughing lightly. I wonder when the last time she did any of this was. It has to be years, decades probably. We order in from a little Italian place around the corner from the house for an early dinner, all of us somehow ravenous from all the decorating, and eat in the living room by the tree while we watch all three *The Santa Clause* movies. It's...well, fuck, it's damn near perfect.

"So..." I say quietly, stroking Ollie's hair where she's passed out on the couch between Hattie and me. She made it through about two and a half movies before she tapped out.

"So what?"

"Are your feelings towards Christmas any different yet?"

She looks at the tree, the hint of a soft smile curling her lips. "Jury's still out, but your ace in the hole here is sure helpin' to tip the scales." She glances down at Ollie, gently patting the girl's feet where they rest in her lap.

"I never promised to play fair, just that I play to win."

"Well, there are still twenty-one days left before Christmas. Plenty of time for December to strike." She glances at her watch. "I better get goin'." I nod and we both ease out from under Ollie. I tuck a thick blanket around her and brush the hair back from her face, my throat tightening a bit when I realize how much older she's looking even since last Christmas. I know everyone says it, but damn it, time really does fly by in the blink of an eye.

I lean down and give Ollie a kiss on the forehead and walk Hattie to the door.

"Well, even if it doesn't change the way you feel about the holiday, I'm really glad you joined us today. It was nice."

"I am too. And it was. I'd give this a solid 9/10 for my first Christmas-related activity."

"Just a 9?" I ask, pretending to be offended.

"I know you well enough to know that I have to leave you something to aspire to." We both grin.

"You aren't wrong."

We pause by the door and when she turns towards me and lifts her face up to look at me, that shift happens again, just like on the couch that day. That heavy electricity hanging in the air around us, a thick, palpable anticipation that makes my heart race. She has to feel it too, right? It can't just be me. Her chest rises and falls in quick, shallow bursts and I think she most definitely does.

The question is, do we do anything about it?

Is it *just* physical for her? Would something just physical between us be a terrible idea? As I glance down at her lips, seeing her tongue slowly trace along the bottom one, as if in invitation, I think it's the best idea I've ever fucking had. Then I think of how messy that could get, how upset Ollie would be if something did happen between us and then we couldn't get back to being friends afterwards—how upset *I'd* be if that happened.

Regardless of how badly I want her, and dear God do I want her, I care about her too much to risk losing her friendship. It's been a quick thing, but I already feel closer to her than I have to anyone in a long time. I'm close with my teammates, like brothers, but this is different. I can't risk not having Hattie in my life for one night of fun—no matter how fucking fun it might be.

A tiny voice whispers, *but what if it wasn't just one night. What if she wants more?*

She's made it clear that she doesn't want to date a player.

But that was before, when she thought you were just a manwhore like Rizzo, the whisper comes again. That stupid fucking voice needs to chill out.

I don't know if she'd still be against dating someone on the team or not. It may be too complicated for her to do that, to date someone where she works. She may not even *want* to date anyone at all right now. She'd told me a bit about her last relationship and I wouldn't blame her if she swore off men all together after that piece of work. It's a good thing the fucker lives halfway across the country. Someone needs to teach him how women should be treated and I'd love to volunteer for that job.

With a Herculean effort, I take a small step backwards and make the smart decision: No. It's too risky. I don't know for sure how she feels and I'm not going to push it, not yet anyway. Before my resolve slips, I open the front door. We both turn to look out and freeze: a thick blanket of snow covers everything. *When the fuck had this happened?* Sometime between getting dinner and the end of the last movie, the sky had absolutely opened up, nearly a full-on snowstorm.

"Oh my God," she whispers. "I've never seen so much snow!" She rushes out onto the porch and down a couple of the steps, boots crunching on the thick layer of snow that's already accumulated there. She holds her hands out and lifts her face upward, laughing as fat flakes land on her nose and cheeks. It's still coming down steadily and doesn't look like it's going to stop anytime soon.

I pull out my phone and check the weather. Sure enough, we're supposed to get another couple of *feet* of snow throughout the night. I'd known that it was predicted to get bad later in the week and we're prepared, fully stocked with supplies and everything, but I didn't think it was supposed to start tonight. I feel like such an asshole because now she's stranded.

She runs back up into the safety of the covered porch, kicking the snow off of her boots.

"It's beautiful," she says, surprising me a little bit. Then she turns and gives me a triumphant look and my brow furrows. "My car is currently buried in snow. December strikes again."

"Getting snowed in with me and Ollie goes in the *December Screwed Me* column? Ouch. You wound me deeply, Mac."

Her eyes go wide. "Oh, no, that's not—"

"I'm fucking with you," I assure her. But then it really hits me: *she's snowed in with us.* For God knows how long. The snow's still coming and they won't be plowing the roads anytime soon, especially not back this far into the community, so a couple of days at least. It seems to hit her at the same time.

"Uh, so, I guess I'm kind of stuck here for the foreseeable future?" She tucks a strand of hair behind her ear, and then her hand goes to the diamond at her throat. She runs the pendant along the chain sometimes when she's thinking...or nervous. Is she nervous now? *Should* she be? I'd talked a big game in my head five minutes ago about not pushing boundaries and not risking things and making the right decision, but now, I don't know if can keep any of that shit in mind with her here with me in this snowed-in little bubble away from the entire world. I'm not an idiot. I've seen Hallmark movies and read romance novels—for some reason being snowed in together always puts the main characters in a tense, lust-fueled battle of wills until they finally crack. *Fuck, fuck, fuck.*

"Well, we've got plenty of room and we're completely stocked with supplies. We've got a generator, so we're good even if the power goes. Ollie will think it's the best thing that's ever happened." We both chuckle a bit at that, and she nods, accepting the situation because, well, what else can she do?

"Slumber party it is then."

"Ooh are you going to braid my hair and paint my nails?" I ask, waggling my fingers in the air and doing my best to fight against the tension that I can feel already building. *Have I mentioned: fuck?*

"I was thinking more Ouija Boards and prank calling cute boys," she says with a grin, sauntering back into the living room.

"I do have all the team's numbers in my phone," I say, locking the door and following her. "Who's your guy? Jules? Mickels? Oh, no, I know—Frenchy. Can't deny that accent is sexy."

She chuckles and rolls her eyes, nodding towards the couch. I pick Ollie up and carry her to bed, tucking Pickles in beside her. She wraps her arms around the dragon without waking, holding him tight to her chest. I kiss her head, turn on the night-light, and gently close the door.

"You're a pro. Didn't even wake her up." Hattie says as we make our way upstairs.

"I've done it a time or two." Ollie had a talent for falling asleep almost anywhere except her bed: the couch, the tent in her playroom, the back porch. I'd even found her passed out in a kitchen cupboard when she was five. I grin and show Hattie to the guest room.

"You've got your own bathroom through there, towels and toiletries are in the cabinet. There are some of my old t-shirts and sweatpants and stuff in that drawer that you're welcome to sleep in." I force myself not to think about the fact that she'll be going commando at some point during this stay while we wash her underwear. I've seen plenty of Hattie's underwear strewn around her house before—her organized chaos isn't contained only to her office—and of course it always put a flirty little image in my mind of her parading around in her boyshorts, but thinking about it now, with her here stuck in the house with me for God knows how long? Well, it's all hitting differently.

She wanders around the room, taking in the décor with a soft smile. It's full of all my hockey memorabilia: framed jerseys, trophies from when I was a kid, media shots and newspaper articles. Sara calls it my *I Love Me Room*. I guess it is, a bit. I'm proud of everything I've accomplished, of how hard I've worked to get where I am, and I like showing it off. Hattie perches on the edge of the bed, pulling one leg up under her.

"Thanks, Shep."

"No problem. I'm the door at the end of the hall if you need anything." Like a midnight orgasm. No...Yes? *No, damn it.* I grit my teeth against my warring thoughts but give her an easy smile. "Night, Mac."

"G'night."

I close her door and lean my forehead against it for a second before pushing off and heading to my own room. I take a shower, my mind wandering like crazy as I step under the hot stream.

Hattie is here.

In my house.

In the next fucking room.

I lean my palms against the tile, ducking my head so the water pelts the back of my neck. I don't try to stop the thoughts. I let them come, hoping that maybe if I give myself a few minutes to just lean into it, I'll be able to make it through these next few days without doing something stupid.

So, I imagine leaving the shower and knocking on her door. I imagine her opening it wide, shock on her face just before I slam my lips to hers. I can almost feel her lips against mine in my mind, and I groan. My hand slips downward and I hiss in a breath through clenched teeth. I grip my cock and glide my hand up and down, slowly, letting my imagination run wild: Hattie's tongue thrusting against mine; my tongue skating over every inch of her skin, biting, licking, sucking; sinking deep inside her, her soft pleas and gasps of pleasure as I thrust; her screams as she comes hard around my cock...

I bite my lip and let my head fall back as I stroke harder, and then I come in a rush, a guttural moan breaking free from my throat. My legs tremble from the force of it and I have to steady myself against the tiled wall for a long minute, catching my breath as the water continues to beat down against my skin.

"*Fuck,*" I mutter, hoping that takes care of that.

It doesn't take care of shit. This snow storm is a special kind of torture. I can't stop thinking about Hattie in the bed just a few yards away. Just down the hall, she's there, alone. I want to do all manner of depraved things with her, but I also just want to *be* with her. I want to fall asleep with her tucked against my chest, my arms wrapped around her.

What in the hell is wrong with me? I know the answer, but it's a stupid, ridiculous fucking answer, so I push it away. We're friends. That's it. I'd told Kasey, one of the athletic trainers, that when she'd asked about the two of us the other day. I wasn't sure *why* she was asking, exactly, but I'd assured her that Hattie and I were just friends, nothing more. Of course I'm not naïve or blind, I can see the potential there. The chemistry between us is off the charts and imagining being with her like that is as easy as breathing.

But it isn't a smart move. I don't even know if she would want that. I don't come alone. I'm a package deal and it's a lot to ask someone to sign on for a new relationship and a potential kid at the same time. It's obvious that Hattie loves Ollie, but being the fun playmate and being the maybe step-mom are way different.

So, yeah, it isn't a smart move, like I said.

So, why am I padding down the hallway towards her room? *This is stupid. This is stupid. This is really fucking stupid.* I pause in front of her door, heart thudding against my chest like a drum. I raise my hand to knock, but freeze. Some tiny bit of control remains intact and I grip onto it like my life depends on it. I grit my teeth and close my eyes. I can't do it. I can't make my knuckles wrap against the wood. I shake myself and quickly back away, silently bolting back to my room and leaning back against the door, panting like I just did line drills.

"Fuck," I whisper, knowing that this was going to be the longest night of my life.

Chapter Nine

HATTIE

I flop back onto my stomach for the third time. Nope. To the back again. It's too hot under these covers, so I kick them off in an annoyed huff. Now I'm cold. *Fuck.* I can't sleep, can't stop thinking about the fact that I'm sleeping in Connor's house, in his fucking clothes. The old t-shirt is soft and smells like him, his detergent mixed with the faintest trace of his cologne, making this all so much worse. I don't know what's wrong with me. I don't know why I'm thinking about him this way when I've been totally fine for the most part in the past two months. Of course, I've known and appreciated how attractive he is all this time, and I'd had wayward thoughts here and there, maybe a few dirty ones, but it hasn't been this...*distracting* until tonight.

Now, all I can think about is the fact that he's only a few feet down the hall. Does he sleep shirtless? Does he sleep in anything at all? I cover my face with my hands and groan. What in the hell is my problem? I've slept in the same house as male friends before. I had guy roomies senior year of college for fuck's sake. And I never laid there pining like a crazy person the whole time, as if I'm unable to be near a penis without wanting to jump its owner in the dead of night.

That's because you didn't want to be more than friends with any of them that stupid voice in the back of my mind says.

I don't think I can go down that road with Connor though. We have a connection, a deep one, there's no denying that, but he's also a single dad and a professional athlete who's on the road half the year, and I'm...I don't know what I am, other than afraid. I don't even know precisely of what. Getting hurt I guess? I don't know. I don't want to try to be more with Connor and then lose him as a friend if we mess it up. And after Josh, I don't know that I trust myself anymore. I hate him a little for making me question that part of myself, to wonder if every relationship is going to turn out as badly as ours did.

But that moment by the door, and the one before that on the couch that first night I came over and he told me about losing his sister and adopting Ollie...there's *something* between me and Connor that's hard to explain, something more than friendship. It's heavy and intense and holds the promise of something terrifyingly epic.

And that's not even talking about the physical.

Watching him chop down that tree earlier was strangely arousing, making me feel hot despite standing in the freezing cold. The way the muscles in his arms and back moved and flexed as he swung the axe. His hair had toppled over his forehead, beads of sweat dripping down his temples. His gaze had been hard and intense, the way it is during games. There was just something so ruggedly masculine about it, something so damn sexy, I could barely stop myself from reaching out to touch him, to brush the hair away from his face, to run my hands down his broad chest as it heaved from the exertion of chopping down the tree.

I'd barely been able to keep my eyes off of him all day after that, watching him hang decorations and lift Ollie to reach the top of the tree, stealing cookies from the plate as quickly as Ollie and I could decorate them, humming quietly to the Christmas music without even seeming to realize he was doing it. Just like he'd said his mom used to do. He'd looked so happy, and I was fairly certain I'd seen him stealing glances my way as often as I was stealing them at him.

But that could just be all physical from his perspective. He might want to fuck, but that doesn't mean he wants anything more. Would I be ok with that? Could I do the friends-with-benefits thing? Normally, yes. But with Connor? No, I don't think I could, because deep down I know that I have feelings for him that would get all kinds of confused if we hooked up. I've been pushing them away over the past couple of weeks, but they're there, I can't deny it. They may be passing, they may never turn into anything, but they're there.

Today had been an amazing day, and I'd felt such a deep sense of contentment, of belonging and family, that it had made it hard to breathe for a minute. I'd let myself imagine, just for a second, that this was my actual life. That Connor and Ollie and I were a *real* family. It fell into place in my mind as easy as taking my next breath. I know how insane that sounds, but that doesn't make it any less true.

But.

There's always a fucking but, isn't there?

But—I'm the one who said friends and nothing more. I'm the one who wasn't sure a relationship with anyone, let alone a professional hockey player, was a good idea. And I'm the one who's terrified of losing Connor. So, not taking the risk and staying just friends is the right choice, really. I know it.

Yet, suddenly I'm tiptoeing down the hallway towards his door, telling myself how stupid it is the whole way. *Stupid, but worth it?* I bite my lip, imagining all the ways it'll be worth it...

Before I can wrap my knuckles lightly on the door, it swings open. Connor stands there and his lips part when he sees me. We both stand frozen for a heartbeat before I move forward, going up onto my tiptoes, fisting his shirt in my hands, and yanking him down to kiss me. He tenses in surprise, but then, his kisses me back with a passion that sets every inch of my body on fire. His lips are hot and hard against mine, demanding everything I have. Has he been thinking about this as much as I have?

He tunnels one hand in my hair and the other slides down my side, landing on my hip and pulling me towards him. His tongue thrusts against mine and I groan, twisting the front of his shirt harder in my fingers. He walks us backwards, his hand moving from my hip to slide over my ass. He squeezes and groans low in his throat, his chest rumbling beneath my hand. I grin against his lips. I had a feeling he was an ass man. I gasp when he yanks the old sweatpants off me, not even slowing his steps, and he chuckles. I maneuverer out of them easily just before he backs into the bed, sitting on the edge when his knees hit it. He pulls me into his lap and I straddle his waist, hissing in a harsh breath when I settle down against him. I can feel him hard as steel, only the thin silk of my panties and his lounge pants between us.

"Mmm," I mutter, wrapping my arms around his neck as he kisses along my throat. I rock my hips as he continues his divine torture, his lips and tongue scorching a path along my skin, his scruff tickling ever so slightly. He runs his hands underneath the hem of my shirt, his fingers brushing over my stomach and slowly inching upward.

"Hattie," he breathes. *Hattie? He never calls me that.* I don't think about it too much, just writhe in his lap as his fingers grip my back as I move. I roll my hips over and over, the friction hitting just the right spots. I can't stop, don't want to stop. My body tenses and I'm climbing, climbing, climbing...

My eyes fly open just as the orgasm rips through me. I dig my fingers into the sheets and bury my face in the pillow, terrified that somehow Connor will hear my panting breaths from down the hall. My heart thunders as I lie there in shock.

"Oh my God," I whisper, brushing damp hair off my forehead. I'd just come—*hard*—from a dirty dream about Connor. I throw my arms over my face, my stomach still fluttering and the orgasm still sending little aftershocks through my core. "Fuck, fuck, fuckity fuck."

This snow storm is going to be the death of me.

❄· ·❄· ·❄

Ollie thinks that the blizzard is the most amazing thing to ever happen. She loves snow, it keeps her beloved uncle from leaving her for another few days, and I'm there to be an extra playmate until everything is cleared up.

"Best day ever!" she yells when we explain why I'm still here and that I'd be staying until the snow let up. I feel the need to make it very clear that I'm staying in the guest room, and hope that Connor doesn't catch the flush of my cheeks. Flashes of the dream flutter through my mind and I quickly busy myself stirring the pancake batter.

As the morning wears on, I recover from my little nocturnal adventure, and decide that it isn't that big a deal. Dirty dreams are just a part of life, a perfectly healthy part, might I add, and Connor is hot as hell—I'm not going to sit here and deny that. So, yeah, it's fine, and once I make peace with that, I relax and the day is fantastic. I have my first official snowball fight, build my first snowman, experience my first bout of near-frostbite in my toes. Ok, so that's a *slight* exaggeration, but I whimper dramatically as the feeling painfully returns to my feet in front of the fire. Connor rolls his eyes as he shoves a mug of hot chocolate in my hands.

"Really?"

"Listen, my toes are used to being nice and toasty, usually shoved in the sand of the gulf coast, alright?" He chuckles but mutters that I'm a baby as Ollie bounds over with a bag of mini-marshmallows. I surreptitiously flip him off behind the little girl's back and grin at her, checking out her offerings.

"Do you want some, Mac-and-Cheese?"

"Oh, of course. You can't have hot chocolate without marshmallows. I think it's against the law, actually." She giggles and dumps about twenty in my mug, but I don't mind one bit.

Eventually the sun goes down and after a little bit of fighting, Ollie finally goes to bed. I had to promise her at least ten times that I would be here in the morning before she finally gave in and let Connor go tuck her in. I'm standing by the back doors, looking out into night when Connor pads quietly back into the living room. He's in worn jeans, a black long-sleeved t-shirt that fits close to his muscled frame, and bare feet. How they aren't freezing, I'll never know. I'd borrowed a pair of his thick, woolen socks earlier and I'm fairly certain that "borrow" is going to turn into "steal" because they're amazing.

"She's out."

"Poor kid, she must have been exhausted. I don't think she stopped for more than ten minutes the entire day."

He laughs lightly. "Sounds about right. How about you? Are you ready for bed, or can I talk you into a drink?"

"A drink sounds good."

He smiles and nods, heading to the kitchen while I turn my gaze back to the glass. The lights strung in the trees and around the yard are on, casting a soft glow over everything. So much snow has fallen since the afternoon that everything is completely smoothed over again, all traces of our snowball fight and snow angels completely gone. The lights glint off of the snow, making the ice crystals glitter like diamonds. I'd never realized how beautiful snow could be. I mean, sure, it's pretty in movies and on postcards, but I always kind of thought that was just camera tricks. It really is breathtaking though. The stars reflect off of the surface of the lake and I can just make out the mountains in the distance, just hulking black shadows against the night sky now. Connor sure did pick a great spot to call home, that's for sure.

He joins me and hands me a glass. I take a long sip and give a little *mmm* of appreciation—Jameson and ginger ale. I'd tried it for the first time when we'd gone to the bar after he man-handled my chair for me, and it had quickly become a new favorite.

"It really is beautiful," I say nodding towards the picturesque scene just outside.

"It is. I've always loved the snow. Don't get me wrong, I'm perfectly content to lounge on a beach somewhere with a fruity concoction in my hand, but snow has just always been...I dunno how to explain it. My happy place I guess?" I can't say that I'm surprised. I feel like all hockey players were polar bears in a former life.

We make our way over to the couch, settling in with a bit of space between us. Though it isn't awkward or anything, it seems like we're both being a bit...cautious after last night. Or I could just be imagining the whole damn thing and I'm the only one who noticed anything at all. Connor has this unflappable air about him most of the time, like no matter what's thrown at him, he just rolls with it, and it's hard to tell what he's really feeling about something. I inwardly shake myself and take another sip of my drink.

"I get that. Water has always been mine. There was a small fishing pond on one of our property growing up, the bayou running along the other, and we'd taken too many trips to the beach to count over the years. My mom was the same way, always loved the water, so I think that's another part of the reason I love it so much—it was always kind of our thing. Even before my dad bolted, mom and I would swing in the hammock right on the edge of the water or take the pirogue out on the bayou, just the two of us." At his confused look, I add with a laugh, "it's just another name for a little boat. But we would go out for hours, exploring and talking. Nowadays, I guess I feel close to her when I'm near the water, any water."

"Ah, so that's why you picked the house on the Sound." I nod and absently run the diamond along the chain around my neck. He nods to it with a question in his eyes. "Mom gave me this on my sixteenth birthday. It's a diamond from my mamaw's engagement ring, actually, that mom had set into a necklace. I pretty much never take it off."

"That's really nice." I smile and he continues, "And what about your dad? You haven't said much about him other than he left."

I huff out a laugh. "He's one of those guys that just never could grow up, ya know? Even after he got married and had a kid, he was still more concerned about going out with his friends or trying to make it as a musician playing local bars than being an adult. He tried his best for those first few years, I guess, but in the end, he just wasn't meant to be a family man. I think he was a little intimidated by mom, too. She was the powerhouse bread-winner. She worked her ass off to get her architectural firm up and running before I was born and by the time dad bolted, she was designing multi-million dollar homes for really affluent clients—like governors and shit—and her waitlist was over a year long. I don't think he could handle feeling emasculated." I shrug a shoulder. I came to terms with all of this a long time ago and it doesn't really bother me too much nowadays. "He tried to come back once, about five years after he left, and mom kicked him off the porch with a shotgun pointed at his crotch."

Connor busts out laughing. "I think I would have liked her."

"I think so too. She was strong and smart and witty. She was a Cajun woman, born and bred and didn't take shit from anyone, total fire in her veins and not scared of anything. I once saw her swat a gator on the nose like it was a dog who was trying to get scraps off the dinner table. Hand on the Bible," I say when he looks dubious. "She was great. I really miss her," I say with a sigh. "But yeah I haven't spoken to my dad since I was...oh, eighteen probably. He got in touch with me just after graduation and I stupidly agreed to meet with him, thinking, I don't know, maybe he'd finally realized the mistake he'd made and wanted to reconnect, like one of those stories you see online or something. Turns out he just needed money."

"What an ass," Connor says.

"He is that indeed. It stung a little, I won't lie, but I got over it pretty quickly. I threw my tea in his face—*very* dramatic, I know—told him I hoped a rabid nutria bit his dick off, and then left the restaurant. Haven't talked to him since."

Connor tries desperately to hold back his laugh, but it doesn't work out so well. He throws his head back and laughs, that deep, husky laugh of his that I love. My lips curl upwards and soon we're both cracking up.

"A rabid nutria? What the fuck is that even?"

Through my giggles I say, "it's kind of like a beaver." He laughs harder and I shrug a shoulder.

"Mac, I swear to God, you are the most ridiculous, hilarious woman I've ever met." I take it as the compliment he means it to be.

We settle down again and talk about this and that, the conversation flowing easily, like always. Eventually, we end up on past relationships. We've touched a bit on them before now, but tonight seems to be the night for deep-diving. I don't know if it's the second—no, third?—drink, or the feeling of being isolated from the entire world, just me and Connor hidden by the snow, but it apparently makes us want to share.

"I haven't been in a serious relationship in...Christ, the last one was in college actually."

"Wow, really?"

"Yeah. Cassidy and I dated junior and part of senior year at Cornell, but it didn't last too long after I got drafted. She couldn't really handle the lifestyle and honestly, I was too wrapped up in it all to care enough to try harder than I did." I give him a know-ing look and he shrugs. "*Reformed* playboy, remember? Anyway, she's married now, has three kids, and seems super happy, so it worked out the way it was meant to. We've stayed in touch a bit after the initial her-hating-my-guts-for-being-an-asshole thing passed. I got them all tickets to the game last time we were in Buffalo, actually. Her oldest son is big into hockey and I gave him a stick signed by the whole team. It was a good time." I smile, liking that he's one of those guys who's genuinely happy for an ex to be happy.

"But yeah, I haven't really dated anyone in a long time. I've had a handful of relationships that lasted a few months here and there since then, but it was never anything *really* serious. Then you know with the whole Ollie thing, dating went on the way, way, *way* back-burner." He takes a sip of his drink, turning and laying an arm along the back of the couch, his hand just behind my head. "What about you? Just the ex in Texas?"

"A few semi-serious boyfriends in high school, college was just lots of fun," I say with a grin, "but Josh was the first real serious relationship, yeah."

I let out a long breath. He knows a bit about Josh, but not *all* the gory details. Connor just thinks that Josh was an asshole and I moved for a fresh start. He doesn't know that the fresh start was needed because I feared for my life. I don't want to burden him, but I decide to tell him everything. I tell him about how we met, how things were great for a while, and then how out of control they'd spiraled. He tenses when I get to all the things that hap-pened after we broke up, his jaw ticking, and his eyes hardening like he's barely containing his rage. He moves his arm from the back of the couch, his fist clenched on his thigh.

"So, that's when I took the job. It came at the perfect time and I just knew that if I didn't get out of Galveston...well, he was never going to stop and, I don't know, I just had this feeling that he was going to lose it soon, in a very *episode-of-Criminal-Minds* kind of way."

He stares into the fire, that muscle in his jaw still flexing over and over. He absently runs the fingers of his left hand over the tattooed knuckles on his right, as if he's imagining using them on Josh.

"Say something?" I finally say, though it comes out as a question. I know that I just threw a whole lot of crazy on him.

"I kind of want to kill the fucker," he says, startling me. He turns to face me. "I'm sorry, but it's true. To treat any woman like that...to treat *you* like that?" He shakes his head, lips pressed into a hard line. "I'm sorry you had to go through that, Mac. Really."

"Thanks. It was...scary," I say, finally able to say the words out loud. I realize now that I haven't really been able to talk to anyone about all of this. I tried to talk to my "friends" back home when it was all happening, but they hadn't really cared, had barely even listened to me, or had defended Josh before I could even get a full sentence out, so I kept the worst of it to myself. I went through all of it completely alone.

But now, I can share it with Connor. Now, I have someone who will not only listen, but actually *hear* what I'm saying, who will empathize with me and let me feel whatever it is I need to feel without saying I'm overreacting or that it isn't a big deal or think that I'm weak. Someone who cares about me enough to want to fucking kill the psycho-stalker ex who made my life a living hell for months and months. Tears spring to my eyes and his widen in alarm.

"I'm sorry, I've just...God, I've never said that out loud. I've never really had anyone to talk to about any of it before, so it just kind of hit me now. It was really fucking scary, Shep. If I had stayed, I think he would have...he would have..."

I cut off as the tears fall and I clap my hand over my mouth, unable to say the words out loud. Connor reaches out and pulls me into his arms. There is nothing sexual about it, it's comfort he's offering, nothing more, and I accept it like a drowning person clinging to a buoy. I let myself think about everything that had happened, everything that *could* have happened, let myself really feel everything for the first time.

When I was in the middle of it, I'd just been focused on the next hour, the next minute, the next second, wondering if he was going to be outside of every building I exited, wondering if I was going to see his car around every corner, wondering if I was going to wake up in the middle of the night with him standing over me. I'd been in a constant state of damage control I guess, just treading water and not really able to think about it all, not fully. Since the move, I've tried not to think about it, trying to just focus on the here and now, the new job and new friendships. Now, it all hits me like a fucking tank. I cry into his shoulder as he rubs his palm up and down my back in a soothing rhythm.

"It's ok, Mac. It's alright. You're safe now. You got away. You don't have to worry."

Eventually I cry myself out and feel so much better. It's like all of that had just been a giant weight sitting on my chest this whole time. I didn't even really realize it was there, but now that it's gone, I feel like I can finally really breathe for the first time in almost a year. I pull back from him and scrub my eyes.

"I'm so sorry," I say with a shaky laugh, "I'm a mess."

"A hot one," he says with a crooked grin but then he purses his lips. "I actually meant that as like *you're a hot mess*, like you always say, not calling you hot. Though you are obviously hot...ah fuck, this isn't working out. Let's try that again. Take two." He rolls his hand in the air in a *come on* gesture.

"I'm a mess?" I say, laughing again.

"Yes, you are. There, that was better."

I disentangle myself from his arms, only now realizing the position we were in. We both decide that this was probably a good cue to call it a night. We head upstairs and stop in front of the guest room door.

"You good?"

"I am now. Thanks for..." Being there? Threatening to kill my terrible ex? Letting me cry all over you like a crazy person? "Just, thanks."

"Of course. I'm always here, Mac. Whatever you need." He holds my gaze for a moment that seems to go on forever, and I'm not exactly sure if he's meaning as a friend or something more. I don't know what I'm thinking, but everything around us seems to fall away. I feel myself rising up on my toes, leaning my face towards his without even realizing it. His eyes widen in surprise and he inhales sharply, but he doesn't move away. I rest a hand on his chest and I swear he stops breathing completely. Time seems to be moving in slow motion as I run my fingers upward, across the soft skin of his neck, through the silky strands of hair that brush the top of his collar. I stare at his lips, soft breaths pushing past them, and move mine ever closer...

Oh my God, what am I doing? With the state I'm in, with everything about Josh very raw and on the surface right now, crossing any lines with Connor would be a *terrible* idea. When—I mean *if*—we ever go there, I don't want it to be because I'm an emotional mess. I shake myself and yank my hand down, taking a step backwards.

"Oh God, Shep, I'm sorry." I run a hand through my hair, shaking my head. "That was...I'm just emotional and a little tipsy," I say with a nervous grin, though I'm trying to hide it. "I'm sorry," I say again.

We're good enough friends that I don't *think* this almost-kiss will make things weird between us, but there's a tiny sliver of doubt creeping in. He clears his throat and leans a shoulder against the wall beside the door, the picture of casual.

"Hey, no problem." A small, crooked smirk curls his lips. "I warned you from the beginning you'd want to kiss me, remember? I'm honestly surprised you've held off this long. It's quite admirable." I laugh and slap him in the stomach, relief rushing through me that he doesn't seem to be weirded out. Unflappable as always.

"Let's just pretend that never happened, shall we then?"

He smiles but it doesn't seem to reach his eyes, though of course I can't be completely sure in the low light of the hallway. The overhead lights are off, the illumination coming from lights running along the baseboards at intervals, almost like night-lights.

"Goodnight, Shep," I say quietly, turning the knob.

"Night."

He heads down the hallway and I watch him go, cursing myself and wondering if crossing a line with him would *really* be so terrible after all.

❄ · ·❄· ·❄

"So, it looks like the snow has cleared off for now. I'm going to shovel the driveway and they're already clearing the roads. You should be all set to leave in a couple of hours."

I shouldn't be disappointed, but I can admit that I am. Just a little. It's been fun playing house with Connor and Ollie, pretending, just for a couple of days, that this is my real life, that we're this happy little family unit. It's been more than fun. It's made my heart ache in a way I don't even really understand, a longing to have all of this and more rearing up inside me so forcefully that it's startling. I force it all away. I know it's just the strange magic of the snow and my biological clock ticking as Kelly had oh-so-tactfully pointed out when she interrupted Nat and I eating lunch a week ago, discussing one of the guys on the team who had just announced that they were having their fourth baby.

So, as much as I've loved it, I can also admit that it's probably a good thing it's all over because if I spend another night here, I know I won't be able to stop myself from doing something stupid. After the almost-kiss the night before and the way I'd stayed up half the night wondering if I shouldn't have just said fuck it and given in, my self-restraint is hanging on by a thread. Not even a thread—a fucking *hair*. When we'd come in from the snow earlier, I'd accidentally walked in on Connor changing in the laundry room, and that hair had nearly snapped completely.

His back was to me, and he'd just been pulling his damp shirt over his head. I'd never thought of a man's back as being sexy before, not really, but Connor's was mouthwatering. Smooth skin and sculpted muscles that moved in intriguing ways as he took his shirt off. More tattoos covered his back—an angel, a Celtic knot, some script that I couldn't make myself stop and read—and I had the intense urge to press my lips against them, run my tongue along the black, swirling lines. I'd dropped the bundle of wet clothes I'd had in my arms and he turned when he heard them thump to the ground. I'd gotten a brief glimpse of the front view before, but it hadn't done it justice, not by a mile. Not by a fucking light year.

I couldn't seem to pry my eyes away from his chest...and his abs...and those daggum dips beside his hip bones. Why do those exist?? They shouldn't exist. It isn't *fair* that they exist. But they might be my favorite things to ever exist. It's complicated, ok?

My gaze flitted upwards again, roving over the tattoos covering his torso, to his chest. A dagger and rose covered the upper part of his left peck, converging into more roses and what looked like a snake wrapping over his shoulder and down his arm. They were works of art, so painstakingly detailed and beautiful. And did I mention sexy?

But then my eyes snapped back to his chest and my eyes widened: a metal bar was shoved through his nipple. I'd known it was pierced, had seen the bar pressing against the fabric of his shirt in the past, but I'd never actually *seen* it before. It was surprisingly...enticing. I had the strange urge to flick my tongue over it, wondered what it would feel like. Would the metal be cold? Or warmed by his skin? Would he like that? Would he tangle his hands in my hair and hold my mouth to him, urging me to keep going, silently begging for more? Or maybe not so silently—

Connor struck me as the vocal type, which made my toes curl in my soon-to-be-stolen wool socks.

He raised an arm to rub the back of his neck and my mouth actually *watered,* the movement so fucking sensual. So sexy. So unfair.

"Jesus be a river," I muttered, still staring, and shaking my head.

"What does that even actually mean?" he asked, and I could hear the amusement in his voice.

"I don't rightly know," I said honestly, "a friend of mine used to say it."

He'd laughed at that, his stomach muscles contracting and adding a whole new layer to the sexy picture before me, but his laughter finally made me lift my gaze up to his. He was smirking, that cocky, crooked smile that melts panties and breaks hearts and makes women want to do really, really stupid things.

"My eyes," he said in an amused voice, tinged with just a bit of sexy flirtation, "are up here, Mac."

"Oh fuck off," I said.

"You're thinking about kissing me again, aren't you?" he teased, crossing his arms over his chest. I rolled my eyes, but was secretly thankful that he could be so nonchalant about the almost-kiss, could let it just roll off of him like it wasn't a big deal.

"You're never going to let me live that down, are you?"

He grinned shamelessly. "Nope," he said, popping the "ope" part loudly. I bent down and grabbed the first thing from the pile—a handful of sopping socks—and hurled them at his face. He caught them easily, of course, but he sputtered as the water splashed over him. I cackled and he wiped his face slowly, giving me one of those looks he got sometimes, playful and intense.

"Payback is a bitch, McNamara."

❋· ·❋·.·❋

Payback comes later when he drops a huge snowball—a snow boulder, really—directly onto my head, sending snow and ice skittering down the back of my coat and shirt. I scream and twist, trying to escape the freezing droplets dripping down my spine, and he and Ollie double over with laughter.

"You look like you're dancing," Ollie giggles, copying my moves and jumping around like a monkey. Watching her, I can't help but join in the laughter, though I do promise my own payback at some point.

"But mine will come when you least expect it," I warn Connor with narrowed eyes. "Sleep with one eye open, Shepherd."

The rest of the day passes with board games and movies and naps by the fire. As promised, the plows have come through, the snow has stopped for the time being, and Connor dutifully clears the driveway. Ollie and I cut out snowflakes to hang around the playroom while he works, and she tells me about everything she's putting on her Christmas list: a mini 4-wheeler, a life-sized T-Rex (I'm not sure she knows what *life-sized* actually means), new ice skates with purple and pink laces, and a handful of other things. I've already picked out a bunch of books for her, but peruse the list for some additional little treats I can toss in, after checking with Connor, of course. I'm not usually a gift giver, but there's no way I can *not* get Ollie a present. That would be a crime against nature. Part of me acknowledges that this in and of itself is a victory for Connor's *Operation: Destroy Dreaded December*, but I won't be admitting that to him.

"What are you asking for?" she asks, bobbing her head to the playlist we made earlier as she pours blue and silver glitter onto her snowflake, getting more glitter on the floor and on herself than the paper.

"Oh, um, I haven't really thought about it."

She looks up at that, eyes wide and mouth open in abhorrent shock. I barely stifle a laugh. "You don't have a list?" she asks, truly incredulous. I shake my head. "Well, we need to make you one, otherwise Santa won't know what to bring you!" Her little face is pinched with determination and worry, and it makes my lips curl. She's so dang sweet, wanting to make sure that Santa has my list so I can have a good Christmas.

So, we make a list. I tell her things to write down for me like books or new sweaters, but the only thing I really want is for this December to truly be different than any others. For most of my life, I had zero expectations or hopes of Christmas being good, and I was honestly ok with that. I didn't really care or mind after a while. But now, with Connor determined to make me have a happy holiday season for once, I actually want things to be different. I *want* to have hope. *Please let this be better, please don't let anything bad happen, please let me just enjoy this time with this great little makeshift family I've found in Connor and Ollie, with Sara and Bobby and Nat and the entire team really. Just give me one fucking good Christmas. Please.*

Ollie pouts when it comes time for me to leave, but I promise that I'll see her again in a couple of days and she reluctantly accepts it and gives me a hug before flouncing off to find Pickles. Connor walks me to my car, not bothering to put on a coat. *Crazy former polar bear.*

"So, does being snowed in still count in the negative column for December?"

I tap my chin, pretending to think it over. "I *guess* it can shift over into the positive side, though my toes may never be fully-thawed again," I say with a mocking scowl. Half mocking anyway. They do seem to be permanently cold now, despite the socks that I did, in fact, steal.

He smiles and folds his arms over his chest. "I told you, I play to win."

"I'll admit I'm kinda lookin' forward to the continued attempts."

"And I'm looking forward to Skating with Santa this week." It's one of the many holiday events coming up at the arena, and I think it's going to be great. A bunch of guys from the team volunteered to do hour-long skating sessions with all the kids who signed up, and of course a special guest will be skating with them: the Man in Red himself. We'd found an awesome guy who has a real beard and custom-made suit and everything. He just so happens to be a former hockey player himself too, so he can handle himself on the ice and we've already shot a bunch of promos of him facing off against Rizz, skating around the rest of the guys, and taking shots at Connor in a custom Vipers Jersey: *Claus* across the shoulders and the number *25* on the back.

"Because of course, I'll be teaching you to skate during it," he adds. My smile falters and the shit-eating grin that spreads across his face makes me want to smack him.

❄ · · ❄ · · ❄

Ice skating: not actually so bad. Sort of. I fall a lot at first, but eventually kind of get the hang of it with a lot of help from

Connor and the rest of the team, and by the end it's actually pretty fun—when I'm not on my ass. They'd taken it upon themselves to decorate one of those little walker things that they have for kids for me to use after the Skating with Santa event. Connor had told everyone that I was a bit of a Grinch (though not the reasons of course), so they decked the walker out with Christmas wrapping paper, bright red and green bows, and a giant reindeer stuffed animal strapped to the front.

"Your chariot awaits, my lady," Rizzo had said with an exaggerated bow before the rest of the guys parted like the Red Sea to reveal the walker. I was in such a good mood after the event—it had been such a success that we'd had to add another round of sessions the following weekend—that I didn't mind the joke. And the walker had actually been really helpful, so I didn't even care how ridiculous I looked.

"See, not so bad, right?" Connor asks, skating backwards in front of me like it's nothing and smiling like an idiot. I get the distinct feeling that teaching me how to skate, sharing this part of his world with me, makes him very, very happy. Which, in turn, makes me very, very happy.

"Not so bad," I agree. I ditched the walker about half an hour ago and haven't fallen again since. I *think* I even look mostly comfortable now, though I won't be winning any figure skating competitions any time soon.

"So, are you up for another *Make Mac Love Christmas* escapade tonight?"

"Hmm, it depends. Does it involve my ass hitting ice all night?"

He chuckles. "No skating tonight, I promise. A giant maze of Christmas lights."

"Ok, that actually sounds really cool," I grin. I'm enjoying the hell out of all of his attempts to turn December around for me, and part of me thinks he may just pull it off. *Knock on wood.*

"Great."

Rizzo skates up then, stick in hand.

"You can't leave until you let me teach you how to shoot a puck."

"Seriously?" I ask, lips curling upward. That actually sounds pretty fun now that I can stay mostly vertical on the ice. Connor smiles and skates off to grab his own stick and glove.

Rizzo shows me the basics and I spend the next half hour hitting pucks at Connor, a bunch of the other guys gathering around and cheering me on—and booing Connor when he stops my shots. I try not to take it personally that he didn't bother to put on a helmet or any pads whatsoever. He's grinning like a freaking lunatic as we mess around and I know that I'm smiling just as much.

"Ok, I think I might really love hockey," I admit as Rizzo gives me some more pointers.

"The fact that you ever doubted the level of superiority of it to every other sport makes me question my high opinion of you, Mac," Rizzo says, his voice mockingly indignant.

"I wouldn't go that far, but I'll admit that I now see the appeal of whacking pucks at people."

He laughs and Connor yells, "Is that really all you got, Mac? Come on, ya hoser!" I narrow my eyes at him, but before I can say anything in response, a bunch of the guys rush him. "Hey! What the—"

He cuts off as they tackle him, a giant dog pile forming that leaves the goal wide open.

"Go!" Rizzo yells in triumph. "Just like I showed you earlier. That's it, move the puck with you as you go. Nice and easy...you got it, Mac!"

Connor tries desperately to crawl back towards the goal with five guys still on top of him, pulling him back. "This is so not fair, you know that right!?" he calls, though he's cracking up.

"All's fair in love and hockey!" Jules yells from the top of the pile. "Get in there, Mac! Light the lamp!"

I can't stop laughing or grinning as I make my way towards the goal.

"Cheaters! All of you! *CHEATERS!*" Connor roars, laughing when Howey puts him in a headlock.

I smack the puck the last couple of feet into the mostly wide-open net and all the guys cheer when it sails easily inside. They leap up from the dog pile and I yelp as they hoist me up onto their shoulders, the sound quickly becoming a ridiculous giggle. Connor rolls onto his back, and props himself up on his elbows to watch the show, his smile wide and gorgeous and so genuine that it makes something twist inside my chest. I meet his gaze and he winks, mouthing *rematch, McNamara.*

I smile back and my God, I think this might be the happiest I've felt in years.

Chapter Ten

CONNOR

Despite the fact that there's a seventy-eight percent chance that I'm falling in love with one of my best friends, December is going off like gangbusters. Hattie has been totally on board with everything holiday-related I've thrown at her, and I think deep down she's desperate to have me succeed, to have December finally mean something more to her than hurt and anger and all around bullshit.

The look on her face when she'd been messing around on the ice with us after the Skating with Santa event had been priceless and I think that may have been the beginning of the end for me. Well, that, and when she'd almost kissed me in the hallway that last night at my place. I think my heart stopped beating for the span of an endless minute when she'd started to lean up towards me, her eyes burning, licking her lips softly as she stared at my own. She'd stopped herself at the last minute, and I'd played it off as if it wasn't a big deal, but it had been like being within an inch of touching Heaven and being yanked back to earth. I can't stop thinking about it, can't stop wondering *what if...*

So, even if I'm feeling...*things*, I'm not pursuing shit on that front, at least not yet. There's still a twenty-two percent chance that it'll pass, that it's just a crush. A major one, but still just a crush. Wait, do adults get crushes? Is there an age-limit cut off for that term? Like once you're past fifteen, they aren't called crushes anymore? What are they then? Passing fancies? *Oh my God, shut the fuck up, Shepherd.*

I shake myself, stopping that stupid train of thought and focusing on the crowd. The whole team is on a float in one of the big Christmas parades in town, and it's seriously a blast. We wave and toss out little goodie bags to the kids, a few of which even have tickets to an upcoming game hidden inside—Hattie's idea of course.

"So, I might have done something stupid," Rizzo says as he smiles and waves to the crowd.

"Might have?"

"Ok, so there's no might about it. I slept with Nat. You know, Hattie's assistant?"

I groan and elbow him hard in the ribs. He grunts but we both keep the smiles plastered on our faces.

"You fucking idiot."

"I know, I know." Despite being a shameless flirt with damn near everyone, Rizzo has never actually hooked up with anyone in the Vipers' organization before. For lack of a better phrase, he knows better than to shit where he eats.

"And?"

"And she told me it was a one-time thing," he says, sounding...affronted?

I turn to him, brows furrowed in confusion. "Isn't that exactly how you like it?"

"No, no, no, you aren't listening. *She* told *me* it was a one off, not the other way around. When we were done, she got dressed, told me it was fun, kissed me, and then bolted."

I laugh. "She pulled a Rizzo on you."

"Yeah, she did. And fuck if it wasn't...hot? I don't know, man, maybe that's not the right word, but I haven't been able to stop thinking about her since. I'm desperate to get a round two. Like can barely enjoy my time with anyone else kind of desperate." He runs a hand through his hair. "What is wrong with me?"

"A lot," I answer, shaking my head, "a lot."

We both laugh and then he grins widely, pointing at a little girl in a Vipers Jersey with a *15* on it—Rizzo's number. "Hey! Someone give that girl two treat bags!"

"Maybe you're just growing up," I offer.

"I've done no such thing!" he says, looking aghast. "Balls. Farts. Boobies. See—no grown-ups here."

"I *mean* maybe you're just getting tired of the game. Maybe you're ready for something more than one-night-stands from Puck Bunnies who just fawn over your abs or fame."

"And chiseled jawline, don't forget the chiseled jawline. And massive co—" He cuts off when I punch him in the stomach, letting out a small *oof.* He laughs as he straightens, but then turns a bit more serious. "I don't know...I'm not saying you're right, but...maybe you've got a point. *Maybe,*" he emphasizes when I give him a knowing look. "But even if that's the case, there's no way that Nat will believe that I want more than just a hook up or fuck-buddies kind of thing."

"Well, sounds like you've got some work to do then, my friend." He groans and I grin, waving to the crowd.

I can finally see the sign for Town Tavern about a hundred yards further up the route—that's where Hattie, Sara, Ollie, and her grandparents are all supposed to be watching from. Ollie has been talking about the parade for weeks and I know she was even more excited when Hattie said she would be watching with the family instead of being up on the float—though she'd been invited.

I spot them and wave enthusiastically, sticking my fingers in my mouth and whistling loudly. Ollie is on her grandpa's shoulders and cheers wildly when she sees me. Or *us*, rather. When I told her that the float was a giant viper wearing a purple, teal, and black checkered scarf and matching hat, a big fangy grin on his face, she thought it sounded like the funniest thing in the world and couldn't wait to see it.

Sara leans over and says something directly into Hattie's ear, and Hattie throws her head back, laughing. God, she looks beautiful with her loose curls spilling out from beneath a Vipers beanie with a glittery black puff ball on the top, tight jeans, and dimples on full display. *Fuck me.*

Ollie snags a goodie bag out of the air when one of the guys tosses one her way, and waves it around her head wildly. She's smiling so big that I can't imagine how her cheeks don't hurt. Hattie's smile falters, her brows drawing down, and she glances around, up and down the side of the street they're standing on, then scanning across the road around the floats. I wonder what that's about, but she quickly seems to shake herself and smiles again as we move slowly past. I catch her gaze and wink, and she sticks out her tongue before cupping her hands over her mouth and cheering loudly. Soon, we're on to the next section of the street, and I'm already thinking about when I'll see her again.

Ok, so maybe it's more like a ninety-percent chance that I'm falling in love with one of my best friends.

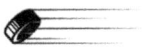

"Hey, uh, can you possibly help me out, man?"

I look up from my phone as I head towards the players and employee's entrance to the arena and see a guy holding a big floral arrangement standing by the door. He's wearing a baseball hat and a jacket with a patch on the front with a bouquet of flowers and some script underneath that I can't quite make out. The name of a flower shop, I assume.

"I can try," I say as I get closer, sliding my phone into my pocket.

"I got a flower delivery here for a..." he checks the card attached to the vase with a black ribbon, "Hallie McNamara." His accent is very southern California surfer and I fully expect him to call me *brah* any second. It sounds slightly off, though I can't quite put my finger on why. "But the door is locked and I can't find a call button or anything."

"Yeah, this is kind of a private entrance. Deliveries and stuff usually go to the front. And I think you mean Hattie."

Something flashes in his eyes, so briefly that I think I must have imagined it.

"Oh," he says, squinting at the card again. "Oh, yeah, you're right, I think those are Ts – Kris's handwriting is awful," he laughs and shakes his head. "Sorry, I didn't realize there was another way in. This is only my third day and I'm new in town. I know, I know, a delivery guy is a pretty stupid job for someone who doesn't know his way around." He looks sheepish. "But my aunt knows the owner and I really needed the job and...well, thank God for GPS, right?"

I huff out a laugh, smiling.

"I feel you. It took me a while to learn my way around too. But, hey, I can't let you in this way, sorry, man. They're pretty strict about security and stuff, but I can have someone meet you at the front entrance once I get inside. It shouldn't take too long."

He looks towards the front, then down at his watch. "Do you know her? This Hallie—er, Hattie—chick? I mean, could you maybe do me a solid and take them in for me and figure out where they need to go? I know it's asking a lot, but to be honest, I was supposed to deliver them earlier, but I accidentally left them at the shop and now I'm late and I really need this job. Aunt Jenny or no, the owner already wants to fire me I think, and this might just be the nail in my coffin."

I grin and wave him off, stepping forward to take the flowers. "Yeah, sure I can take them in, no problem."

His shoulders sag in relief and he smiles, a slash of pearly whites beneath his thick beard and mustache...and I swear there's that flash in his eyes again. Something dark and burning, but in a heartbeat, it's gone, his expression totally casual, showing nothing but gratitude. I give myself an inward shake. *I think I need sleep.*

"Thanks, dude. You're completely saving my ass right now. I totally owe you one."

"It's no problem, really. I'll make sure she gets them."

He nods and jogs off towards a black delivery van parked a few spots down. I head inside and take the elevators up to the offices instead of down and make my way to Hattie's office. She's at a meeting with a potential new sponsor, so I leave them on the table in the corner. I wonder who they're from, but know that it wouldn't be polite to snoop. I *might* glance at the card as I shift the vase back a bit on the table, but all I see is her name scrawled across the front in admittedly messy handwriting.

I shrug, figuring I'll ask her about it later, and head down to the training room before I have to get ready for the game.

Chapter Eleven

HATTIE

"Tell me not to sleep with Rizzo again," Nat begs from her perch on the table next to my flowers, leaning over to smell one of the blooms. I glance up from my screen and grin at her.

"From what you told me, you didn't really do much sleepin' the first time around."

She throws a notepad at me and I duck, laughing.

"I'm serious! I don't think I can hold out much longer. I swear me telling him it was a one-and-done somehow made him *more* interested. He's hinted at wanting another hook up since it happened, but now he's being weird—he asked me to dinner. Like a legit *dinner date*." I raise my brows. That is very un-Rizzo of him. "Right?! That's what I thought!" she exclaims, reading my mind. "I know it's just a means to an end, another night in the sack, but still."

"Well, what did you say?"

"I told him...I'd think about it." She groans and puts her head in her hands. "I'm not going to be able to hold out much longer. When I knew it would just be one night of fun and then we'd be adults and just see each other at work like normal, it didn't seem like that big a deal. I could handle that. But with him actively trying for another round?" She puffs out her cheeks and blows out a long breath. "It's a completely different ballgame that I am not equipped to play. I mean, you've seen him! I do not think with my brain when he's around, I think with something else entirely and it very, *very* much wants me to accept his invitation. Actually, it just wants me to say fuck dinner all together and tell him to just take me to a hotel."

I can't help but laugh at that. "Well, would it really be so bad if it wasn't a one-and-done? I mean, plenty of people have steady fuck-buddies."

"Yes! Or, well, no. Maybe? I don't know! I was ok being a notch in his skyscraper-length bedpost for one really, *really* good night, but continually just being one in a rotation of countless women? I don't think I could do it." She pinches the bridge of her nose. "Ugh, let's change the subject. Who sent you flowers? The parade float guy? He seemed *very* smitten with you."

Brian *had* flirted when we were working on the float design and everything—and I'd flirted back a bit, admittedly—but it was harmless and nothing had ever come of it. Would I have accepted if he'd asked me out? I honestly don't know. He was super cute, funny, and sweet, but when I thought about going out on a date with him, it wasn't *him* I pictured sitting across from me at dinner or holding my hand as we walked down the street or leaning in to kiss me good night. No matter how hard I tried, someone else's face always popped up instead.

"They aren't from the parade float guy, thank you very much." I hit send on my last email and head over to the table, shifting the flower arrangement a little. "Well, I guess they *could* be—I don't actually know who they're from—but I doubt it." Brian had actually ended up getting *Bobby's* number at the end of the float build. He was an equal opportunity flirt and the two had gone out on a few casual dates. Bobby said that it was fun, but they decided that they had friends vibes, nothing more.

I'd initially had the crazy thought that the flowers were from Connor and I'll even admit to how my heart had stupidly leapt at the thought, but when I'd texted him, thankfully catching him before he had to head out to the ice to start warming up, he'd explained that he'd brought them inside, but they weren't *from* him. So, the sender is a mystery. Connor joked that I have a secret admirer, and while that sounds potentially romantic or sexy on the surface, as someone who had an unwanted shadow for several months, I can decidedly tell you I want no part of that. If someone wants to tell me they're into me, they need to just come out and say it.

I don't actually think it's that though, I think they must just be from one of the many charitable organizations or sponsors I've met with lately. It wouldn't be the first time I've received gifts of flowers after meetings. I decide to try to track down the florist tomorrow and see if they can tell me anything. Until then, I'm just enjoying the pretty addition brightening up my office.

"Hell, maybe I'll call float guy then. Maybe he'll get my mind off Rizzo and his giant—"

"Ok, ok, come on, you," I cut her off with a laugh. I grab my bag and turn off the light. "Let's go grab Bobby and head down to the game." I lace my arm through hers and as we walk down the hallway, I lean in and say in a low voice, "But, uh, explain exactly what you mean by *giant...*"

❄· ·❄· ·❄

The game is going great. We're up by one and Connor has been a rockstar in the net. All the guys have been absolutely ruthless and I think I've seen more fights break out in this one game than I have in all the others combined. I'm in my customary spot right by the glass, my voice nearly hoarse from all my screaming and cheering. I smother a smile as Rizzo skates by, catching Nat's gaze. She holds it, even bites her lip, and I elbow her in the ribs.

"Shit, I was doing it again, wasn't I?"

"Yup," I say with a laugh. A nasty hit causes yet another fight and I wince as I turn to Bobby. "Ok, so am I just imagining it, or is tonight's game a bit more, uh, volatile than usual?"

"Definitely not your imagination," Bobby confirms. "So, Rizzo and Connor both used to play for the Kodiaks, and they left at the same time to come here. I guess some of the guys still hold a grudge about it—which is so stupid, but whatever—and every time they play, it's a freaking gongshow." I'd learned that *gong-show* usually meant a game that just gets plain old rowdy: fights, penalties, shit-talking. Usually lots of goals, too, and so far that's all tracking for tonight. Connor is doing fantastic, but the Kodiaks are relentless and really freaking good. We're still up by four, but it's a crazy game so far.

"Two years ago," Bobby continues, "there was a huge brawl, like a clear the benches, everyone on the ice throwing punches kind of brawl. It was crazy."

Nat finally yanks her gaze away from Rizzo and I smile into my beer. "Ooh yeah, I remember watching that one with my ex! It was brutal."

"Dang, that's nuts."

"Yeah, this particular game is always *very* bloody."

He ain't lyin'. I don't think I've ever seen so many players having to leave the ice to get bandaged up. I catch Connor's eye during a timeout and he winks, despite the intensity of the game. Since the snow storm, things with us have been...different. Well, actually, things with *us* have been completely normal—we've joked around and gotten coffee and binged *Criminal Minds* like always. It's the way I'm thinking about him in my head that's been different, the way I can barely keep my hands to myself, the way I can't go two seconds without thinking about him in a way that is very not-friendly. Or extremely *overly*-friendly, depending on how you look at it, I guess. I think about that near-kiss way too often and ninety-nine percent of the time, I regret stopping myself. I mean, I know it was the right call, but to actually know what it feels like to kiss Connor? To know what his lips feel like, what he tastes like? I almost groan just thinking about it.

And it isn't just the physical. I...damn it, I have feelings for Connor. I don't know the depth of them yet, and I'm not sure that it's enough to risk our friendship, but I can't deny that they're there. I have no idea what to do about them, or if there even *is* anything to do about them, so I've decided to do the mature thing, and just ignore them.

Nat and I are quite the damn pair when it comes to pretending we don't want the men we want. *Lord help us.*

The game resumes and I try to stop thinking about anything not hockey-related. We almost score again, another fight breaks out, and a few guys land themselves in the penalty box. Lather. Rinse. Repeat. I roll my eyes after what seems like the twentieth fight of the period.

"And they say that women are dramatic?" Bobby laughs into his beer and Nat goes on a nacho run. "Oh, and cotton candy!" I call after her as she jogs up the steps.

The crowd boos over a bullshit call, and two of the Kodiaks make a break towards our goal, Jules and Roman hot on their heels. I hold my breath as they near the goal, watching as Connor prepares for the shot, waiting with that quiet, intense stillness he has.

But then someone goes down. I can't even really tell what starts it, can't tell if it's a red jersey or a black one that hits the ice first, but somehow there's suddenly a pile of bodies careening towards Connor. I tense as they collide, nothing on earth able to stop them or even slow their attack. The sound of the collision echoes through the space, seems to vibrate down into my bones. The entire goal shoots backwards, slamming into the wall behind it with a loud crack. Bodies tumble, limbs sprawl, and a helmet flies across the ice.

My heart seems to stop in my chest as my entire body goes cold.

The helmet is Connor's and he's not moving.

Chapter Twelve

HATTIE

Connor is lying there on the ice, not moving, and I can't breathe. Why isn't he moving? *No, no, no.* He's ok, just a little stunned. He's ok. He has to be ok.

I'm on my feet, hands pressed against the glass as if I can reach through it and get to him. The entire arena falls into a stoic, almost eerie silence as twenty-thousand people seem to hold their collective breath, but my heartbeat and blood pound so loudly in my ears, I almost wince.

Medics make their way out onto the ice, and everything suddenly feels like a dream. This can't be happening. This can't be real. I stare wide-eyed, completely immobile as they check him over.

He still isn't moving.

Why the fuck isn't he moving yet??

"Hattie?" Bobby lays a hand on my arm.

I try to swallow but can't. My stomach twists painfully, my body feeling weirdly numb, too hot, and too cold all at once. How is that possible? Someone brings out one of those boards, like at a football game, and everything seems to freeze, suspended in a horrible, terrifying moment in time: they use those boards when someone might have a spinal injury.

And then I'm pulling away from Bobby's touch and sprinting up the stairs, barely able to even see. He calls out behind me, but I don't stop. I run and run, my thighs burning as I make my way to the top. I trip once, going down hard, cranking my knee against the edge of a step and biting my lip. I taste blood, but I don't care. I pull myself up, ignoring the concerned fans who offer me helping hands, and burst into the main concourse of the arena, nearly stumbling and barely righting myself at the last second before I bite the dust. I mumble apologies to people along the way that I bump into, but I don't slow down. I sprint around to the other side but there are too many damn people. I think I scream at them to get out of my way, but I can't be sure. Nothing seems real. I don't feel like I'm in control of my body, like I'm outside of it somehow. Why are there so many people? I need them to move, I need a clear path. I need to get to Connor. *Connor, Connor, Connor.* His name thunders through my mind over and over, like the beat of my heart. *He has to be ok.*

I finally see the door that leads down to the lower levels. A security guard is always posted out here during games, and when Luis sees me, he immediately opens the door with his access card. I fly down the stairs and around the corner towards the training room, cursing December up and down as I go. This can't be happening. December has always been bad, but this is just too much. It can't do this to him because of me. *I'm* the one who's supposed to suffer for whatever reason, not anyone else. *Not him.*

God, please let him be ok. Please, please, please.

I freeze when I see them at the end of the hallway. They've got him on a gurney now and are wheeling him towards the door leading outside to a waiting ambulance. Why did it take me so long to get here? Why couldn't I have run faster? What good is all the stupid cardio I do if I can't even get to him in time??

I stumble forward, eyes wide in horror, feeling like I might vomit. *Oh God. Please, please, please.*

"Hey," I yell, or try to. It comes out in a choked whisper. "What's happening? What's wrong??" I demand of no one in particular. They don't seem to hear me. They don't pause, so neither do I. My vision blurs as tears well, threatening to spill. "Hey!" I yell again, louder this time, desperate for someone to answer me.

Someone steps in my path, gripping me gently by the shoulders. I look up to find Jules there, a bandage on his forehead and dried blood smeared down his temple and cheek, his light brown hair streaked with it.

"Mac, hey, it's alright."

"Wh-where are they taking him? What's happening? Is he ok?" My voice trembles and I can feel my hands shaking at my sides. I try to move past him, but he holds me in place.

"Mac, you're bleeding. Are you—" *Fuck this.*

"STOP!" I shriek, cutting Jules off, and a moment later, to my surprise, everyone does. With a rush of relief that's nearly painful, I realize that they didn't stop because of my scream. They stopped because Connor had raised a hand to *make* them stop. I almost sob but somehow hold it back, a strangled gasp coming out instead. Jules releases me and I rush forward. The EMT standing near Connor's head shifts out of the way as I approach, making room.

"Oh my God, Connor," I whisper when I finally lay eyes on him. They've got him in one of those braces that prevents him from moving his head too much and there's a dark bruise already forming on his right cheek, blood coating on his neck from a cut

I can't see, staining his hair a deep crimson. I feel like I can't breathe again and my arms and legs feel like they're made of jelly. I lean forward so I can look at him and make sure he can see me.

"I'm ok, Mac. I'm alright." His brows furrow a bit as he stares at me. He looks surprised and confused and maybe a little touched? I might be imagining things. I'm very close to losing my shit completely, so it's extremely possible.

"He lost consciousness and took a hard hit to the head and neck, so we're taking him to the hospital to get some scans and be sure everything's alright," the EMT beside me says in a soft, kind voice. I swallow hard and I think I nod in acknowledgment.

"He's...he's ok though?"

"*I'm alright,*" Connor says again, lifting his hand to grip mine. I squeeze as hard as I can and his lips quirk up on one side, a ghost of that crooked smile that gets me every time. I can tell he's in pain though, regardless of how alright he claims to be, and seeing him strapped to the gurney like this makes it nearly impossible for my mind to believe that he could really be ok.

"You're bleeding," he says, concerned. "What the hell happened?"

Before I can answer, the EMT clears his throat. "We need to go," he says gently. I stare into Connor's eyes for one more long moment, conveying...I'm not sure what. My mind is a mess and all I know is that seeing him hurt has been the scariest moment of my life.

I nod, squeeze his hand one more time, and step away so they can wheel him out. That small step backwards and releasing Connor's hand is one of the hardest things I've ever had to do. It feels wrong on so many levels. Jules steps up beside me, wrapping an arm around my shoulder in a friendly way and I lean into his side, not even caring how gross he is at the moment, drenched in sweat and covered in blood.

"He'll be alright, Mac," he says quietly.

I stare long after the door shuts behind them, my hands clenched into fists. My pulse is still racing and I feel a little dizzy. Bobby's words from earlier echo in my mind and I see red as fury blazes in my chest, swift and hot and totally unexpected.

"Did they do this on purpose? Because of the rivalry or bad blood or whatever?? They wouldn't...I mean, they wouldn't have *tried* to..."

Jules' brows fly up in a surprise. "No. No, no, no," he says vehemently. "We get heated out there because of it, but no one would ever do something like that on purpose, Mac, I promise."

I nod, the fury fizzling out almost as quickly as it had come, leaving me empty and cold and dizzy. I turn to face him, blinking several times to get my vision to clear.

"What about you? Are you alright?" I nod towards his forehead.

He waves me away. "Ah, I'm fine. Didn't even need stitches. Kasey got me all glued up, I'm good to go." He studies me for a minute, brows drawing down as I blink rapidly to stop the hallway from swaying. "Uh, you're looking a little pale, Mac. Why don't we sit down for a second, ok?" For a rough and rowdy Bostonian, he can actually be exceedingly sweet. My legs do feel like they're going to give out any second, so I let him help ease me down onto a nearby bench. "Sit tight, I'll be right back."

He leaves and comes back with Kasey and she hands me some kind of sports drink. I take a few sips, not really tasting it, but the cool liquid does help settle me a bit. I wipe my mouth with the back of my hand, and wince. When I look at my hand, it's streaked with red. Huh?

"Hattie, you've got a cut on your lip. I'm going to get the blood off so I can see it more clearly, ok?" Kasey says in a soothing voice. She has a great bedside manner. She would have been a great doctor. I nod and she gently wipes at my mouth and chin with a damp cloth. I wince a little but the pain is pretty muted. "Ok, it's not too bad. The bleeding has already almost stopped, but I want you to hold this on it for a few minutes. That should do the trick." She studies me and I blink rapidly, trying to focus on her, but everything is going a little pear-shaped.

"Is she ok?" Jules whispers.

"Hey, Hattie? Look at me, try to focus on me alright?" I shift my gaze to hers, trying to do what she's asking, but all I can see is Connor. Connor not moving. Connor strapped to that board. I sway and Kasey's grip on my shoulders keeps me upright. "Alright, I want you to put your head between your knees, ok? It'll help with the dizziness. It's probably just all the adrenaline." I do as she asks, leaning over and putting my head in my hands. "There you go. Slow, deep breaths, ok?"

I know I'm being ridiculous, but seeing Connor like that really freaked me out. I can't even explain why, exactly, other than that it feels *wrong*, like a part of me is strapped to that fucking stretcher right now.

"Keep an eye on her," Kasey says, "I'm going to grab an ice pack for her neck. It should help." I hear her footsteps fade away down the hallway.

"First big injury you've seen, huh?" Jules asks.

"Yeah," I say thickly, though that's not even half the reason I'm so upset. I've seen brutal hits before during football games, had friends wheeled off the field just like Connor, but tonight was so different.

"I understand. The first time I got knocked out, I think my ma nearly had a coronary. It's scary shit."

I lean back against the wall and take a deep, settling breath, letting it out in a long whoosh. I stay that way for a long minute before Jules cuts into the silence.

"So, what do you call the things that you push around the store? Like when you're buying groceries."

I crack open one eye and find him grinning at me. This is one of Jules' favorite games. He loves asking me what I call certain things and usually thinks my "southern" answers are hilarious. I muster a half smile for him.

"That's a buggy," I say, shaking my head.

He laughs. "A *buggy*," he says, trying to mimic my accent, but it just comes out sounding ridiculous. "I love it. Hey, Connor really will be alright. We can't be the Sin Bin without him, yeah? So, he'll be alright and we'll all be carrying on again in a few days."

I let out a long exhale, actually feeling a little better. I meet his eyes and smile, letting him know how much his kindness means to me.

"Thanks, Jules."

"Forget about it," he says, waving me away again. He needs to get back up to the ice, and I need to get my shit together. I've got to handle the Reindeer Toss event as soon as the game ends, and, as much as I'm dying to go to the hospital, I know that they're just going to say that they can't tell me anything since I'm not family. One of the other guys on the team could probably swing it, but they're mini-celebrities around here, especially at the hospital. Not only has the ortho team at Seattle Sacred Heart operated on half of the players, but the guys do a ton of charity work in the attached children's hospital.

So, when Kasey comes back with an ice pack for me, I take it and agree to stay put for just a bit longer until my color looks more beach bum and less Casper the Friendly Ghost. Then I put on my metaphorical big girl undies and do what I need to do.

I focus on the event and doing my job with a smile, though worry for Connor gnaws at the back of my mind. I somehow block out the worst of my panic while I work, and everything goes great. After what feels like decades, everything is finally done and I head to my car. I'm determined to camp out in the waiting room of the hospital whether they'll tell me anything or not, but Rizzo catches me in the parking garage.

"Coach just heard from the hospital—Connor's fine. Mild concussion and a cracked rib, but nothing else bad internally. A couple of stitches for a cut on his head, but it's superficial. He's gonna be sore as hell for a couple of days, but he's alright."

I close my eyes and let out a shaky breath. When I open them, Rizzo is studying me in one of those rare moments of seriousness that he has. I've come to learn that Rizzo plays up the cocky, ridiculous, playboy thing—and he *is* those things, don't get me wrong—but he's also kind and caring and has a lot of depth beneath the surface. It's one of the reasons I haven't told Nat to run far, far away from him. There is much more to Anthony Rizzo than meets the eye.

"Are you ok, Mac?"

"I...no," I say, honestly. "No, I'm not." Tears well again, even though I know it's ridiculous, and then Rizzo wraps his arms around me. I let myself cry for a couple of minutes, let myself just have a moment here to let the fear and relief all mix together in a little break down. Rizzo doesn't seem to care, just lets me cry it out. After a bit, I pull away, sniffling, scrubbing my eyes and nose. "Sorry. It was just...a lot seeing him like that."

He smiles and simply says, "I know," but the way he says it makes me think he's meaning something completely different than agreeing that seeing a friend hurt is hard. He doesn't push though and I'm beyond thankful for that because honestly, I wouldn't even know what to say. I need time to figure out what the hell is going on in my head and my heart right now.

"Night, Rizzo."

"Night, Mac."

Chapter Thirteen

CONNOR

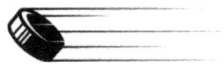

Waking up in the hospital is never a good feeling, but it's even worse when I know how worried Hattie was and how upset Olls will be when I'm not home in the morning. I know I shouldn't complain because that hit could have turned out so much worse. I got lucky as fuck to get out of it with just a concussion, a cracked rib, a bunch of bruises, and a couple of stitches. A guy I played with in high school took a hit like that once and wound up paralyzed from the neck down.

So, yeah, I know how lucky I am. I also know that the utter terror I saw in Hattie's eyes was nothing I ever want to see again. She'd been pale as a ghost, those stormy blue eyes wide and stark. That look...well, it made me think that maybe she felt more than just worry for a friend. And I'd be lying if I said that the thought didn't make my heart thunder in my chest.

They're keeping me for observation for the night but I should be released tomorrow afternoon unless anything crazy happens. I'm just about to get up and search the whole floor for a landline or a cell phone I can borrow when Rizzo comes in.

"Hey, fucker," he says in greeting. He's grinning but I can see the tension around his eyes and at the corners of his mouth. *He was worried.* Hell, *I* was fucking worried. I saw it all happening like it was in slow motion, but there wasn't a damn thing I could possibly do except close my eyes and brace for impact. I felt the collision, felt myself being propelled backwards along with the net, and my helmet fly off. I felt a blinding pain in the back of my head and neck and then total blackness. I woke up halfway down the hallway to the training room, not quite sure what had happened at first.

"I'm assuming the words "visiting hours" don't apply to the great Anthony Rizzo?"

He gives me an admonishing look. "Please. Like anyone could possibly say no to me."

"Except Nat," I point out.

"Listen, asshole, do you want food or not?" He holds up a white paper bag, shaking it a little as he comes to the bed. "If you do, then I suggest you stop pointing out things that may or may not be facts."

I grin. "Oh fuck, I love you." I lunge for the bag and tear into the bacon cheeseburger. He chuckles but pulls out a second one, setting it on the small table for when I'm done with this one, and then a third for himself, joining me for a midnight snack—or, more accurately, a one-thirty a.m. snack. I didn't realize how hungry I was until the scent of the food hit me, but now I'm ravenous. I never eat right before games, so the last thing I had today was a late breakfast with Ollie this morning. Er, yesterday morning, I guess.

"How are you feeling?" he asks after handing me one of the sodas from the carrier.

I shrug and immediately regret it, shifting uncomfortably to take a long gulp of my drink.

"I'm alright. Sore. How'd the game turn out?"

"We won." I nod, happy that we pulled it out and annoyed that I wasn't there to help my team. He pats a small duffle bag that he tossed on the bed. "So, I got you some clothes and your phone and spare charger from your locker. And I've already checked in with Sara and told her I can come by in the morning to help with Ollie if I need to or if she's upset. I told her you'd call or text her once I got your phone to you."

"Thanks, man. I appreciate everything." I take another long drink and ask, what I hope is nonchalantly, "What about Mac?"

Rizzo gives me one of those knowing looks of his. He hides it well, but Rizzo is far more observant and intuitive than people realize. Which, of course, is just how he likes it.

"She's alright. I let her know that you were ok as soon as Coach told us. She's tough, but she took it pretty hard."

I exhale roughly and run a hand through my hair, wincing again in pain and cringing at how disgusting it feels. I wonder if they'd let me take a shower or not and, reading my mind, Rizzo offers to give me a sponge bath. I flip him off, laughing, but it trails off, my expression growing serious. Hattie's fearful face flashes across the forefront of my mind and my chest aches.

"She looked so scared," I say quietly.

"She was. She was fucking terrified, man. Jules told me that she nearly passed out after they wheeled you away."

I wonder if it's too late to text her but decide that I don't really care. If the roles were reversed, I know I'd want her to text me. Honestly, if the roles were reversed, I don't know that I would be handling it well at all. The thought of seeing her hurt, of not knowing if she was ok, sends a jolt of unease through me, so acute it makes my stomach twist painfully. I lean my head back against the bed and close my eyes.

"So, are the two of you just going to skate around it forever, or what?"

I slide my eyes open, though with a bit of difficulty. I don't know if it's the meds they gave me or just everything coming to a head, but I'm suddenly completely wiped out, despite only having woken up a few minutes ago. I meet Rizzo's steady gaze. I could deny it, but what's the point. Rizzo knows me better than almost anyone else in the world, sometimes even better than I know my-self.

"It's complicated," I say instead, which isn't a complete lie. It's a bit of a cop out, granted, but not a lie.

He calls me on it, of course. "Try again." He crosses his arms over his chest and gives me an expectant look.

"I...I'm just not sure either of us is ready to take the leap, even if we might want to." Knowing that I have feelings for Hattie and that I want her more than I've ever wanted another person doesn't change the fact that it might not work out if we try. It might not be the right time or she may not be ready. Hell, *I* may not be ready. I've never tried to date anyone while being a single dad and I have no idea if I know how to balance all of that. Of course, Olls already loves Hattie and part of me knows that Hattie would make the situation as easy as breathing, but the fear is still there. The uncertainty is too much for me, at least for the moment, but I decide to really take a look at everything once I'm out of this God forsaken hospital bed.

Everyone here has been great, but I'm a terrible patient. I'm very much of the rub some dirt in it generation when it comes to injuries. I've played with broken fingers and cracked ribs, stitches and pulled muscles. I don't like being out for the count and I really don't like being taken care of. I'm the one that should be taking care of everyone else. Plus, hospitals bring back too many bad memories of Hannah's short battle. She chose to go into hospice at the end, not wanting to die in a strange place without her family nearby, but before that, there had been quite a few hospital stays and I don't like being here one bit.

"I understand that," he says, seriously. Rizzo isn't one to mock or make light of shit like this. "Well, when you figure it the fuck out, you let me know. Until then, I can still try to get in her pants, right?" His grin returns and his eyes glitter with amusement.

"You don't stand a chance, jackass." My lids are growing so heavy I can barely keep them open, but I have to send a message before I pass out.

Connor: I'm ok. Going to sleep in this terrible hospital bed now. I'll call you in the morning.

To my surprise, she texts back immediately. Shit. Was she up, just waiting on word from me? Or just so worried she couldn't sleep?

Hattie: Don't ever scare me like that again. I'm so glad you're alright.

Connor: I'm sorry. But I promise I'm alright. And I'll make it up to you.

Hattie: You owe me coffee for an entire year.

I chuckle, but can't manage to type out a response to that before sleep finally swallows me up.

I slowly blink open my eyes, confused for a minute where I am. This is most definitely not my bed which I've come to believe is the most comfortable one in existence. I paid way too much to make sure that was the case. It takes a second for the room around me to come into focus and another couple after that for my mind to catch up. *Oh, right. Hospital.* My neck and face and ribs are sore, and I've got a headache, but overall, I'm not too worse for the wear.

"Mornin', sunshine. You look like you got rode hard and hung up wet."

I whip my head to my left to see Hattie sitting in the chair by the window, a cup of coffee from our favorite spot in her hands. Talk about a sight for sore eyes. She's in leggings and an ice blue sweater that hangs loosely off one shoulder, and her hair is in one of those messy braids she likes. *Gorgeous. Completely gorgeous.* She gives me a warm smile, but I can see the worry beneath it, and her eyes are red-rimmed and a little puffy. Guilt settles in my chest like a heavy weight. I feel like a total jerk. Not that's it's actually my fault, but still.

When I don't answer immediately, she clarifies. "You look like shit."

My lips curl up. "Not possible, Mac."

She laughs, though it sounds a bit shaky, and comes over to the bed, swatting at my leg. I shift over a bit so she can perch on the edge.

"How long have you been here?" I ask, rubbing my eyes. She pours me a cup of water from the small table beside her and hands it over. I sip it gratefully as I stare at her, brow arched in question. She chews her lip for a second before answering.

"Six a.m." she admits. "I...I was up already," she adds, looking down at her hands.

"Mac," I say quietly, the word coming out somewhere between chiding and gutted. That's how I feel. Gutted. She stayed up all night worrying about me. She gives me a half-smile, one dimple peeking out, and hikes a shoulder.

"How are you feeling? And don't you dare lie to me, Connor Shepherd."

"I would never dream of it, ma'am," I give her a small grin, "I'm alright. Pretty sore, but overall I'm ok, I swear."

She lets out a long breath, staring down at the bed. She picks absently at the blanket before saying quietly, "Con—Shep," she corrects and my eyes narrow slightly. She almost called me Connor. She never does that. Except she did last night, didn't she? Right before they wheeled me out to the ambulance. *Adding that to my think-about-later pile.*

"When you were on that ice and not moving I..." I reach out and put a hand over hers to stop her fidgeting. She glances up to meet my eyes. "I was *terrified*. I don't think I've ever been so scared in my life."

"I'm sorry." It's all I can think to say. I can't promise her it'll never happen again. But she doesn't seem to need me to say anything more. She studies me for a long minute, and once she seems to decide I'm really ok, the stress melts away and she smiles at me, a real smile this time, the one that makes my pulse race and my own lips curl upwards. *Those God damn dimples.*

"I thought December was pulling out all the stops to beat you at your game."

I scoff. "It'll take more than a little collision in the goal to do that. I'm playing to win, Mac. Nothing's going to stop me."

"Good," she whispers just as a nurse comes in, followed by a parade of doctors over the next few hours. Hattie sticks with me through the duration and after what seems like forever, I'm released into her capable hands.

"Is this really necessary?" I complain as she wheels me through the hospital towards the parking lot.

"Hospital protocol," she says, but I can hear the shit-eating-grin in her voice from behind me. "Oh, wait, I almost forgot." Before I know what's happening, she's got her phone out in front of us, snapping a selfie of me in the damned wheelchair and her grinning like a lunatic. "Annnnd that's getting sent to the entire team. Done."

"I hate you. I take back every nice thing I've ever said about you."

"You lie like a rug, Shep." Her twang makes me laugh and we finally leave the hospital, me ditching the blasted chair as soon as we clear the front doors.

Ollie nearly tackles me when Sara brings her home, but it's worth the stab of pain when she wraps her arms around me and tells me that she missed me. It was only one missed morning, but still. I squeeze her back, letting out a shuddering breath as everything that could have happened hits me all over again.

"Aunt Sara said you got hurt," Ollie says in a quiet voice, and I can hear the worry.

"Only a little," I promise her. "I'm ok. The doctors fixed me right up." She lets out a long breath but nods, quickly moving on from me to telling Hattie all about her day at school while Sara and I chat.

"How was she last night?"

"She was great. A little upset when you weren't here this morning, but when Rizzo showed up to take her to school, she couldn't have cared less that you were gone." I smile at that, loving how much Rizzo—and everyone, really—loves Ollie.

"Thank you for staying the night. For everything."

"Of course. You know we're always here for both of you." She looks at Ollie, an indulgent smile on her face. "You letting us stay in her life has been a Godsend, Con. To have this little bit of Chris back...well, I refuse to get all sappy here, but suffice it to say we love you both and are happy to do whatever you need."

My throat feels a little tight at the thought. I know exactly what she means. Seeing little bits of Hannah in Ollie makes me feel like she's still here with us somehow and helps ease the hurt when the days are hard. Sara scrunches her nose up and I can tell she's trying not to cry. She likes to pretend that she isn't a giant softie, but she literally cries at soup commercials—always claiming that there's something in her eye, of course.

"So, anyway, where do we stand on the whole you asking Hattie out thing? Because I stand by my former statement: if you don't, I *so* will."

I give her a playful shove and she winks before darting off into the kitchen to grab something to drink. *Where the fuck* do *I stand?* I honestly don't know, but it seems like things between Hattie and I are back to normal. I think. I'm still not quite sure what the night before meant—was it just the first time she'd seen a friend hurt like that? Was it more than that?—and won't until I have more time to digest everything. But for now, I'm happy to see that she seems happy.

The rest of the day passes with Hattie giving me shit and making jokes about me being an invalid and a few of the guys stopping by to check in. So many, in fact, that Hattie and Sara order a ton of pizza for everyone and it kind of turns into a party.

My neck hurts and my entire body feels like it went ten rounds with The Italian Stallion, but looking around at everyone gathered here, the family that's become mine by chance and choice, I smile.

Today is a good fucking day.

Chapter Fourteen

HATTIE

Tonight is the organization Christmas party and I'm still out shopping for a dress. I don't know why I thought waiting until the last possible second was a good idea, but here we are. Granted, I've been a little bit preoccupied the last few days with work and then Connor scaring the absolute shit out of me and me subsequently trying to wrap my head around all of that, but still. Now I'm out scouring the racks in a panic.

All I Want for Christmas is You starts blaring from my back pocket and I roll my eyes, but smile. In his quest to get me to love all things Christmas, Connor had made all of my main contacts' ringtones holiday songs. Even my text messages come in with a "Ho! Ho! Ho!" I have to admit, I kind of like it. This December on the whole has been almost nothing but *good* so far. Great even. All of the events at work have gone amazingly well, there was a Christmas flotilla on the Sound last night, just like we used to have at one of the marinas back home, and Ollie's Christmas program at school had been the most chaotic and adorable thing I'd ever seen. I'm waiting for the other shoe to drop, but I'm cautiously optimistic that this year might finally be the year that December doesn't royally dick me over.

I fish my phone out and answer without a greeting.

"How fancy does everyone usually get for this shindig? Or is it more of a hootnanny? They're very different things, ya know," I tell Connor seriously.

His deep chuckle resonates from the speaker and my eyes slide shut. God, I love his laugh. It has been nearly impossible to not say fuck the risk and just dive into this thing with Connor the past few days. I've managed, but it's been difficult as all hell because I've been feeling *all* the things. I can't delude myself into believing that it isn't something real or just a passing crush or only a case of wanting to get in his pants (though of course, I really, *really* do) anymore.

Seeing him hurt had shifted things so completely inside my head and heart. Before he'd woken up in the hospital, I'd watched the steady rise and fall of his chest, the light fluttering of his eyes behind his lids, and had simply thought *mine*. I'd never had such a feeling before, such a weird, random, but completely certain thought. Not with Josh or any other guy I've ever dated. Sure, I knew I liked them or loved them even, but I never just felt deep in my heart that they were *it*, that a piece of a puzzle was clicking into place. That with him, the picture finally made sense.

But with Connor...

Of course, I haven't actually voiced any of this to him because, well, I'm slightly chicken shit and he's had so much going on with the whole almost-winding-up-paralyzed-or-dead thing and recovering afterwards, that I didn't think it was a good time to throw this on him too. I know that he's attracted to me, I know that he likes me, maybe even more than in a friendly way, but I don't know if he would actually want to take that leap with me. It's all extremely complicated and I've chosen not to think about it too hard right now. I will after things settle down a bit. Maybe after the party or after New Years, maybe that could be my resolution: coming clean about my feelings. For now, I push it away and focus on finding a freaking dress for tonight.

"Hmm, not quite black-tie, but definitely dressy. Is upscale-cocktail a thing?"

"It is now."

"What are you doing?"

"I'm dress shopping for something upscale-cocktail apparently."

"Ah, and how's that going?"

I pull out the skirt of a flowy green number, but let the fabric flit through my fingers. "Ehhh."

"Well, whatever you pick will be a winner." After a long pause, he adds, "Go with something blue."

I don't know why, but my stomach flutters at the thought of wearing something that he'd like, that he *asked* me to wear.

"Hey, I gotta run. I'll, uh, see you there, alright?" he says, clearing his throat.

"Yeah, I'll see you."

We hang up and I renew my search, a bit of excitement pulsing through my veins. I try another store and spy a glittering, midnight blue dress in the back and beeline for it. A wide smile spreads across my face as I pull it from the rack.

Perfect.

I try it on and, thank God, it fits like a glove. I find some strappy blue stilletos that match perfectly and head across the little square towards the coffee shop.

"Hattie!" I turn, trying to pinpoint where the voice had just come from in the overwhelming crowd, and spot Kasey. I smile and wave, waiting for her to make her way through the throng of people out holiday shopping.

"Hey, Kasey. How are ya?"

"I'm good. Trying to find something to wear tonight."

I laugh, holding up my bag. "I left it to the last minute too, but Angelica's has some winners for sure."

"Oooh, I'll check there next."

"Hey, I haven't gotten a chance to thank you for the other night. For helping me to not pass out into a lump on the floor," I say with a grin and a wrinkle of my nose.

She laughs and waves me off. "Of course, don't even worry about it. Those injuries can be super intense and adrenaline makes the body do some crazy stuff." I give her a nod of thanks, grateful that she doesn't think I'm stupid or weak or something for getting so worked up. Her phone rings. "Oh I gotta take this but it'll only be a second, promise."

I nod and look around while she chats with someone. I smile as a little girl, maybe two or three, toddles her way up to the big Christmas tree in the middle of the square, holding out a chubby hand towards one of the big blue ornaments. I'm just about to shift my gaze back to Kasey when something catches my eye on the other side of the square, just beyond the tree. Something burnt orange. *A longhorns hat.*

My heart thuds against my chest, and my entire body goes cold as people pass in front of where I thought I'd just seen...*No. No, it couldn't be.* I strain to search through the crowd, but the man and the hat are nowhere to be found. My heart is still racing and the memory from the parade rears up, that feeling of being watched.

No. I'm just being paranoid, I tell myself. *This is ridiculous.*

"—ttie?"

I turn back to Kasey, shaking myself. "I'm so sorry, what?"

"You zoned out there for a second," she says with a laugh.

I glance over my shoulder again, back to where I thought I saw him, where I would have sworn for a second that I saw Josh. Nothing there. *A million people in the world have orange hats, Hattie. Get a grip.*

"I'm sorry, I just thought I saw someone I knew."

Her eyes narrow a little in concern. "Are you alright? You look a little pale."

I force myself to shake off the sick feeling that wormed its way into my stomach and is clenching my heart like a fist, and wave her concern away, plastering a smile on my face.

"I'm fine, I just haven't eaten anything today—unless three cups of coffee counts as eating?" We both laugh a bit. "I'm so sorry, what were you saying before I got distracted?"

"Oh, I was asking...well, you and Shep...?"

My brows draw down. "Me and Shep what?"

"Are you two...dating?"

Now my brows shoot upward. "Oh, no. Definitely not. We're just friends." I blurt out the line that I've repeated so many times in my head automatically, but even as I say the words, they taste like a lie.

She smiles. "Ok, that's what he said too, but I just wanted to be sure, especially after the other night..." I don't know why a swift jolt of disappointment goes through me at that. Of course he would say we're just friends. We *are* just friends. *Stop being stupid.*

I keep my smile firmly in place. "Nope, totally just friends. I mean, really good friends, but that's all. Why do you ask?"

"Oh, I was going to try to set him up with one of my girl-friends. I think they'd get along great, but I just wanted to make a thousand percent sure I wasn't stepping in the middle of some-thing with you two."

My stomach twists painfully at the idea, though it's stupid and unfair. I make sure I sound nonchalant when I respond. "Oh, yeah, definitely. Go for it. That'll be—" *terrible* "—great."

"Awesome. Well, I better finish shopping or I'll be coming to the party in my pajamas." She grins and I try to return it but it feels brittle. "I'll see you later!"

"See ya," I mutter as she saunters off towards Angelica's. I watch her go, not really sure how I feel about her setting Shep up with someone, but really, I don't have a right to feel *any* way about it. Like I said, technically, Connor and I *are* just friends...because I've been too scared to tell him I want more. Now Kasey is going to set him up on a date and the fire that lights under my ass is honestly a bit embarrassing. So, that's it. I'm going to tell him now, fuck waiting until January. I have enough faith in our friendship that we can bounce back and sweep any awkwardness under the rug if he doesn't feel the same, just like we did when I almost kissed him that night.

It'll be fine either way. Totally and completely fine. *Then why do I feel like I'm going to puke at the thought of bringing it up?*

Before I spiral down the wormhole of freak-out, I head to my car. I'm so focused on Connor and confessing my feelings, I don't even search the crowd for that damned Longhorns hat again.

Chapter Fifteen

CONNOR

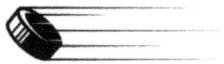

The Christmas party is always a good time. It's in the ballroom of a swanky hotel that overlooks the Sound, and the organization books out the entire top three floors for everyone to stay the night if they want. Ollie is at her grandparents' house tonight, so I plan on crashing here so I don't have to worry about drinking and getting an Uber all the way home.

I knot my tie in the floor-length mirror, and pull my suit jacket on. I turn this way and that, making sure everything looks good. *Not too shabby.* I'd be lying if I said I wasn't doing it all with Hattie in the back of my mind, wondering what she might think. I've been having a major internal debate tonight, have been all fucking day, actually. I keep telling myself that it's a stupid idea, but I think I'm going to broach the subject of being more than friends. God that sounds so fucking juvenile and cliché and stupid, but whatever. I'm tired of pretending that I don't feel things for her, things that friends don't feel for each other. Sure, there's risk, but the reward could be worth it and more. *Go big or go home, right?*

Still, I'm not completely sure when the right time is, or if there's ever a right time. I keep flip flopping. *Yes, it's a great idea.*

No, it's fucking stupid. It's worth the risk. No the fuck it's not. I feel like a dog chasing his tail. I'm never like this and I don't know how to handle it. Annoyed and frustrated, I try to force the argument away from the forefront of my mind, telling myself to just enjoy the evening, and if the time is right, I'll know it.

I head down to the ballroom, the elevator ride taking a bit of time from the thirty-fifth floor. By the time the bell rings and the doors slide open, I'm feeling more like myself. I nod to the security guards posted at the end of the hallway leading to the ballroom to keep fans away from the event, and they incline their heads, stepping out of the way so that I can pass.

"Hey fucker," Rizzo yells out as I enter the ballroom. As always, it's decorated beautifully: a huge Christmas tree in one corner decorated all in gold and red, red and gold tablecloths, an ice sculpture in the shape of the Vipers' emblem. A small dancefloor is set up on the far end of the room, a DJ table not far off in the corner. For now, Christmas music plays in the background, but by the end of the night it'll be a full-scale club scene. The back wall of the room is floor to ceiling windows, looking out over the water. It's seriously gorgeous...and also romantic. *So, maybe the right time could be tonight?*

I join Rizzo and a handful of other guys at the bar. I order a Jameson and ginger ale and we do the first of many toasts of the evening. I mingle, saying hello to spouses and dates, catching up with various members of the organization, but my eyes are constantly scanning the room, looking for Hattie.

Finally, she comes in and *holy shit*—she looks amazing. Better than amazing. *And she fucking wore blue.* My request had escaped my lips before I could stop myself earlier, knowing how good she would look in it, how it would complement her golden skin and make her blue eyes shine brighter. Never in a million years would I have thought she would find a dress that fit her so God damn perfectly, though. It's a glittering midnight blue, long-sleeves and short, showing off her toned thighs. It hugs her every curve, making my mouth water, and *the heels*. She's got on high, strappy, Fuck Me Heels that make me want to do just that. I rub a hand over my mouth as lust slams into me hard and fast. *Christ.* I don't think I've ever wanted someone so badly before. No, scratch that, I don't think—I fucking *know*.

Her hair is up in a loose knot at the base of her neck, but tendrils hang down around her face. It's messy, yet polished, and man, does she look stunning. Someone else comes in behind her, calling her name, and she turns, letting me catch sight of the back of the dress.

Fuck. Me.

It's completely open, only a tiny string of glittering blue connects the two sides across her nape, and dips down to the small of her back, showing the mouthwatering, tiny dimples on either side of the base of her spine. Thumbprints is what I've called them in the past. Fuck if I don't imagine resting my thumbs there now as I take her from behind, seeing her arch her back, hair tumbling over her shoulder as I thrust and yank her backwards...Fuck. I shift my stance and clear my throat, pushing the thoughts away as firmly as I can. But it doesn't work. Not even close. I imagine running my tongue down her spine, ripping the dress off of her, and continuing downward, turning her to face me...

My mouth waters. My cock pulses. *I'm in fucking trouble.*

Rizzo whistles low and elbows me in the ribs. "Holy shitttt. Mac looking good enough to eat tonight."

"Shut the fuck up, Rizz," I grumble. "Where's Nat?" I ask pointedly, and he scowls. The two of them have been playing a strange game of cat-and-mouse and I'm honestly not even sure which is which at this point.

"I'm not going to try again. I've made up my mind."

I smirk at him. "Yep. Right. I *totally* believe you."

"Whatever man, go get Hattie or I will," he says in challenge, one blonde brow arched upward. Why does he look like a fucking model even when he's making that stupid expression? I punch him in the shoulder, down my drink and leave the glass on the high top table before making my way towards her. She's still facing away from me as I approach, talking to a few people in marketing or accounting I think, and without even thinking, I place my hand on the small of her back as I step up beside her. She gasps quietly, but smiles when she sees it's me.

"Hi," she breathes.

"Hey." I nod to the others, exchanging greetings and handshakes, and they eventually move away, leaving Hattie and I alone.

"You look beautiful," I tell her honestly, knowing beautiful doesn't even really cover it. "Glad you, uh, found a dress finally." Do I sound nervous? I feel like I sound nervous. My pulse is racing and my heart is pounding and my tie suddenly feels as if it's strangling me. Is it hot in here? It's definitely hot in here, right? Can they open the doors to the patio? *Jesus. Calm down, Shepherd.*

"Oh this ole thing?" she tosses out nonchalantly, with a grin. I chuckle and her grin fades slightly, her throat bobbing as she swallows and her eyes slowly travel down my body. She clears her throat softly. "You look great too."

Her gaze meets mine and it's back, that feeling like we're right on the edge of something. It feels...combustible. It's like in a movie where they light a fuse and it slowly snakes its way towards the giant pile of explosives. Once that spark hits, we're done for. And right now, I'm totally ok with that, dying for a match to light the entire thing up.

We've somehow edged closer to each other, and she reaches out to straighten my tie, her fingers lightly trailing over my chest when she finishes.

"Do you want to dance?"

Her eyes widen slightly. "A hockey star who can dance?"

"Oh, I have many, many skills, Hattie McNamara," I reply, offering her my arm.

"Well, I'm used to two-steppin', but I can give this a try." She smiles and it's a little different tonight. Coy? Sultry? Sexy as hell.

Though I now have an image seared into my brain of her dancing at a country bar in cut-offs and a plaid shirt tied up under her breasts (yes, I'm aware that's a stereotype, but I don't care), I guide her to the dance floor and pull her close. She places one hand on my shoulder, sliding the other into my waiting hand out to my right. I rest my other on her hip, my fingers brushing the bare skin of her back and making her inhale sharply. Her heels make her only a head or so shorter than me tonight, so she only has to glance up a bit to meet my gaze. We start to move as someone sings *Have Yourself a Merry Little Christmas*, and she gives me a surprised, but excited look, when I actually know some footwork.

"You didn't believe me?" I ask in mock indignation.

"I had my doubts, I'll admit." I chuckle and pull her a little closer to me as we move together, like we've done it a thousand times before. Our bodies seem to be completely in tune with each other and I nearly shudder when she moves her hand so that the tips of her fingers brush the back of my neck, gently sifting through my hair. I know it sounds like something out of a fucking movie, but I swear it's like the rest of the room fades away and it's just me and Hattie and the feel of her body against mine and the look in her eyes.

"You really do look beautiful," I say softly. Her eyes seem to burn, the blue bright in the twinkling lights hanging all around us. She swallows hard once before something shifts and a determined look settles over her face. She stares at me intently, her fingers still gently playing with the hair at the back of my neck, and I fight to keep my eyes from sliding shut.

"I need to tell you something. Or ask you something, I guess. No, tell." She scrunches her nose and we both laugh lightly. I pull her even closer, running my fingers up her spine. I feel like we're right on the edge of a cliff and whatever she wants to tell me might push us right over the edge, but I'm ready to freefall so long as she's beside me. She lets out a long breath and meets my gaze again. "Connor, I—"

"Shep!"

And just like that, the spell is broken and Hattie springs away from me, putting distance between us as Kasey heads our way, waving. *Hattie called me Connor. Just like she did the other night...Does it mean something?* I get the feeling that it does, but before I can figure out what, exactly, or have time to process how disappointed I am that we'd been interrupted, I realize that another woman is walking beside Kasey, a tall platinum blonde with shining hazel eyes in a silk crimson dress that drapes over one shoulder, leaving the other bare.

"Hey Hattie," Kasey adds with a smile when the two women reach us.

"Hey," Hattie says, smiling. She looks flushed and is studiously keeping her eyes from meeting mine. She looks like she's just come out of a trance, that look of determination gone and now one of uncertainty in its place. Of course, to everyone else, she just looks like normal Hattie, genial and sweet. "Looks like you found a dress. I love that color on you!"

Kasey runs a hand over the front of her emerald green dress. "Oh, thanks. You look—*wow*. That's about the only word for it." Hattie grins and inclines her head in thanks and then turns her gaze on the blonde. The ever-polite southerner wanting to include the stranger and not be rude, of course.

"Hi, I'm Hattie," she says, giving the blonde a little wave.

"Oh, right, sorry," Kasey says, shaking herself. "This is Emery. Emery, this is Hattie, and this is the guy I was telling you about, Shep." Hattie stiffens ever so slightly beside me. *Oh. Ohhhh. Fuck.* Kasey had mentioned setting me up with one of her friends a week or so ago, but I didn't think she was going to bring her *tonight*. I don't want to be rude, so I extend a hand and smile.

"Nice to meet you, Emery."

"You too. Kasey has told me a lot about you."

"Well, you should only believe about half of it." We all laugh a bit and I glance sidelong at Hattie. She's smiling, but it's...off. Brittle. It's the fake one that she puts on sometimes when she's not in the mood to deal with people, but she'd never be outwardly rude or cruel to anyone. Does it bother her that I'm apparently on a blind date right now? Is it wrong of me that I'll take it as a good sign if it does? I don't have any desire to be on a blind date tonight, especially not when I'm almost certain that things were about to change between Hattie and me. What was she going to say? What did she need to tell me? I don't really know how to escape the situation in the moment though, so I just go with it, telling myself that I'll talk to Hattie about it all as soon as I can get her alone.

"So, what do you do?" I ask Emery, starting on the small talk.

"I'm a doctor over at Mariners' Memorial."

Kasey rolls her eyes and interjects. "She's being modest. She's a surgeon. A *pediatric* surgeon. She literally saves sick kids daily." I think Hattie turns a bit green at that. Emery smiles demurely, waving it away like it isn't a bit deal.

"Wow, that's amazing," I say, honestly. We do a lot of work with the children's hospitals in the area, I'm surprised I've never seen her before. Answering my silent thought, Kasey explains that Emery just moved back to the area a couple of months ago.

"And she has a son, about Ollie's age," Kasey adds, grinning like she's just won the Matchmaker of the Year award. "I bet they would have a blast together."

"Oh, I—"

"I'm so sorry to interrupt, y'all, but I think Bobby and Nat just walked in, I'm going to go say hello," Hattie says, her tone is sweet as always, but her voice is tight. "It was really great meeting you, Emery. Kasey, Shep, I'll see y'all in a bit." With that she hurries off and I can't stop myself from staring as she goes, my fingers flexing at my side, remembering the feeling of her soft skin beneath them.

Chapter Sixteen

HATTIE

Seeing Shep on a date is like a punch to the gut. It shouldn't be, but I can't stop the feeling. It isn't even jealousy, though I guess that's a part of it, it's just...well it fucking *hurts* to see him with someone else. He'd seemed surprised when Kasey and Emery had walked up, so I don't think he knew that he was going to be set up tonight, but some ridiculous, illogical part of my brain is mad at him for it. I'm well aware that it makes no sense.

I try to keep my distance at first, but we just kind of keep getting thrown together—we're friends after all and everyone knows it, so it's only natural that we hang out all night. Me, Connor, and his freaking date. *Joy.*

Just as I try to sneak off to get some fresh air on the patio, Rizzo yanks me over to a table with him and a handful of other people while Connor and Emery standing on the other side of the high table. Rizzo studiously tries to ignore Nat, but fails miserably, and despite my sour mood, I can't help but smile. She meets my gaze, mouths *shut up*, and then tries to hide her own smile in her drink.

"And I think we need a toast to the newest member of the Vipers' Sin Bin!" Rizzo says to the table, raising his glass. Everyone else joins in. "You may talk funny, but we like ya anyway."

Everyone laughs and I elbow him in the ribs. "Seriously, I think I speak for everyone here when I say that we are so glad that you took this job. We love you and thanks for keeping us out of Jersey!" Voices ring out around the table:

"Hear hear!"

"To Mac!"

"Fuck Jersey!"

"*Please* say darlin'!"

"Not *everything* is bigger in Texas!" Rizzo adds with a waggle of his brows and everyone laughs and cheers, clinking glasses and sloshing liquid all over the place.

I meet Connor's eyes and he smiles one of those heartbreakingly beautiful smiles that makes my breath catch. He raises his glass at me, and I smile back, something passing between us that I can't explain. Despite being surrounded by people, it feels like Connor and I are the only ones here.

But then, Emery leans in and whispers something in his ear, resting a hand on his arm in a flirtatious way, and the moment passes.

I do my best to act normal after that, to smile and laugh and give the guys shit, but inside I'm feeling like I want to cry and scream and muss Emery's perfectly polished chignon. I know I'm being ugly, can practically hear my mom's voice in my head telling me just that, but I can't seem to stop it.

I'd been about to tell Connor...well, I don't know what, exactly. It's not like I'd rehearsed anything or planned it, but when I'd seen him there, looking devastating in his dark suit, hair styled in that not-quite-messy-not-quite-sleek way that looks perfect on him; when he'd held me close as we'd moved to the music, our bodies perfectly in time; when I'd seen the way he'd looked at me—something had just snapped inside, the dam completely collapsing. I wanted to tell him that I wanted him, that I wanted more than just friendship with him, hell, maybe even that I love him, but then Kasey and Emery had shown up.

And Emery is perfectly sweet and beautiful and she's a single mom so she knew exactly the type of struggles that Connor goes through sometimes raising Ollie alone and she's a former college soccer star and a freaking pediatric surgeon saving babies left and right and I can't even hate her if I want to! *Damn it!* Kasey had been right: they were hitting it off. They're both smiling and laughing and Emery's even doing that subtle flirty thing where you touch the guy's arm ever so lightly while you give him *that* look. She's most definitely interested in him—I mean, who in their right mind wouldn't be?—but is Connor interested in her? I can't make myself study him too closely to find out. I think I'm scared to see it if he is. I *think* he'd been caught in that spell with me on the dance floor, had been feeling the same thing I had, but he'd recovered so quickly after Kasey and Emery showed up, that maybe I'd been just seeing what I wanted to see.

I know I *should* be happy for him. I mean, it's not like he and Emery are getting married tomorrow or anything, but if this could be the start of something for him, I should be happy. We've talked about how he's been thinking about getting out there and trying dating again, *really* trying it now that Ollie was settled into her new life with him. Hell, I've even played wingman for him at bars, getting him numbers and hyping him up. It hadn't bothered me to think about him hooking up or dating any of those girls...but that was different. That had been *before.* Now, the thought of it makes me clench my hands into fists, feeling so green with jealousy you may as well call me Shrek.

Despite feeling terrible and wanting nothing more than to go to my room and curl up in bed, I make myself laugh and crack jokes and make toasts with everyone like it's any other day. And the party really is great and I am having a good time, but I'm also barely keeping it all together.

"Care to dance, Mac? I promise to be on my best behavior," Rizzo says, one hand over his heart, one in the air like he's taking an oath or something. I huff out a laugh. I glance over to see Nat dancing with Nowski, so I shrug.

"Sure, why not?"

So, we dance and then I dance with Jackson, then Bobby, then Jules. All the while, Connor dances with Emery. *It doesn't matter. It's fine. I'm fine.* But then Goose yells, "kiss!" and I realize that they're staring at Connor and Emery, who have managed to dance their way under a hanging sprig of mistletoe, and suddenly I'm not fine anymore. I'm so far from fine, I'm not even in the same time zone anymore.

Emery laughs and shrugs, giving Connor a look that says *well, I guess we have to.* His eyes land on me just as Emery's lips meet his, her palm resting on his cheek. My eyes fly wide and my hand flies to my necklace, gripping the diamond so tightly it cuts into my fingertips. I feel like there's something stuck in my throat, like when you try to swallow one of those giant multi-vitamins and it gets caught. I feel the color drain from my face as the entire place erupts in cheers and Connor's eyes pull away from mine, and I think I might puke. I mutter something to Jules about needing some air and I slip away from the crowd, sprinting to the bathroom.

I hide in a stall for longer than I care to admit, trying to get a grip on my emotions. Why the hell am I so upset? I assured Kasey that Connor and I were just friends, I practically *told* her to set Connor up with Emery. I can't be upset about it now. But seeing her kiss him, seeing him kiss her back? It felt like a knife to the chest. It's stupid and illogical and my own fault for not saying anything to Connor about how I felt before, but it doesn't make it hurt any less.

"Hattie?" Nat asks softly, her voice echoing through the large room.

"In here," I sigh, opening the stall door and walking out to meet her, my heels clicking loudly against the marble floor.

"You alright?" she asks, studying me as I lean heavily against the counter where several crystal bowl-shaped sinks sit at intervals.

"Totally fine, why wouldn't I be?" She gives me an *oh come on* look and I let out a rough exhale. "Not really, no. But, it is what it is." She purses her lips and I quickly shift the conversation before she can ask any follow up questions. "And what about you and Rizz?"

She crosses her arms over her chest stubbornly and scowls. "I don't want to talk about it."

I laugh at that, lightly at first, but it soon becomes a full on belly laugh, the kind that makes your sides hurt and you think you might pee your pants a little. Nat joins and soon we're both wiping tears from our eyes.

"My God, we're a pair, aren't we?"

"Shit, my mascara," she says between gasps, eyeing the mirror, "I wonder if Rizz would like to fuck a racoon this evening."

"Ya know, I wouldn't put it past him," I say, making us both laugh harder.

We eventually settle down, fix Nat's mascara, and head back into the ballroom. I actually feel a little better. Not good, but better. We head to the bar and order drinks, and Connor steps up beside me.

"Mac, can I—"

"Bobby! You owe me a dance!" I call. I give Connor an apologetic look as I rush over towards Bobby, dragging him onto the dance floor.

Connor tries to catch my eye several more times through the evening, but I always manage to find someone else that needs my attention, or suddenly realize my glass is empty or someone else's is, so I go to grab refills, or I pretend to want to check out the scenery from the patio. It's cold as all get out on the patio, but I'd rather freeze my ass off—literally—than be around Emery and Connor while they laugh and flirt and Emery can't seem to keep her hands to herself. I know I'm not being fair, but I honestly don't know what to say to Connor right now. I might just blurt out everything that I'd wanted to tell him earlier. I might throw my drink in his face. I might cry.

So, avoiding him at all costs is really the best choice until I can wrap my head around everything. The night slowly shifts from elegant holiday party to hockey players at the club. The lights go low and the dance floor lights up with spotlight and strobe lights, the DJ kicking the music up a notch. A lot of people take this as the cue to make their exit and I decide to join them. I tell Bobby good night, try and fail to find Nat, and don't even say goodbye to Connor. I just head towards the door with one last wistful glance at him as he laughs with the guys, head thrown back and looking carefree and gorgeous...and Emery staring at him like he hung the moon.

"You leaving?" Rizzo asks, startling me.

I nod. "I think I'm all partied out for the night." He follows my gaze and I curse, forcing myself to stop staring at Connor and turn to look at Rizzo instead. He looks at me thoughtfully, seeing more than he lets on, but doesn't say anything about it. *Bless him.*

"Well, allow me to accompany you. I need to grab something from my room." He holds out his arm, like a gentleman in a movie, and I can't help but laugh. I wrap my arm around his and we head towards the door.

"Is the thing you need to grab from your room your balls to just suck it up and go after Nat again already?" I murmur quietly, leaning in to him.

His mouth drops open. "I...I mean, it isn't...I tried...*She's* the one who..." he sputters and I grin.

"Figure it the fuck out, my friend," I say, patting his chest sympathetically.

"Back at you, Mac," he says pointedly.

"I wish I could," I mutter as we leave the ballroom, the doors swinging shut behind us.

Chapter Seventeen

CONNOR

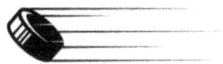

Tonight has been a whirlwind and I don't even know where to begin dealing with it all. Emery is really great. Beautiful, funny, smart, ambitious, a single mom—the whole package, really. But just before she'd come up with Kasey, Hattie had been about to say something, and I just know that it was something big, something that might change everything. All night, I've been trying to get her alone for a second, to get her to talk to me, or at the very least, to gauge her real feelings about my impromptu date, but she's been...not elusive, exactly. She's been laughing and joking and having a good time like usual, but I can never quite get her to look me in the eye and I get the feeling that's by design.

That is, until the kiss. It all happened so fast, I didn't even really realize what's was going on until it was basically too late. It was just an innocent kiss under the mistletoe. It didn't really mean much of anything, but the look in Hattie's eyes just before Emery's lips pressed to mine made my heart clench and a sick feeling rise up in my stomach. She looked...stricken, her blue eyes flashing with pain, her face paling. The room erupted in cheers and jeers and when I pulled away from Emery, Hattie was nowhere to be found.

I need to talk to her to figure out what's going on. If she *is* upset that I'd been set up on a blind date tonight, if what I think I saw on her face during the kiss means what I think it did...Well, I think it means that we have a big conversation that needs to be had. But, what if...

Fuck, what if the whole Emery thing, or, more acutely, the *kiss* with Emery thing, had made Hattie think better of the whole idea? Made her decide that whatever she'd been about to say or do wasn't such a good idea after all? Did everything I want slip through my fingers somehow without me even realizing it? I want to scream in frustration, though I do my best to act normal on the outside. Whatever is going on with Hattie, or between the two of us, I need to figure the fuck out. Emery is great, and in another situation, I'd probably be interested, but not now. Even the kiss under the mistletoe hadn't had any kind of spark. It was fine, but I don't want fine. I want fire and passion and connection. I...fuck, I want Hattie, *only* Hattie, plain and simple.

I search the room yet again, but can't seem to find her. After the kiss, I got the distinct impression that she was avoiding me, and I get that, but I need to talk to her. The need is acute, nearing panic, and I can't even explain why. I just get the feeling like I'm racing against the clock, like I only have a finite amount of time to fix this tonight, to get shit back where I want it. We'd been so fucking close, I know it.

I check the patio again, but no luck, and she's not responding to any of my texts.

"Hey, have you seen Hattie?" I yell to Jules over the music. The party is in full swing now, seeming more like a night club than an elegant Christmas gathering.

"I saw her leaving a few minutes ago with Rizzo."

I rear back as if I've been slapped. *No. No fucking way.*

"Rizz? You're sure?"

"Yeah man. Arm and arm like they were walking down the aisle or some shit." He laughs, stumbling a bit. "Rizz walking down the aisle. Can you imagine that!? Not in a million fucking years." He shakes his head, laughing again before pointing to someone across the dance floor and grinning. He claps me on the shoulder and walks away.

Hattie left with Rizzo, but...it couldn't have been what it looked like. I feel sick, but before I can really process any of this shit, Emery comes back from the restroom.

"I think I'm done dancing..." she says, giving me a very pointed look, and it takes me a second to realize what she's saying. I don't know why I'm surprised: she's been pretty flirtatious all night. Touching me every chance she gets, not hesitating at all to kiss me under the mistletoe, even in front of so many people. She's a single mom out for the night with a pro athlete. Not saying there's anything wrong with her wanting what she's wanting, not at all, but I'm not the one to give it to her. The old me would have absolutely taken her up to my room, enjoyed the hell out of a night with her—and then probably never called her again. But I can't do it.

"It was really great meeting you tonight, but I'm just..." I let out a long breath, deciding not to sugarcoat anything. "This just isn't going to work out, I'm sorry."

"Oh." She looks a bit surprised, but recovers quickly. "It's alright, it was worth a shot," she hikes her shoulder, "and, it was a night out with a bunch of professional hockey players, so it's a cool story, at least." She smiles and then tilts her head. "It's Hattie, isn't it? The reason this isn't going to work, I mean. It's because you're already hoping something works out with her?" I don't have the energy to deflect, and honestly, I don't want to lie about it, not anymore.

"Yes, it is. I'm sorry."

"Don't be. The way you two look at each other...Well, I'm not surprised." She doesn't seem upset or anything, giving me a warm smile. I return it, glad I haven't managed to screw up *everything* tonight and that she isn't leaving wanting to throw a drink in my face or anything.

"Do you need a ride home or anything? I can call you a cab or...?"

"I'm good," she says with a smile. "It was really nice meeting you, Shep." She leans in and gives me a quick kiss on the cheek and then heads over to where Kasey is dancing with Bobby and a few of the guys from the team beneath the flashing lights.

Shep. She calls me Shep, just like everyone else...but Hattie had called me *Connor* earlier—and I fucking liked it. It was like some secret between just the two of us, something reserved only for her, because with her, I'm a different person than I am with anyone else. She lets me be completely myself. No reservations, no worries, just *me.* Good, bad, ugly—she accepts it all. *Fuck. I really am completely in love with her.*

The thought staggers me and I feel like I need to sit down. I knew I had feelings for her, had even thought that I *might* have been falling, but now it seems so fucking obvious. I'm completely in love with her...and she might be fucking someone else right this second. I clench my fists and grind my teeth as the thought fills me with a fiery jealousy that I have no right to feel. I check my phone and still no response from my last text.

Part of me denies that she's up there with Rizzo. I know that Rizzo suspects how I feel and know that he would never do that to me...but I also know that mistakes happen when alcohol is involved and the decision-making starts happening below the belt. I know Rizz is all mixed up with his shit with Nat, and Hattie...well, she may very well be pissed at me or hurt or a mix of both. If the two of them decided to distract themselves from their own perspective emotional shit for a while by falling into bed together, they technically had every damn right to.

Suddenly *very* done with the party, I say my goodbyes and head to the elevators, loosening my tie as I go. Though it wasn't exactly my fault, I feel like I ruined something tonight, and the thought of Hattie with Rizz makes me want to puke or put my fist through the nearest window—or both.

"Fuck." I interlock my fingers behind my head and stare up at the two-story foyer. The elevator dings and I sigh, lowering my hands and my head.

And she's there.

Hattie is there in the elevator, staring at me like a deer in headlights. We both seem frozen, time stilling all around us, everything else becoming a bit hazy. All I can see is Hattie. It's just like during games. Everything else quiets around me, goes slightly blurry, and all I can see is the puck. It becomes my sole focus, my sole purpose. In those moments on the ice, it's all that matters.

And, here, in this moment, Hattie is all that matters.

"Connor," she whispers.

That's all it takes. Something inside me cracks and I cross into the elevator. I reach out to cradle her face and my lips crash to hers. *Finally!* Her lips are soft and warm, moving in time with mine. I groan as I tilt my head, deepening the kiss, thrusting my tongue against hers. I've been thinking about kissing Hattie for weeks and now that it's finally happening, I'm in fucking heaven. *This*, I think. *This is what kissing someone should feel like.* Fire and passion and a connection unlike anything I've ever felt. One of her hands grips the back of my neck, holding me tightly to her and the other rests on my chest. Can she feel how erratic my heartbeat is?

I press her back into the wall of the elevator and she gasps when I arch my hips against her, her fingers tangling in my hair. I barely have any control over my body, the need for her rearing up like an animal inside me. Hell, part of me wants to fuck her right here and now in this elevator, but thankfully I have enough control left to stop that from happening. *Barely.*

"Hattie," I whisper against her lips and her breath hitches. She's not Mac now. She's Hattie. *My* Hattie.

I step back long enough to smash the button for the top floor with probably too much force, and then I stare at her. She's breathing hard, eyes wild in a way I've never seen before. Surprising me, she closes the distance between us, wrapping her arms around my neck and pulling my face down to hers once more. I twist so that when she shoves me backwards, my back hits the side wall instead of the door. She sucks lightly on my bottom lip and I groan, settling my hands on her hips and pulling her hard against me. Fuck, I don't think I've ever been so hard in my life. I move my hands around to her ass, palming the pert flesh, kneading and holding her hard against me and making her moan, the sound making my cock pulse, desperate to be buried deep inside her.

By some miracle, the elevator doesn't make a single stop on the way up, and when the bell rings and the doors open, we finally pull away from each other, panting.

"If you want this to stop, tell me now," I say, voice low and hoarse.

"No," she whispers, trailing her fingers over my lips. "I don't want this to stop."

"*Thank fucking God.*" I hoist her up into my arms, making her yelp and giggle, but she obediently wraps her arms around my neck as I storm out of the elevator and down the hallway towards my room. I gasp in surprise and bite my lip, barely stifling a desperate moan when she leans in to nuzzle my neck, kissing and licking in a way that nearly makes me drop her, my knees going weak. I somehow manage to get the key out of my pocket and into my door, and we tumble inside. I walk us to the middle of the room and set her on her feet, slowly lowering her body down mine, the bottom of her dress rucking up her thighs

I run my knuckles lightly over her cheekbone before cupping her nape and pulling her lips to mine again. Slower this time, less frenzied, but it's a barely contained fire. It will burn out of control soon enough. So I know I need to tell her this before things get out of hand. I pull away enough to speak, but can't seem to make myself move an inch farther.

"Hattie, I'm usually a little...uh, aggressive in the bedroom."

"Just like on the ice," she says, breathless. It isn't a question.

I pull back further so I can look down at her. I arch a brow and she gives me a smile that's half lust-drunk, half sheepish.

"I just had a feelin' you would be," she says with a hike of one shoulder.

"You've thought about it then?"

A sexy little smirk settles over her lips. "More than you could *possibly* imagine."

Fuck. My chest constricts and my cock practically throbs. I groan, pinching her chin gently between my thumb and forefinger.

"You are *killing*, me, woman." She chuckles and bites her lip, not-so-subtly arching her hips forward. My eyes slide closed. Fuck, the feel of her against me...*Christ, I am in* big *trouble.* I need to get this out before I lose my mind. "But yes, like on the ice. So, if there's anything you don't like, just tell me. Anything that gets too intense or too rough or—"

She cuts me off with a kiss.

"Connor," she whispers against my lips, making me shudder in contentment. Hearing my name on her lips like this makes something inside me burn. "I want *everything* you can dish out."

I jerk back, needing to look at her to make sure I heard her correctly. Her smile isn't sheepish now. No, it's downright sinful. Confident. Eager. My pulse races and my body trembles with want and anticipation. She reaches forward and jerks my tie the rest of the way off, tossing it to the floor, and slides my jacket off my shoulders. She yanks open the front of my shirt, a few buttons scattering off, thumping quietly to the carpet around us. She pushes the fabric away, her fingers brushing my skin on the way and making me inhale sharply. *Want her hands all over me.*

She stares at my bared chest for a long moment and I let her. The look on her face is a mix of fascination and hunger. She reaches forward and runs her hands up my stomach, my muscles tensing at her touch. That seems to delight her because she does it again, making my lids go heavy in pleasure, a low, rumbling moan escaping my lips. Her hands are soft and warm and I've wanted them on me so fucking badly, been dreaming of this for so long. She glides them up to my chest and her fingers skate over the metal bar through my nipple.

"This is...intriguing," she says, voice low and a bit breathless. I grin.

"If *that's* intriguing, you're in for an eye-opening night, sweetheart."

She jerks her gaze up to meet mine, eyes wide and mouth gaping.

"You don't mean..." I arch a brow, giving her a salacious grin, and she swallows hard. Her breaths come in rapid bursts, and her pupils expand, black nearly overtaking the blue. She seems very, *very* curious now. Curious and excited and I can't take anymore.

I slowly walk her backwards until she hits the wall. I lean in slowly, using a single finger under her chin to tilt her face up to mine. Just as my lips meet hers, I slide my hand downward, my fingers caging her throat ever so slightly. She gasps, but before I can pull back to make sure she's alright, her gasp turns into a moan and she shifts her hips forward against me again. I apply the tiniest hint of pressure against the sides of her neck, just enough that she knows I'm there, and wait for her reaction. Her pulse beats wildly beneath my fingers and her hands fly out, gripping my hips and yanking me towards her, fingers digging into the small of my back. I smile. *She likes it.*

I pull back and meet her gaze. "Turn around," I whisper.

She obeys and I lean in to plant a kiss at the top of her spine. She shivers and I do it again, and again, slowly making my way across her back. I release the small clasp holding the dainty crystal string and gently push the sleeves of her dress down her shoulders as I kiss her neck. The little sounds of pleasure she makes are driving me wild. A moan here, a gasp there, a whimper thrown in for good measure. I can't wait to make her scream, to cry out in pleasure so loudly that her voice is hoarse tomorrow.

I remove the pins holding her hair up and can't stop myself from rocking my hips against her ass as it tumbles free. I gather the silky strands and toss them over her left shoulder, leaving her back bare. I lean in to kiss her neck again and she tilts her head to the side, giving me better access to her throat. I grin, making a mental note of all the places she seems to especially enjoy being kissed.

She gasps when I shove the dress all the way down her arms, freeing her breasts, but she doesn't seem shy or nervous about it. Oh no, she seems so very far from shy or nervous. She reaches back to thrust her fingers through my hair, holding my lips to her throat as I reach around her and palm her breasts. She groans loudly and arches her back, pressing them into my hands.

"Fuck, Hattie," I whisper in her ear. I knead and rub, her pebbled nipples grazing my palms. I run my thumbs over them and she whimpers, rubbing her ass against my throbbing cock. When I roll them between my thumbs and forefingers, pinching lightly, she cries out, arching forward again, practically begging. "So sensitive," I chuckle against her neck.

"Connor," she breathes. "God, that feels good."

She has no idea what that term means, not yet at least, but I plan to show her by the end of the night. I shove the dress the rest of the way down her body, stepping back so I can admire the sight of Hattie McNamara in nothing but a black silk thong, a tiny bow resting at the top of her ass, and her sexy heels. I run a hand over my mouth.

"Mercy," I say gruffly. "Hattie, you have the most luscious ass I've ever seen." I reach out and run my hands over it, unable to stop myself. She wiggles in my grip and I chuckle.

"Turn around," I demand, voice pitched low.

She turns without hesitation and I take another minute to appreciate the view of her from the front. *God almighty.* I step forward and kiss her again—*hard*, tongue thrusting against hers in a tangle of desperation, teeth clashing, her nails digging into the skin of my arms where she grips me so tightly, like she thinks I'll disappear if she doesn't hold on to me.

I'm going to lose my mind before the night is done. One of her hands moves from my arm, snaking between us and fumbling with my belt buckle. I grasp her wrist to halt her.

"Eh, eh, eh," I tsk quietly before biting her lower lip, drawing a desperate, almost animalistic moan from her lips. "Not your turn yet, Hattie." She inhales softly at that, eyes blazing, and I kiss across her jaw and down the delicate column of her throat, before dipping my head to her breasts. I place soft kisses across one swell before flicking my tongue over her jutting nipple. She cries out and bucks her hip forward, digging her fingers into my hair. I do it again, twirling my tongue around and around, until she's squirming. I grin before taking her nipple between my lips, sucking lightly.

"Ah!" she yells, "*Fuck!*" I trail a hand downward, running my fingers along the silk of her panties. She thrusts her hips towards my hand, silently begging. Another time, I might *make* her beg...and the thought of Hattie begging for me to touch her, of hearing her tell me exactly *how* and *where* she wants my fingers or my tongue makes my cock fucking throb to the point of near-pain, but that's for later. Right now, I want nothing more than to give Hattie anything and everything she wants. I thrust my hand beneath the material and dip a finger between her lips. I groan around her nipple.

"So fucking *wet.*" The words come out low and rough with need. She merely moans in response and I move my head to her other breast as I spread her moisture upward, rubbing the pad of my finger over her clit.

"Oh God," she whispers, legs already shaking. *Oh baby, I haven't even started yet,* I think with a wry grin. I keep up my torture, moving my finger around and around until she's writhing, and then I slide a finger inside. She moans, fingers tightening in my hair, nails digging into my scalp. She's fucking soaked and tight as hell and God I could come right now. I need to taste her, want her on my tongue so badly I can't think of anything else. I kiss down her stomach and remove my finger as I fall to my knees in front of her. As sexy as the thought of her in nothing but these heels is, I need her out of them for now. *Don't want her turning an ankle when her legs give out in a few minutes.* I smirk at the thought. I reach down and unclasp the strap around one ankle, gently lifting her foot to slide the heel off while she grips my shoulders for balance, then repeating the process.

I lean in and plant a soft kiss on her left hip and then meet her gaze as I hook my fingers in the strings resting on her hips and tug her panties down. She bites her lip as she watches, and staring up at her from this angle, knowing what I'm about to do to her, seeing the blatant want in her eyes is possibly the sexiest thing I've ever seen. I somehow tear my gaze from hers long enough to look at my prize.

Fuck. Me.

Smooth skin; glistening lips; a small butterfly tattoo on her hip; her legs quivering with anticipation—this can't be real. I must be dreaming or hallucinating or something.

"You know," I whisper, running my hands up the outside of her thighs, "Rizzo said you looked good enough to eat tonight." I look up and meet her eyes. "I couldn't agree more." Her lips part on a soft gasp and I lean forward to get my first taste of Hattie.

"Fuck!" she cries as I run my tongue along her pussy. My eyes slide closed in utter bliss. God, I've imagined this, thought about it alone in my bed more times than I care to admit. Going down on a woman has always been something I've enjoyed doing, but *dear God*, I could do this all night. She feels so good on my tongue, tastes so fucking good, and I want to taste her forever. The way she moves, the way she moans, it's so damn sexy. Over and over, I lap my tongue along her drenched pussy before flicking it over her clit, circling before sucking gently.

"Oh God...Connor...*holy shit...*"

"Spread your legs," I whisper. She obeys and I hike one of her thighs over my shoulder, opening her wide to me and giving me all the access I need. I lean back in, licking in earnest, doing everything I can to drive her crazy, but changing things up when I sense she's on the verge. I want this to last. I need this to last. God, I don't think I've ever been so turned on. She digs her nails into the back of my head and grinds her pussy against my face. I fucking love it, but I need her still, so I pin her hip to the wall with one hand, gripping the thigh on my shoulder with the other, forcing her legs open even wider. Her muscles tremble and I can tell she's close again.

"I...oh God, Connor, don't stop. *Pleasepleaseplease.*" I glance up her body and see her head thrown back, eyes squeezed shut in bliss as she pants, her chest heaving.

"Hattie," I say in a low voice. Her lids spring open and she glances downward, sweat beating across her forehead. "Eyes on me, baby." She gasps quietly, looking surprised and confused and maybe a little bit shy, but also incredibly aroused. "Remember, you tell me if any of this is too much, yeah?" She swallows hard but nods slowly, biting her lip. I smile a slow, sensual smile.

"Then," I say again, lacing as much sensuality as I can into my voice, "Eyes. On. Me."

I slowly lean back towards her, keeping my gaze locked on hers to see if she obeys. She does and I hold her gaze as I lick her pussy, long and slow from the bottom of her opening all the way to her clit. She whimpers and her breath catches, but doesn't break my stare.

"Good girl," I whisper.

"*Oh God.*" Her eyes fly wide and her expression is...bewildered? Has no one ever said those words to her before? Is she surprised that she likes it? Because I have zero doubts that she does by the way she's writhing, the way her eyes seem to burn with desire. I've always been a talker, so I keep going, testing to see what she does or doesn't like.

"Watch me while I eat your pussy, Hattie. Watch me while I make you come on my tongue."

"*Fuuuuuck,*" she breathes, but the look in her eyes tells me that she's ready to play. Oh yeah, she's definitely down with the dirty talk. The thought floors me and I smile as I set back in, licking and lapping and sucking, and all the while, she watches raptly, and I can't stop myself from reaching downward and stroking myself over my pants. God, my cock is throbbing, I want her so fucking badly.

"Mmmm," she moans as she watches me stroke. I arch a brow and she bites her lip, giving me one of those half sheepish-half sultry looks. So, Hattie might just like to watch, too. One more thing added to my mental file, one more thing added to the mile-long list of things I want to do with her. Her expression changes to one of shock and near-ecstasy as I release her hip and thrust a finger inside her while I lick her clit.

"God, yes, Connor! Yes, yes, yes. Just like that...oh God..." I add a second finger, curling them forward as I move them in and out and suck gently on her clit. "Oh *GOD!*" She screams and I can feel her orgasm ripping through her, can feel her pussy clenching my fingers in tight pulses. I groan and remove my fingers, quickly replacing them with my tongue. I want to taste her climax, want her to ride my tongue through it.

"That's right, baby," I nearly growl against her flesh. "God, you taste so fucking good."

Her eyes slid shut in the midst of her orgasm, but now she pries them open, watching me again. It's so fucking hot I can barely stand it.

"Co-Connor," she whispers between panting breaths. Her legs are trembling and she feebly attempts to push my head away. I could make her come again, but there are other things I need more, so I pull away, kissing the inside of her thigh where it still rests over my shoulder, before gently placing her foot back on the floor. I stand before her, tracing my thumb over her bottom lip.

To my surprise and supreme delight, she throws her arms around my neck and slams her lips to mine. Some women don't like kissing after that, which is totally fine, but it's always been a bit of a turn on honestly. She goes up on her tiptoes and I run my hands down her sides, over her hips and then lift, urging her legs around my waist. Then, I'm walking us towards the bed, lying her back and following her down, settling my body over hers.

Chapter Eighteen

HATTIE

Oh. Dear. God.

I can't quite believe this is happening. Me and Connor. Together. *Finally.* When I'd seen him standing there outside the elevator, staring up at the ceiling, every bit of resolve that I'd built up throughout the night to put my feelings aside had dissolved like sugar in the rain. When our eyes had met, that was it. I couldn't pretend anymore. No matter what happened, no matter the fallout, I couldn't pretend anymore that I don't want him, that I don't...that I don't *love* him.

Because I do.

I know it deep in my bones, in my soul. And if he doesn't feel the same, then I'll deal with it, but for now, I can't stop this from happening. I need him, need to be with him, even if it's only for one night. One perfect, blissful night.

He settles his body over mine and I feel like every last nerve ending is on fire. I just got off—with quite possibly the biggest orgasm of my fucking life, by the way—and I already want more, *need* more. He's beyond sexy, and beyond skilled, and I can't even imagine what he might have left up his sleeve. I've never been with a man who talks very much, let alone demands things, and damn if it isn't just what I've been craving without ever knowing it.

When he told me to watch him? *Jesus, Mary, Joseph, and the Great Pumpkin.* It was the hottest, dirtiest, sexiest thing that's ever been said. *Actually* watching him? *Dear God in Heaven.* I don't even have words for how erotic it was, but I want to see it again, over and over, on repeat for forever. I feel like I can finally be free in bed with Connor, like I can finally have everything I've ever wanted but was never able to ask for. And I realize now that the reason is because I *trust* Connor in ways I've never trusted any other partner before. I feel safe with him, safe enough to let myself completely go, to be in the moment and not worry about anything but the feelings and sensations and the complete and utter connection between us.

His lips are soft and warm against mine, but demanding. The man knows how to kiss, that's for damn sure. He starts to knead my breast again and I moan into his mouth, thrusting my tongue harder against his with my desperation. He gives an appreciative half groan, half grunt type of noise from deep in his chest and it sends shivers down my spine. He starts subtly thrusting his hips, his cock rubbing against me in a teasing glide that's driving me crazy. I rub my hands over his back, his shoulders, his stomach. I can't stop touching him, want to kiss and lick every tattoo on his sinfully perfect body.

When my hand brushes his belt buckle again, I whisper, "I think it's time for this to go." I can feel his smile against my lips just before he pushes himself up, standing beside the bed. I lean up on my elbows and watch raptly as he runs one hand through his hair and undoes his belt with the other, whipping it through the loops and out with one hand. A jolt goes through me. I can't possibly explain why, but that was somehow *extremely* arousing. *What is happening to me?* When he'd stroked himself earlier while he was going down on me, it had been hot as all hell. Explain that to me. Explain why it made me impossibly wetter to know that he was so turned on by doing that to me, that he couldn't keep his hands off himself, to see him moving his palm up and down, wishing it was my own.

He slowly unbuttons his pants and then slides the zipper downward. My pulse is racing, my heart pounding in my chest so hard that I can't believe it hasn't crashed right through. He slides his pants and boxer-briefs down and all thoughts fly out of my head. I stare, my mouth going dry and my fingers clenching the sheets. He's thick and hard, his cock straining forward, and *oh my.*

Connor is *pierced.*

I don't know why I'm so shocked. I mean, he hinted earlier that this was the case, but actually seeing it...

Wow.

Wowie.

Wowza.

I don't even know what to think or say. He stands and lets me stare, bless him, though if I looked as good as he did naked, I'd stand there and show off too. He seriously looks like a Greek God brought to life. How is he real? *Is* he real? Part of me suddenly wonders if this is all some insane dream or something. But I don't think even my dirtiest, sexiest dreams could have conjured Connor's pierced dick.

There's a barbell seeming to go straight through the head, a silver ball on both ends. Because he's so tall, I have a good view of the underside too and *oh dear God*: a row of small metal bars runs up the bottom of his shaft. Though I've never actually seen one, I know what a Jacob's Ladder is. *Why...why is this so* hot*? Why do I want to run my tongue over them?*

I have to touch him. I need to run my hands over every inch of his body, but most definitely over those piercings. Unable to stand it any longer, I shift forward, crawling to the edge of the bed and raising up onto my knees. I reach out and run my fingers over the piercing through his nipple before leaning forward and giving it a tentative lick. He gives a hoarse moan, so I do it again, enjoying the feel of the cool metal against my tongue.

"Fuck, Hattie," he huffs out.

"Does it feel good?" I ask, honestly wondering, though the question comes out a little more sex-kitten than curious one.

"Oh yeah."

I pull back and glance up at him as I slowly trail my fingers down his stomach, over each hard ridge of his abs, the muscles tensing beneath my hands.

"And what about these?" I ask as I run a single finger along the underside of his cock from base to tip, fascinated by the ridges formed by the barbells beneath his skin. His hips buck forward and his jaw clenches as he shuffles his feet apart, widening his stance.

"Christ," he says through gritted teeth.

"It doesn't hurt for them to be touched?"

"The opposite," he whispers hoarsely. I'm surprised. When my hair gets caught around my cartilage piercing and pulls, it definitely doesn't feel good. I can only imagine what kind of...um...*pulling* might happen with these piercings. He looks down at me intently and I bite my lip as I touch the piercing through the head. His chest rises as he inhales deeply, and I wrap my palm around his cock, slowly and carefully stroking, enjoying the sensation of the piercings as they rub over my skin. I lean forward and lick his nipple again and he palms the back of my head, gently—but firmly—holding me to him. I grin and circle my tongue over and over before sucking gently. I want to know everything that turns him on, every touch, every spot, every motion that drives him wild. Eventually I pull away.

"And, um, *during*...it doesn't...I mean, it isn't uncomfortable for you?"

"Oh, sweetheart, uncomfortable is the total wrong word for it." He leans down and kisses me softly, pulling away to murmur, "And I'm not the only one who gets pleasure out of them." I swallow hard, trying and failing to imagine it, though my body reacts as if I completely understand exactly what he's saying. My breathing becomes quick and shallow, goosebumps spreading over every inch of my skin, my pussy and nipples both throbbing. I want his mouth on both again, but I want something else even more right now.

I lean up and kiss him, wrapping one hand around the back of his neck and continue stroking his cock with the other. He said it doesn't hurt when the piercings are touched, so I stroke harder. His hands fly to my hips, fingers gripping me tightly, small grunts and groans emanating as I move my fist, up and down, up and down, running my thumb over the head. I wonder what the metal would feel like against my tongue. Just when I decide that now is an excellent time to find out, he slides his hand from my hip to between my thighs. He quickly slides two fingers inside me, making me gasp against his mouth in surprise and pleasure. He pumps them in and out as I stroke him, moving my hand faster, gripping him tighter. I can't help but worry it might hurt him, but it seems to be the opposite, just as he said. His cock seems to throb in my hand and I feel a bead of precum beneath my thumb on my next sweep over the head.

He shifts his hand so that his heel presses against my clit and I cry out.

"Ok?"

"Yessss," I hiss, eyes sliding closed and head falling back as he works his fingers in and out, putting just the right amount of pressure on my clit. He leans down to kiss my neck, licking and— I jolt as he bites down at the spot where my shoulder meets my neck just as he curls his fingers, not hard, but enough that I feel it, and *oh my fucking God* does it nearly make me come. I can't even begin to wrap my head around this.

"Jesus!" I moan-yell.

"Actually, it's Connor," he says against my skin and I can hear the smirk in his voice, "but it's a very common mistake." *Cocky bastard*, I think with a smile. A smirk of my own spreads across my face when he lets out a choked moan as I move my hand downward, cupping his balls and tugging gently. "Fuck, Hattie!"

A second later, I'm on my back and he's above me, lips slamming to mine in a searing kiss. He pins my wrists to the bed on either side of my head and grinds his hips against me, not trying to slide inside, but making sure I know he's there—and driving me crazy in the process. I arch my hips upward, wanting him to thrust inside, needing him to fuck me so badly I think I might die. As if reading my mind, he starts to pull away.

"Need to get a condom. Hang on."

A crazy notion pops in my head, one that is now cemented there with no hope of it leaving. I don't want *any* barriers between us. It might be weird but I don't really give a fuck. If he's down then...

"Wait. You...well, I mean, are you, ya know...clean?" He freezes.

"I am," he says slowly, as if his mind is circling around what I might really be saying, but refuses to land on it. "I was always safe back when I was hooking up, but I also got tested regularly just to be sure. Completely clean and I haven't been with anyone in over three years." He's holding himself completely still and I don't even think he's breathing. Oh yeah, he knows what I'm getting at and it seems like he's in shock.

"I am too. And I'm on birth control." I'd immediately gotten an IUD after my miscarriage. Seeing Josh's reaction had made it clear he was not someone I wanted a future with. So even though I wasn't consciously ready to accept that and end things at the time, part of me was aware enough to know I needed to take every precaution I could not to end up pregnant again, tethered to him in any way.

He levers himself up onto straightened arms, staring down at me with a serious expression.

"Are you saying what I think you're saying?"

I bite my lip and nod. "I mean, if you want...?"

"Christ," he says, almost to himself.

"Actually, it's Hattie," I say with a smirk, using his earlier quip. His lips curl upward and a devastating smile, one that's tinged with a sensual mischief and my stomach does a nice little flip. The dirty promises that smile holds. *Lord help me.* I'd told him I wanted everything he could dish out, and while that's still completely true, a part of me is a little afraid of what all that could entail. Afraid in the best possible way, like that nervous terrifying anticipation right before you jump out of the plane when you go skydiving. That exhilarating fear of the unknown.

He reaches down and grips his cock, and my entire body trembles in anticipation. My eyes fly wide as he runs the head up and down my pussy, never pushing inside, and his piercing sends ripples of unexpected pleasurable sensations through every inch of me.

"Mmm," he mumbles. "So fucking wet for me, Hattie." He meets my gaze as he continues to move his cock up and down, and I desperately move my hips, trying to get him inside. "Do you think you can take it?" I nod eagerly and he smiles. "That's my girl."

Why do those words make my thighs quiver and my pussy impossibly wetter? *Dear God.* Do...do I have a *praise kink*? I've read about them in some of my romance novels, but never really thought much of it in real life. But now, hearing Connor say the words in that low, husky voice...

Fuck.

Me.

Yep. There is a ninety-eight percent chance that I'm now hooked on Connor praising me in bed. *Who knew?*

He slowly slides his cock in and *fuck* it feels good. He hisses and the muscles in his chest and arms bunch with tension, his jaw clenched. My hands fly to his hips, gripping tight as he moves.

"God damn, Hattie. You're so tight."

He's big. Not like fear-for-my-life kind of big, but big enough that it's uncomfortable at first. He gives me time to adjust, though, not moving again until he knows I'm ready. I wiggle a bit and then it's better and I nod, letting him know I'm alright. He settles over me, holding himself up on straightened arms, and slides forward in one quick thrust and I cry out, arching my back upward.

"Alright?" he grates, stilling, sweat beading on his forehead and chest. I nod, and he moves back to thrust again, still slowly. I can tell he isn't even all the way in yet, and I start to question if I *can* actually take it all, but with each move, he slides a little further inside, my body adjusting to him. He's moving slowly, giving me time to get used to everything, but I can tell he's dying to move, to *really* move. A couple more long, slow thrusts, and I'm dying for him to move too. I can *feel* the piercings as he slides back and forth, the ridges rubbing me inside in a way I never could have imagined. The ladder is amazing, but *dear God* the one on the end hits the perfect spot that I don't think has ever been hit before, that I wasn't even sure existed until this moment.

If he keeps this up, or, heaven help me, when he *really* starts moving, I think I might actually come this way. It's rare that I get off during sex, honestly—which is *completely* normal, by the way. Not that it hasn't felt good in the past, great even, but it doesn't typically end with me reaching the big O. That usually comes from tongues and fingers and toys. But I'm already feeling closer to an orgasm in the first few minutes with Connor than I ever have before, so that's gotta be a good sign, right? The possibility sends a rush of excitement through me, making my heart beat impossibly faster.

When he thrusts once more, he finally shoves all the way inside, our bodies as close as they can possibly get and it's pure ecstasy. He waits for a second, leaning his forehead down against mine, seeming to just need a moment to wrap his head around everything that's happening.

"Hattie," he whispers, saying my name like a prayer. He kisses me softly and I rub my hands over his back, holding him to me, trying to convey without words what this all means to me. He lets out a shuddering breath.

That anticipation blooms in my stomach again when he pulls back, staring down at me with something unreadable in his eyes. Unreadable, but undeniably sexy.

"Are you ready?"

"*Yes*," I say, but it comes out like a plea. His lips curl at the corners.

"Then, buckle up, sweetheart."

Chapter Nineteen

CONNOR

I've lost count of how many times we've fucked tonight, how many times Hattie has come, how many times I had to pinch myself to believe it was all *actually* happening.

I'd been a bit worried it would be too much for her, that I should ease into things a bit more, but she'd only ever spurred me on, *begged* for more. I'm rarely surprised in the bedroom. I can usually read people pretty well and can gauge how they might react to things. Never in a million years would have thought sweet, little Southern Belle Hattie McNamara was an insatiable, dirty-talk-loving, adventurous, sex goddess.

When I'd first slid deep inside her, I nearly came right then and there. I pride myself on lasting, but there I was, ready to lose it after one pump like I was fifteen again in the back of my dad's old truck with Kelly Johnson. I managed to hold out, running plays in my head and thinking of practice drills until I somehow got a grip on myself. Then, the weight of the moment had nearly felled me. It wasn't just the physical aspect of finally being buried so deep inside Hattie that our bodies were all but fused together. It was so much more than that. It was connection on some insane, soul-deep level that I couldn't even understand. It was the feeling of relief and contentment, of feeling for the first time that I was exactly where I was meant to be, the utter *rightness* of the situation washing over me like a soft, caressing wave.

Then I'd pulled back and the look in Hattie's eyes had brought on a carnal, primal kind of lust that I could barely comprehend. After that, it had been a whirlwind of sweat-slicked bodies and cries of pleasure; biting; scratching; kissing until my lips were sore and hers were swollen; going until we couldn't possibly go anymore.

And in between those bouts of the greatest sex of my life, I'd pull her into my chest and kiss her damp temple, gently run my fingers down her back as we caught our breath. *That* was new. I was never really big on the whole afterglow thing before. I was never an ass who just immediately got dressed and ran out the door, but I never felt the need to cuddle or nap with my previous partners. If things got especially...heated, there was always a bit of aftercare, but it wasn't like this. With Hattie, it was so completely different on so many levels.

Now, she's dozing with her head on my chest, early morning light streaming in through the bottom of the curtains, and I don't think I've ever felt such utter contentment. We didn't do much talking last night—well, not that kind anyway, though plenty was said and I'm already starting to get hard just thinking about Hattie telling me exactly what she wanted, how she wanted it, begging, *demanding*...I shake myself—so, I'm not sure what she's thinking or what last night meant to her.

What did it mean to me? I let out a long sigh. It meant fucking *everything*. But, if she doesn't want this to be more than just one great night after the Christmas Party, if she wants to just blame it on high emotions and alcohol, I'll find a way to be ok with that.

I have to be. She's too important to me for any other alternative. So, I'll grit my teeth and bare it, pretend that I'm fine never touching her again, even if I'll be dying a little inside every fucking second.

I lightly trace my fingers down her spine and she shudders, a soft moan passing her lips. She's still mostly asleep, and I know exactly how I want to wake her up. I smile at the thought, cock already jumping to attention. All I know is that it is a damn good thing stamina is very important to my job, otherwise there's no way I would have been able to keep up all night—and be ready to go again this morning after only an hour or so of rest.

I dip my fingers between us and start to slowly rub her clit. Another moan and she raises her leg, giving me better access, though she doesn't move her head from my chest. Too exhausted? I chuckle but gently start fingering her, moving nice and slow, getting so deep in her hot little pussy. Everything about her turns me on in ways I can't even wrap my head around. Her breaths start to come faster, tickling my chest, and her fingers clench where one hand rests over my stomach.

"Mmmm, Connor..." I keep pumping my fingers until she's nice and wet. She yelps in surprise when I lift her body upward in one quick movement, settling her thighs on either side of my face. Now she's far from asleep, eyes wide with interest and arousal. I grip her hips and pull her downward and then, I feast on her, nice and slow, taking my time to enjoy every lap of my tongue, every taste of her, gently licking her pussy over and over. I know she's got to be sore, so I take care to keep everything nice and soft. Her head falls back and her soft mewls drive me crazy. She's so responsive. So sensitive. So fucking sexy.

"Connor...don't stop..." she whispers, voice rough with sleep and from her screams the night before. She starts to rock her hips, grinding her pussy down on my face and I fucking love it, can't get enough. I keep things slow though, even when she's writhing with need, keeping her at the razor's edge. She whimpers when I close my lips around her clit, sucking gently while I reach up and palm her breasts. "Oh Godddd." Her hands cover mine and we move together to massage her flesh, before her hands move upward, piling her hair on top of her head.

"Connor, I'm...I'm close..."

She grinds her hips faster, desperate to come. I pinch her nipples—hard—as I move my tongue just a tiny bit faster and she screams, tunneling her fingers into my hair and holding my face to her dripping pussy. When she explodes on my tongue, my eyes slide shut in pleasure, my own hips arching upward in response. She shudders above me as I lap up every last drop, about to start right back up again, but before I even realize what she's doing, she's sliding downward. She turns her back to me and glides down on my cock without warning.

"Oh, fuck!" I grate as she starts to ride me. This view is...*Jesus fuck* it's hot. I can't decide what part of her I love most, but her ass is definitely up there. *The things I want to do with it one day*...I bite my lip and try to force the thoughts away. Watching her slide up and down, seeing my cock disappear inside her...I reach out and grab her ass, kneading and squeezing and yanking her down harder while I buck my hips upward. *So much for gentle.* But if Hattie wants hard and fast, if she wants to ride me, then who the fuck am I to argue?

"That's my fucking girl. Ride my cock, Hattie. Ride it hard." She moans loudly, and my lips curl upward. Hattie likes to be praised. And fuck do I like praising her. I swear to God last night when I called her a good girl, she came almost instantly.

"Oh God. Right there," she pants. "That feels so fucking good. I love your cock so deep inside me, Connor." I grit my teeth. Not only does Hattie Jane McNamara like being dirty talked *to*, she likes to do the talking as well—and I *love* it.

"Then fucking take it deeper, baby." I yank her down hard and thrust my hips up, and she screams out.

"GOD!" Her head falls back and I keep up the rhythm, arching upward as I pull her down, her hips twisting and rolling. She grips my legs, nails digging in and I know she's getting close. She cries out as she comes, and I can feel her contracting around my cock, tight little pulses squeezing me over and over. It's too fucking much. I dig my heels into the mattress and buck upward twice more before I join her over the edge, grunting something unintelligible even to my own ears.

I lift her off of me, and she melts into an adorable little orgasm-riddled puddle. I grab a towel from the floor and clean us both up. Once I settle back in, she maneuvers enough to rest her head on my stomach, her body sprawled boneless across the bed.

"I never woulda thought that forgetting my floss would lead to all this," she says eventually, voice rough and breathless, holding my hand when I lay it over her stomach.

I chuckle. "Is that why you were in the elevator then? I wondered for all of thirty seconds during the night."

"Hmm, thirty seconds? Was your mind otherwise occupied perhaps?" She turns her head to grin at me, her hair tickling my stomach, and then continues, "But yeah, I was going to see if the front desk had any floss when I found you."

"Well thank God for your superb dental hygiene, then."

"Hear hear!" she cheers, raising her fist in the air. I laugh and she lets out a long sigh. "I don't think I can walk. I mean literally. Every muscle in my body feels like it's made of jelly. I don't think I can move from this bed."

"Well, why on earth would you wanna do that?"

She laughs. "We can't stay here forever, Connor." She flips so she's on her stomach, gaze meeting mine. I reach out and brush her hair away from her face.

"I like when you call me that," I say softly. She smiles and pushes up to her knees, scooting up the bed so she can lean in and kiss me. I don't know if now is the right time for the big conversation or if I should let her take the lead. I don't want to push her, but I need to know what this all means.

"Hattie, last night..." She stiffens and pulls away, expression guarded. Does she not want to talk about it? Or is she worried about what I might say? I run my hand through my hair, exasperated with all the questions and the second-guessing. I think it's time to just lay it all out on the line and see what happens. "Hattie, last night was one of the best nights of my life." Her lips part and her eyes go wide. "But not just because of the mind-blowing sex. That part was fucking amazing, don't get me wrong, but..." I let out a long whooshing breath. Fuck it's been a long ass time since I've had to confess my feelings to someone. I think I'm rusty.

"I don't want it to just be last night, Hads," Her lips curl at the new nickname, "I want more with you. I want us to be...*us*. Together." Her lips curl upward and I shake my head. "I'm really bad at this, aren't I?"

She grins, those dimples making my heart clench. "I finally found something that Connor Shepherd sucks at. Other than pin ball, of course."

My mouth gapes and I narrow my eyes at her. "You fucking *cheated* and you know it!"

"I did no such thing! I tripped and stumbled into you. It's not my fault you let little ole me break your grip on the machine so you didn't beat my score." She gives me big doe eyes, feigning complete innocence.

"Rematch. Rematch right fucking now." I start to throw my legs off the bed but she grabs me, giggling, and pulls me to her for a soft kiss. When we pull apart, she runs her thumb over my bottom lip.

"Go back to the part about you wanting to be *us*. You were doing better than you think."

I chuckle a bit, but exhale roughly. I just need to know.

"What do you want, Hattie? I need to know what you're thinking, what last night meant to you."

I actually hold my fucking breath while I want for her to answer. She holds my gaze for what feels like an eternity but then she smiles, one of those smiles that could bring a grown man to his knees, and my chest twists.

"Last night meant...everything, Connor. I want *us* too." The breath I'd been holding comes out in a loud *whoosh*, making her laugh. "When I saw you with Emery last night, it felt like someone had punched me right in the stomach. I felt sick. I would have stood by and been your friend through it all if you'd wanted to be with her, but it would have killed me on the inside." It feels like my chest is going to explode. I reach out and run my fingers through her hair. It's a tangled mess and I make a mental note to get her into the shower as soon as we finish this very important conversation.

"I may have even thought about yanking her hair out," she says scrunching her nose in that adorable way she does.

I chuckle low and deep and she sighs in what I think is contentment. "Well, I'm glad you didn't resort to violence, but I would put my money on you any way. You're scrappy." I boop her nose and she pokes me in the ribs. I laugh but then sigh, growing a bit more serious. "Someone told me you left with Rizzo, and when I thought that you two were...God, I nearly lost my mind."

"Were you jealous?" she teases.

"Fucking green with it," I tell her honestly. "But it was more than that. It was like this cold, numb feeling right in the middle of my chest, like I'd lost something I'd never actually had, but I couldn't be whole without it." I shake myself. "I can't explain it right."

She leans in and kisses me again.

"I know exactly what you mean."

I cup her face, gently brushing my thumbs across her cheeks. "So...you're in?"

She places a hand over my chest, right over my thundering heart.

"I am *all* in, Connor."

Chapter Twenty

HATTIE

Hattie-1, December-0.

Well, really, in the grand scheme of things it's like Hattie-1, December-too many to count, but whatever. I have one in the win column for once and that's all that matters. Christmas is in about a week and despite a few false starts, I haven't been this happy in...well, maybe ever. Connor and I have officially started dating and we're in that disgustingly blissed-out phase where we can't keep our hands off of each other and everything is new and I can't stop smiling like a moron.

It's all happened crazy fast. I mean, I've only known him for like three months really, but I don't care. It wasn't love at first sight with Connor, but it was connection at first meeting which I think is just as monumental, maybe even more so. We had the opportunity to get to know each other, learn all the ins and outs and quirks, learn to trust each other completely without all the pressures of being a couple. Now that connection that made us friends has turned into so much more. No one has dropped the big L-bomb yet, but I've been close a few times. I don't think it would freak him out because I'm pretty positive he feels the same way, but I'm still playing that card close to the vest for now.

For the first time in recent memory, I'm actually excited for Christmas. Making cookies for Santa, reading *The Night Before Christmas*—both the original and the Cajun version that Connor had found online and thought was the greatest thing he'd ever seen—watching Ollie fight sleep on Christmas Eve to try to catch the big man coming down the chimney, seeing the wonder in her eyes when she sees everything waiting for her beneath the tree in the morning. God, I want all of it so badly, it startles me.

Ollie hadn't really thought much of the fact that I was now sleeping over more often, even when it wasn't snowing, but she seems to love the fact that I'm now "Uncle Con's girrrrlllllfriiiiee-eennnnddd" —I think partly because she just likes to say the word "girlfriend" like that, all drawn out and high pitched. I don't know if she actually even knows what it means, but she seems happy and likes having me around, so until that changes, I'm not going anywhere.

"I miss you," I say, pouting. The Vipers are in Denver and it's the first time in two weeks that Connor and I haven't been together. I mean, even before we officially started dating, we rarely went a day or so without seeing each other, but now it's different. I miss falling asleep with him and waking up with him...and I'd be lying if I said I wasn't missing him physically. That man's body is a drug and I am completely addicted, absolutely no chance of rehab in my future. I swear it's like every second that he isn't on the ice, that I'm not working, and that Ollie isn't around, we're ripping each other's clothes off. Hell, sometimes we don't even bother with that. A memory of him fucking me against the wall in my office at the arena springs to mind, making my lips curl. He'd merely unzipped and yanked my panties to the side beneath my dress. He'd covered my mouth with his big hand, silencing my screams, and don't even ask me to explain why it was so damned sexy.

Another time, I'd sucked his dick under the desk while he'd been doing a podcast interview on the computer in his home office. It had taken me a little bit to get used to his piercings when taking him with my mouth, but I couldn't deny that I loved the way they felt on my tongue now that I'd gotten it figured out. Now *that* had been a fun little game—his need to win any challenge (i.e. keeping his shit together on camera so no one was the wiser about what was happening) and his need to lose himself in the pleasure of it all warred within him, his entire body tense with it. At one point, I'd sucked him as deep as I could go and tugged gently on his balls and he'd broken into a coughing fit to hide his guttural moan.

As soon as he'd clicked off the camera, he'd leaned back in the chair so he could watch—which he loved to do—and promised payback later—which I couldn't wait for.

"Eyes on me, baby," he'd rasped, wanting me to watch him watching me. "God, you're doing so fucking good. I love your mouth on my cock, suck it deep in that hot little mouth." I'd whimpered and slipped my free hand into my panties. "*Good girl*," he whisper-moaned. He came on my tongue while I finger fucked myself and it had been just about the hottest thing ever. Until what had happened next when he yanked me up and bent me over the desk...

I shiver at the memory, goosebumps erupting over my skin. In all honesty, I probably *need* a little break from all of it, but that doesn't mean that I *want* one.

He chuckles and leans back against a brick wall.

"I like hearing you say that. Makes me feel all warm and fuzzy inside."

"Oh fuck off, Shepherd."

He looks indignant. "I was being serious! But fine, be rude." He glances around before adding quietly, "maybe I'll make you beg me to forgive you when I get home..." Another little shiver runs through me and he grins, knowing damn well *exactly* what such a simple sentence just did to me. He likes making me beg sometimes, and I can't even pretend that I don't like it just as much.

I let out a long exhale. "An-e-wayyyy," I exaggerate to change the subject. "You at the stadium?"

He does that guy head-jerk-nod-in-greeting-thing to someone walking by, another player I assume. "Yeah, I'm about to head into the locker room to get ready."

"Well, good luck. I'll be watching the game in that little black lacy number you like so much..."

He scrubs a hand across his jaw and groans. "You are a cruel woman, Hattie McNamara."

"Don't start games you can't win, Connor." I smirk as I hit the clicker to unlock my car.

"You heading home?"

"Yeah, gonna grab something to eat and then..." I trail off as I get closer to my car, reaching for the handle on the driver's side door, but something, I can't even say what, makes me freeze.

"Hattie?" he asks, brows furrowed. "What's wrong?"

"I...I don't know. Something feels wrong," I frown, dropping my hand and taking a step backwards. I glance around, but I don't see anything weird—no one lurking in the shadows, no unmarked vans parked nearby. I even bend down and check under my car, but there's nothing there. Even so, the hairs on the back of my neck stand up and my pulse races, my skin prickling uncomfortably. What the hell? Why is my body reacting so weirdly for apparently *no* reason? It's like some instincts I don't even understand are warning me about...something. But *what?* The whisper of an answer tickles against the back of my mind, but I can't quite grab onto the thought and then it's gone like smoke on the wind.

"Wrong? Like what? Are you hurt?" Connor asks, pushing off the wall and looking concerned.

"I'm not sure. It just...I don't know, something doesn't feel right." I have no idea what's wrong with me, what could possibly be making me feel so strange, but there's just something deep in my bones telling me that something is up. *Wrong, wrong, wrong,* my mind whispers, the words thudding in time with my racing heart.

"Hads, go back inside and get Rand or Larsen or one of the other security guys to walk you back out to your car and check things out, ok?"

"No, it's ok, I'm ok..."

"Hattie," he says, his tone brokering no argument. When I glance back at the screen, his eyes are burning with something cold and intense and terrifying. He looks like he wants to come through the phone and rip whatever is scaring me apart with his bare hands. "Do it."

"Ok," I whisper, whipping my head back and forth as I jog the short distance back to the doors. I'll admit I feel better once they close behind me, the lock clicking into place. No one can get in these doors without a key card. "I'm inside," I tell Connor, though he can probably tell already, but I'm nervous and on edge and just need to talk to him, even if it's stating the obvious.

"Are you alright?"

"What's wrong?" I hear someone ask in the background. *Rizzo?*

"Not sure yet. Hattie, are you ok?"

"Yeah, I'm ok. I...maybe it was nothing. I'm being stupid." Even still, I make my way back to the front of the arena where one of the guys is always at the security desk.

"No, you aren't. Your gut was trying to tell you something, your mind warning you before you could even process why. It's better to be safe than sorry. There are always a lot of break-ins and stuff around the holidays. Maybe someone was checking cars for open doors."

"Yeah, maybe..."

"What's going on, Shep?" Rizzo asks again, sounding uncharacteristically serious.

"Hattie was walking to her car in the parking garage and felt like something was wrong. I told her to go back in and get one of the security guys."

"Fuck, is she ok?" A second later, his face is in the screen next to Connor's. "Are you ok?" he asks me directly.

"Yeah, I'm ok," I say with a small smile. Rizzo had been happy, though not at all surprised, that Connor and I had gotten together. I believe his exact words were "well it's about fucking time, you idiots." I'd already been pretty good friends with Rizz, but now that I'm officially dating his best friend, we've gotten closer and he acts like I'm his sister. "It was probably just my imagination running wild. I did watch Halloween the other night, so maybe I just freaked myself out with that," I add, trying to make light, but it doesn't quite land.

I finally make it to the security desk and I feel my cheeks heat slightly when Rand smiles at me. "Hey, I'm about to talk to Rand, I'll call you back after I get to the car, ok?" I almost say *love you, bye*, but barely stop myself. Connor looks like he would rather chew crushed glass than get off the phone with me right now, but nods in acceptance, and I quickly end the call, sliding the phone into my back pocket.

"Hey, Miss Hattie," the older man says with an inclination of his head. Rand is a former Green Beret and head of security for the entire arena. He's in his late fifties, but he's in ridiculously good shape—he does triathlons for crying out loud—and you'd never guess his true age by looking at him. His hair is jet black, streaked here and there with gray, with a thick beard and mustache to match, and kind blue-gray eyes. We've become friends of a sort since I started—I usually bring him a coffee when he's on the morning shift, and he brings me a slice of pie anytime his wife makes one.

"Hey, Rand."

"What can I do for you tonight? I didn't realize you were still here."

"Yeah, I had a bunch of things to catch up. But, um...ugh, I feel so stupid asking this, but will you maybe walk me to my car? Or have one of the other guys on shift do it?" He goes instantly on alert, his eyes turning serious.

"Are you alright?"

"I'm fine, really, and it's probably nothing but," I let out a long breath, "when I was walking out to my car a minute ago, I just felt like something was up, you know? Something felt wrong. I was on the phone with Connor and he told me to come back in and get one of y'all to walk me back out and check things...I'm sorry," I finish, feeling so incredibly stupid.

"Hey, don't you be sorry. Connor was right. It's better to be safe than sorry. Let me call Luis and Lynch, hang on one second, ok?"

I nod and fiddle with the strap of my bag while he radios to the other guys. Within a few minutes, Luis and Lynch arrive, another younger guy in tow but I can't quite remember his name. He's new and I've only met him once. Something with a J maybe? Jason? Jackson?

"Justin,"—*Justin! I was close*—"you stay here at the guard desk. You two, with me."

With that, the four of us head back towards the parking garage and though I'm incredibly embarrassed and feeling like I'm making a big deal out of nothing, I have to admit that I do feel much better being escorted to my car by three huge, and, in Rand's case at least, deadly guards. I hang back with Luis while Lynch and Rand do a sweep of the area.

"I'm sorry," I tell Luis again, "but I do appreciate y'all doing this."

"Don't be sorry. This is our job and we want you to feel safe. Plus, it was getting stuffy inside anyway—the cool air feels nice." He smiles warmly at me and I grin back, nodding in thanks. Unsurprisingly, they don't find anything amiss. They even check inside my car, under the seats and in the back, before giving me the all-clear to hop in and head out. I make a mental note to bake them some cookies tomorrow.

"Thank y'all!" I call out the window as I drive off. They all wave, but Rand has that serious look on his face, and I can tell he's not going to let this drop. I have a feeling he's going to pull security footage as soon as he's able, just to check.

I still have that off feeling, but I trust the guys and know that they've checked everything. My car is safe. I'm safe. But I need Connor, so I use the hands free to call him back.

"Hads," he breathes, sounding stressed. "You ok?"

"Yeah, I'm good. Rand, Luis and Lynch all came out and checked for me. Nothing amiss but...Con, can I stay at your place tonight? I know Ollie is with the grandparents, but...I don't know, I'm just still weirded out and I don't want to go home." I love my place, but I feel safer at Connor's, even when he's not there.

His place is somewhat secluded with all his acreage on the water and surrounding forest, but it's still within a gated community, and visitors have to be on a list at the guardhouse to get inside. Plus, he also has a huge, mechanical, iron gate at the end of his driveway that can only be opened with a security code, though he rarely ever shuts it, and a fence running the perimeter of the property.

"Of course, babe. Close the gate behind you tonight too, ok?" I should have known he'd read my mind about the gate. I swear sometimes it's like we share a damn brain. Though he's trying to hide it, his voice sounds strained.

"I'm sorry I'm not there, baby." I can just imagine him running his hand through his hair in irritation and my lips curl upwards on one side.

"It's ok. Seriously, it really was nothing, I'm just weirded out. No more scary movies for me," I say lightly, trying to ease the mood a bit and make him feel better. It probably really was nothing, maybe just a local paparazzi photographer hiding in the shadows, trying to get a few pics of the Vipers' sexy goalie's new girlfriend or something stupid like that.

I hear someone calling his name in the background. "Shit, sweetheart, I gotta run, I'm sorry."

"It's fine, I promise. I'm going straight to your place now and then I'm going to do naughty things in your bed while I think about you." I grin at his low moan.

"You're the devil...but as they say: pics or it didn't happen." I can thankfully hear the smile in his voice now.

"You're such a perv."

"And you love it."

"You aren't wrong," I say honestly. "Ok, good luck, babe. Text me after."

We hang up and I head to his place. I'm on the permanent guest list these days and the gate guard smiles as he waves me through. I finally make it to his driveway and, for the first time, close the gate behind me. Once inside the house, I lock the door and set the alarm system, and send him a quick text to let him know that I'm there and all locked up tight.

I shuck my coat, boots, and socks, and crank the heat up, making myself at home and feeling better already. I rummage through the fridge and find some leftovers from last night's supper, and eat them standing at the island while I text Nat and Bobby in our group chat about this and that. Bobby is in Canada visiting his grandparents for the holidays and Nat is at some function for her dad's company, though she begs me to come up with a fake emergency to get her out of it in the next thirty minutes. She hates going to these things and her relationship with her father is...strained to say the least, but she still goes. It was actually at one of these things that she and Rizzo first hooked up, so, I guess they aren't *all* bad.

I decide to take a hot bath before the game starts, maybe send a few teasing photos to Connor, but I need a drink first. After I pour a glass of wine, I head towards the bedroom, rolling my head on my shoulders to work out the tension there. I let my mind wander back to the parking garage and the strange feeling. What had it been? I frown as I try to walk through everything: I walked towards my car but nothing looked off. The doors were closed and the windows were up, it was still parked in exactly the same (somewhat crooked) way it had been when I'd come back from a meeting earlier in the afternoon. I'd gotten closer, reaching for the door handle and...

The wine glass slips out of my hands and shatters at my feet. My vision blurs and I barely notice the stab of pain in my foot as a shard of glass slices my skin. I glance downward, but hardly even register the blood pouring over my foot, staining the wood floor. I can't breathe, can't move.

I know what had felt so wrong, what had made that unexplainable unease climb up my spine. I try to swallow past the lump in my throat, try to focus over the roaring of the blood in my ears, but I can't. I can't do any of it.

Because the reason I'd frozen by the car:

I'd smelled Josh's cologne.

Chapter Twenty-One

HATTIE

I tell myself over and over again that I must have imagined it, but I can't quite make myself believe it. I read somewhere once that the sense most closely tied to memory is smell. I *know* that smell and, given how our relationship ended and the months following, that smell was sure as shit tied to my memories and brought with it a fear so acute it was nearly paralyzing.

Normally, you could brush that off, saying that plenty of guys could wear the same cologne, but not in this case. Josh wore Tom Ford Neroli Portofino. It costs almost nine-hundred dollars a bottle and has a *very* distinctive smell. I can't even imagine the odds that someone else happened to be wearing it and also had been hanging out near my car.

I didn't tell Connor about my suspicion. I don't know why, exactly. Maybe partly because a piece of me believes that if I don't voice the thought, it can't be true. It's like when you're a kid and you think there's a monster in the closet, but you just pull the covers up over your head thinking: if they can't see me, then they can't get me, they can't be real. It's stupid, I know, but here I am. I let out a long breath as I drive towards my side of town. I'll tell Con when he gets back from the trip in a couple of hours, but for now, I need to get a few things from my house.

Just a quick trip and out, ten minutes tops. It'll be fine, I tell myself. I won't lie—I'm scared of Josh and what it might mean if he went to the trouble of tracking me down and coming here...but I am also my mother's daughter and I refuse to let him come into my town, to my *home*, and make me afraid of my own shadow. Fuck that shit. I'm going to grab my stuff—grab what I'm fairly certain will give me some pretty hard evidence to take to the cops, if he's kept up with his old habits—and then I'm going to take matters into my own hands. I will not let him win, not this time.

My phone dings and I check my message while I'm stopped at a redlight:

Connor: Just landed.

I type out a quick response before the light changes again:

Hattie: I'm grabbing some stuff from my place and then heading back to your house. See you in a bit <3

As I pull onto my street, my heart starts to beat wildly. There's no guarantee that Josh even knows where I live, and even if he does, what are the odds he's just lurking nearby, waiting for me to come home? I drive past the house the first time, making the block, and watch intently to see if anyone follows me. Nothing.

"God I really am paranoid."

This time, I pull in the driveway, idling for a few seconds while I scan the house, the yard, the street behind me in my mirrors. I don't see anything odd or out of place, so I take a few deep breaths, and jump out of the car and up the front steps. I stand just inside the foyer for a long minute, straining my ears to hear the sound of footsteps or breathing, but I don't hear anything except the low hum of the heater. I swallow past the lump in my throat and force myself to move into the living room.

My lips quirk slightly at the tiny artificial tree I'd let Ollie put up beside the fireplace, momentarily easing my panic. It's decked out in multi-colored lights, pink tinsel, glittery ornaments, and a crooked star—and I honestly love it. It's the first tree I've had in years and the day she came over and we decorated it was the day I knew that little girl had a piece of my heart that I'd never get back.

I just need to get this done, grab my stuff, and go wait for Connor to get home. He'll pull me into his arms and make me feel like everything is ok. I stand for a long minute in the middle of the living room, half expecting Josh to step out of the shadows like the boogie man or something. When he doesn't, I shake myself and grab an old baseball bat out of the hall closet and check every room in the place. Nothing. I exhale roughly and head into my bedroom, propping the bat on the edge of the footboard and pulling an old shoebox out of the shelf in the closet.

I dig around under some pictures and random jewelry and finally fish out my old cell phone. I'd kept it even after I'd blocked Josh and gotten a new number, just in case, though I haven't looked at it since I moved. I head back to the bed, plug it in, and let it charge for a few minutes. While I wait, I stuff some clothes, my laptop, phone charger, and some new lingerie that I'd bought a few days ago into a weekender bag.

The phone screen glows to life, having enough juice to at least turn on now while still plugged in. I power it up and take a deep breath before I go into my blocked messages. Then I gasp in stunned horror, one hand flying to cover my mouth. There are *hundreds* of messages. I scroll through, my stomach lurching the more I read.

-Hattie, I love you, come on. I'm sorry. I'm so sorry, you know how I get sometimes, but I need you.

-I fucking hate you! You stupid bitch, you'll never find another man as good as me!

-WHERE DID YOU GO?? FUCKING ANSWER ME BITCH!!! HOW DARE YOU FUCKING LEAVE ME. I'LL FUCKING FIND YOU, HATTIE. THERE'S NOWHERE YOU CAN HIDE.

-YOU'RE MINE. YOU'RE NOTHING WITHOUT ME.

On and on. Multiple messages almost every day. I'd been so, so wrong about everything. How could I have been so fucking wrong?? I truly thought he'd finally just move on once I was gone, that the obsessive, possessive claim he had on me would fade away if I wasn't *there* for him to focus on. If there was no outlet, I figured he'd just...stop. I'd seriously underestimated his mental state, the depth of his feelings, of this sickness in his head. He'd been hiding it all so well. Even when I saw the truth of it, I only saw the tip of the fucking iceberg.

In the last three weeks, the messages had gone from screaming obscenities and threats to calmer messages—but entirely more terrifying.

-You don't know the mistake you've made, Hattie. We belong together. I'll make you see it. I'll make you understand. Only you can quiet the loudness inside my head, baby. I'll find you and we'll fix it.

-You belong to me. No one takes what belongs to me. You thought you could run off and I'd just let you go without a fight?...but you know what? I think you want me to fight for you. This is a test. This has all been a test to prove how much I love you. I get it now, baby. I get it and I'll pass the test, I promise.

The next message confirms what I already know to be true, despite part of me trying to deny it. My mouth goes dry and my ribs feel like they're closing in against my lungs, slowly squeezing, squeezing, squeezing.

-Seattle is too cold for my beach girl...

He's here. He found me. I hadn't imagined being watched at the parade that day, hadn't imagined seeing him at the square when I was talking with Kasey. *Oh God, oh God, oh God.* That meant that he'd been here in Seattle, watching me, for *weeks*. My palms are so sweaty I almost drop the phone, but my blood turns to complete ice when I get to the most recent message, from last night. Just a single word:

-Soon.

I'm just about to call the police and bolt from the house as fast as possible when the hair on the back of my neck stands on end. Before I can even breathe, a voice drawls from the doorway.

"Merry Christmas, Hattie."

Chapter Twenty-Two

HATTIE

✳ · ·❄· ·✳· ·❄· ·✳· ·❄

The phone slips from my fingers, clattering to the floor. My entire body shoots through with tension, my fight or flight or freeze instincts deciding on the latter as my muscles lock in place. My chest rises and falls rapidly, but no air seems to be making it through. I don't know how, but I force myself to turn around.

I already know what I'm going to see, but even still, what little breath I have in my lungs goes out in a whoosh: Josh is standing in the doorway. Part of my mind is convinced I'm dreaming, that this can't possibly be real, but the other part is screaming at me to run, to fight, to do *something*. But I just stand there, frozen in terror. He's dressed in black boots, dark jeans, and a black sweater, his brown hair long and shaggy, his normally clean-shaven face covered in thick scruff. His skin looks pale, almost sallow, and there are dark circles under his eyes as if he hasn't slept in days. His brown eyes are both wild but terrifyingly focused all at once, and they're locked on me with the intensity of a snake that's preparing to strike.

He's got a small stocking from the mantle in one hand and—I suck in a ragged breath—a huge knife in the other, the kind Crocodile Dundee would carry, mocking all other knives for their puniness. *Fuck, fuck, fuck.* This isn't good. Josh is admittedly a spoiled little rich kid who grew up with nannies and butlers, but he's a spoiled little rich kid from *Texas*. He knows how to hunt and is perfectly capable of using that knife.

"Since when does Hattie McNamara decorate for Christmas?"

"Wh—" I have to swallow three times before I can finally actually speak, and even then, my voice comes out shaky and small. "What are you doing here, Josh?"

As if I hadn't spoken, he runs a thumb over the fuzzy top of the stocking.

"You hate Christmas," he says absently. Then he glances up and his gaze hardens, something dangerous flashing in his eyes. "But a few weeks with the hockey player and you're Mrs. Fucking Claus." His voice trembles with fury, quiet and intense, and my heart beats wildly in my chest, thunders in my ears. He's been watching me. Been watching *us*. A fierce protectiveness rears up at the thought of him hurting Connor or Ollie, even fucking looking at them. It helps push away the panic, anger filling the space in my chest instead.

"Why are you here?" I ask again, voice louder and hard as ice this time, surprising myself. Josh's brow wings upward. *Guess it surprised him too*. I glance surreptitiously as possible at the bat still leaning against the end of the bed. Can I grab it before he can reach me? *Fuck, probably not.*

He drops the stocking to the floor and steps into the room, his boots trampling the felt and fur. He slowly twirls the knife and I can't help but eye the bat again. He follows my gaze, lips curling upward and he gives me a chiding look, like I'm a kid who got caught trying to steal cookies. He grabs the bat and tosses it to the other end of the room and I jump at the sudden clatter as it bangs against the wall and then the floor. He takes another step forward and I step backwards, bumping into the nightstand.

"Did you like the flowers?" he asks, voice silky.

"What? What are you talking about?"

"The flowers I sent you. Your favorites, of course," he smiles at me, that same old charming smile. "Did you think I would forget something like that?"

It takes me what seems like a long time to figure out what in the hell he's talking about, but then it hits me: the lilies. They hadn't been from a client after all. Vomit rises in my throat as realization hits. Josh had been the one with the flowers in the parking garage. He'd tried to get inside. He'd...oh God, he'd talked to Connor. Josh could have attacked him, could have killed him. Even though nothing happened, I still feel lightheaded at the terrifying possibility.

"How did you know I was home? How did you get in here?" I ask, changing the subject.

Josh scoffs. "As if I didn't have cameras on the place the first night I got to town and found you. I've just been waiting for the right moment, for a time when you were here alone and your neighbors weren't snooping about. You should really invest in a security system, Hattie," he tsks, "and a better lock for your back door."

He'd been watching me all this time, could have come into my house at any time and killed me or...touched me. I barely fight back the bile that rises in my throat, but I push it away. I push away the fear and the sense of violation, and focus on the anger. I grit my teeth. *Fuck this asshole.*

"Why are you fucking here?" I snap.

His smile slips and his eyes flash dangerously. Within a breath, he's a different person. The change is utterly terrifying.

"I'm here," he sneers, "to remind you who you belong to, Hattie."

His words send an icy shiver down my spine, but I make myself move. I turn and grab the lamp, yanking the plug from the wall as I turn back towards him. He's there, right in front of me, but I don't hesitate as I swing the lamp as hard as I can at his head.

"Fuck!" He grabs the side of his face and I push past him, desperate to escape. If I can get out of this house, I can run for it. I'll run all the way to the police station if I have to. I run five fucking miles a day, I can outrun Josh, who can't stand cardio and looks right now that he's surviving on a steady diet of Jim and Jack and not much else. I can do this. I just need to get to the door.

I'm halfway through the living room, almost to the foyer, when Josh slams into me from behind, wrapping his arms around my waist like a defensive lineman. We go down hard and I scream as pain laces through my elbow and knee when I hit the hard floor. We slide a few feet and I struggle to get him off of me, but then he yanks my head back and I feel the tip of the knife at my throat and my struggling stops. I freeze, tears sliding down my cheeks.

His breath is hot and harsh at my ear and I can tell his teeth are bared when he whispers, "That wasn't very nice, baby. I think all this time up north has made you forget your manners. I'll help you remember them."

I swallow hard, feeling the edge of the knife nick my skin when my throat moves, and squeeze my eyes shut.

This is it.

This is the end.

I'm going to die.

Chapter Twenty-Three

CONNOR

Something is off. I don't know what, but there's a weird, uneasy feeling churning in my stomach. It's been there since last night when Hattie had freaked out in the parking garage. I know that it turned out to be nothing, but...I don't know. I've always been a firm believer in trusting your instincts, in our ability to innately know when something isn't right. If Hattie had such a strong reaction in that parking garage, there was a reason for it.

Which is why I can't wait to see her, wrap my arms around her and ease my mind. It was probably just a carhopper checking for unlocked doors, but I'll still feel better once I'm back with her. I'm headed back from the airport now and Hattie should be done grabbing her stuff and already back by the time I get home. God, I can't wait to see her, to kiss her, to play out in person everything we'd talked about and teased throughout the day yesterday in our texts. My lips curl upward as I imagine it, already having to shift in my seat. *The mouth on that girl,* I think with a grin. She'd seemed subdued after the game, but I assumed it was just from still feeling freaked out about her parking garage ordeal and being exhausted—we've admittedly been running each other ragged physically and staying up way too late most nights, and work has been crazy hectic for her. I decide to pamper her tonight: hot bubble bath, candles, her favorite wine, a massage—and *not* the kind with a happy ending. She deserves a night of relaxation and being treated like a queen.

My phone rings and I assume it's Hattie, but it's Rand's name flashing across my screen. He's the head of security for the Vipers and we've actually gotten pretty close over the years. I lost Hannah and he lost his son in a car accident within two weeks of each other, and we just kind of bonded over it and found solace in each other. It's an understated, quiet friendship, but an important one to both of us. We've even gone ice fishing up at his cabin in Oregon a handful of times. Maybe that's why he's calling now, to plan another trip. He's a big, burly, former special-ops guy, and was a private security guy after that for people and in places he can't even talk about, and just the sight of him is enough to immediately calm most rowdy fans in the rare instances altercations break out during games.

"Hey, Rand," I say cheerfully, answering with the hands free.

"Hey, Shep, how you doing?"

"I'm good, man, how about you?"

"I'm alright," he says, his voice sounding a big strained. Could just be the time of year. The holidays are always hard when you've lost someone.

"You planning an Oregon trip soon?" I ask, a bit of hope in my tone. I really enjoy our trips and I'd love to bend his ear about my relationship with Hattie.

"I wish that's why I was calling, but this is about something else, Shep." My chest tightens, something cold settling in my bones.

"What's going on?" I ask, my entire body tensed with alert without even really understanding why.

"It's about Hattie, about the incident last night." I tighten my grip on the steering wheel and my heart starts to beat faster. "I took a look at the security footage after Hattie left. There *had* been a man near her car before she exited the building. He didn't try to open the car, didn't put anything on it or under it, didn't even peek in the windows to see what was inside. He eventually put his hand against the driver's side door for a minute, looking...I don't know, relieved maybe? His shoulders kind of sagged. Anyway, then he just walked off. Again, not threatening exactly, and not illegal by any means, but it still just struck me as odd."

"I agree," I somehow manage to get out. My throat feels thick because I know there's more. Something that can't equal anything good. He wouldn't have called or sounded so serious if there wasn't more to this story. I try to keep my speed under control, but I'm desperate to get home, to get to Hattie. "What's going on, Rand?"

"So, I sent a still from the security footage to an old colleague of mine to see if anything popped on the guy. I just had one of those feelings." Rand's feelings were like clockwork and it would be a cold day in hell before I ever questioned them.

"And?" I ask in a low voice.

"There are several warrants out for him."

"Warrants? For what?" *Holy shit.*

"Some pretty heavy stuff. Breaking and entering, assault...attempted murder."

"Murder?!" I yell. "What the fuck?"

"I'll send you the full report, but listen, I tried to get ahold of Hattie to tell her all this and see if she knows the guy or if he's tried to contact her, but I haven't been able to get through." That cold feeling spreads out through my entire body. I try to tell myself that it's fine, she's probably not answering because she's working out or in the shower or something equally innocuous. She's fine. She has to be.

"Can you send me the picture of the guy? Maybe I've seen him hanging around at games or something."

"Of course. Sent."

I pull off on the shoulder and grab my phone. When I open the message, rage erupts in my chest.

"Mother fucker," I mutter, bringing the phone closer to my face to be sure I'm seeing what I think I am.

"Shep, you ok? Have you seen him?"

"I talked to him," I mostly whisper in disgusted astonishment. "He was trying to get inside the building a few weeks ago as a flower delivery guy. With flowers *for Hattie*. I fucking had him right there, Rand."

"Hey, there's no way you could have known."

"What's his name?" I ask, my right hand tightening into a fist so tightly my knuckles turn white beneath my tattoos.

"Josh. Josh Alcott."

The bottom drops out and I can't breathe as everything comes together in a resounding clash inside my head.

"That's...oh fuck, Rand, that's Hattie's psycho ex-boyfriend, Josh. He was stalking her before she left Texas."

"Fuck," Rand grounds out.

Then a thought hits me and my heart thunders loudly in my ears, my rage suddenly burning ice cold as fear slithers up my spine: was Hattie actually back at my place? I haven't heard from her since she told me she was running by her place, and Rand hasn't been able to get ahold of her...

"I gotta check something. I'll call you right back."

I don't wait for a response before I hang up and pull up my security system app. I pull up the feed of the driveway and garages and my entire body goes numb, that icy fear reaching outward and seeming to coat my entire body.

Hattie's car isn't there.

I peel back onto the road, tires spitting gravel and squealing as I cut across both lanes and pull a slightly illegal and definitely unsafe U-turn, and fly like a bat out of hell the other direction. I call Hattie again, holding my breath.

"Come on, Hads, pick up." I'm probably overreacting. She's probably fine. But when the phone just rings and rings and eventually goes to voicemail, a sick feeling settles in my gut, heavy and sour and poisonous. So I call again. And again. And again.

But she never answers.

Chapter Twenty-Four

HATTIE

✳ ·✳· ·✳· ·✳· ·✳· ·✳

I try yet again to free my hands from the plastic ties, but all I'm doing is slicing my wrists to pieces even more. I'd seen a Clipper video about getting out of these things, but it only worked if your hands were bound in front of you. Josh, of course, has mine zipped securely behind my back. My shoulders ache from the strain already, my muscles burning.

I'd really thought I was done for after he tackled me in the hallway, but Josh had merely yanked me up, tied my hands, and tossed me on the oversized chair by the fireplace, the one Connor had moved in here for me. My eyes water at the thought of Connor, of never seeing him again, but I try to focus on nothing but Josh and how the hell I can get out of this situation.

I have no idea what Josh plans to do with me and every time I ask, he either deflects the question or doesn't even seem to hear me. He keeps flip flopping between acting like a doting boyfriend and an angry psychopath seconds away from losing his shit, and I honestly don't understand what's happening. He's obviously drunk, but there's something else going on too, like he's fighting different voices in his head. Thankfully, at least one of those voices seems to *not* want to slice me up like a Christmas ham with his giant knife, so that's a plus, I guess. But I have the distinct feeling that one wrong move will set him off and the other voice, the one that seems to be full of bitter, scorching rage, will take charge and I won't like what happens then.

Josh stokes the wood in the fire, building up the flames so a rush of heat washes over me.

"There, is that better? I know my girl doesn't like to be cold." *Doting boyfriend voice back in charge apparently.* He smiles at me, and I can see the ghost of the handsome man beneath all of his fatigue and desperation. There's the large cut across his eyebrow from the lamp I smashed into his face, a smeared line of dried blood across his cheek. "See, baby? I can take care of you. I know I didn't do it right before, but I can fix it now. I'm passing your test."

I want to scream at him that me moving across the country without a word or leaving a trace of where I'd gone wasn't a fucking *test*, it was a desperate attempt to escape him, but instead I just say, "Josh, you need to untie me." I try for a calm, placating tone, but I don't know how well I'm managing it. "Let's just talk—"

"Talk?!" he roars, springing up from the fireplace and whirling on me, eyes wild with rage. *Doting boyfriend gone.* "I tried to talk to you for months and you refused. *Months*, Hattie. You left me and thought you could just disappear and that I would just *let* that happen?" He leans in close, making me shrink back into the chair, desperate to get away from him. He reeks of stale tequila and cigarettes and I don't think that he's showered in days. "And then when I finally track you down, I find you here, *fucking some God damn hockey player?!*"

"I wasn't—" But I don't finish my sentence. Josh backhands me hard enough to send my entire body tumbling into the side of the chair. My ears ring and I see stars for a second, my cheek burning like it's on fire. Tears immediately spring to my eyes and I taste blood where I bit my tongue. I gasp as he yanks me back upright, gripping my face hard, fingers digging into my cheek and probably leaving bruises.

"Don't. Lie. To. Me," he whispers in an icy voice. He points an accusatory finger at the lingerie strewn across the floor where he'd dumped my bag. I could tell him that I wasn't actually fucking Connor when he first got here to stalk me some more, but there's no point. "You think I haven't seen you with him? You think I don't know why you're packing lingerie to take back to his place, you little slut?!"

I swallow hard as he pulls the knife back out of the holster at his belt, wondering if this is the time he loses it completely. I squeeze my eyes shut and try to pull away as he runs the flat edge lightly down my face, but he's still gripping my face and I can't move. I force myself to open my eyes again and he finally releases my face. I work my jaw and wince at the pain.

"Tell me I was better, Hattie," he says in a deadly cold whisper, twirling the tip of the knife on the pad of his thumb. "Tell me you didn't like fucking that asshole." I don't say anything, but flinch backwards when he screams, "TELL ME!" He's getting close to the edge, I know it. Is playing along the right call? It's really my only choice. My mouth feels like sandpaper so I have to swallow several times before I can get the words out.

"You were better, Josh. Of course you were. I didn't like fucking him. I—I thought about you the whole time. I was just trying to make you jealous so that you'd come for me." I want to vomit. I feel disgusting playing into his sick little fantasy, but if it keeps my heart beating and my blood flowing, I'll do it.

His face shifts, the rage and tension melting off, and his lips curl into a slow smile. "I knew it," he whispers. "You can never love anyone like you love me, baby."

"No one," I agree.

Before I can even brace myself, his lips are hard on mine. I scream against him, but the sound is muffled against his mouth. I jerk my head away and he steps back, smiling.

"Oh, Hattie. The things I have planned for you..." He leers at me, eyes roving over my body in a way that makes terror fist my heart. *Oh God, he's going to...he plans to...*I choke back a sob and bile burns my throat. I have got to get out of here, have got to figure something out.

My phone starts buzzing yet again and Josh sighs, pulling it out of his pocket. His face twists in rage as he looks at the screen.

"Connor. *Again.* If I didn't know any better, I'd think he was obsessed with you, Hattie Jane." He smiles widely, like it's a funny private joke, like we're sharing a laugh about it with him using his pet name for me. "I met him, you know. Talked to him." I already know this, but hearing him say it still makes me jolt. "I was trying to get inside to deliver your flowers. I knew you weren't there, of course, but I wanted to see where you worked, see how hectic your office is," he grins at me, like we're sharing a funny joke about my work habits, "to prove to you that there's *nowhere* you can go that I can't follow, Hattie."

I take a deep, shaky breath at the idea of Josh finding his way into my office, touching my things, being there without my knowledge. It's such a violating feeling, it makes my skin crawl and my pulse race.

"I'm sure one of those other hockey imbeciles would have let me in eventually, but *he* came along, and I couldn't pass up the opportunity to talk to him, to see how he reacted to someone mentioning your name." Josh's eyes darken, looking cold and terrifying. "He was *so* helpful, agreeing to take the flowers to you for me. He had no idea who he was talking to, the fucking idiot." He tilts his head slightly as he studies me. "I should have killed him right there," he says as if it was an afterthought, a missed opportunity. My chest constricts painfully and I can't seem to see for a second.

Before I can say anything to that, my phone buzzes again, a text this time. His face settles into a mask of rage mixed with deranged glee as he reads the message.

"Your new little boy toy is on his way here right now." My stomach flips. Would Josh really try to hurt Connor? To...*kill* him? In a fair fight, I would bet a million dollars on Connor taking Josh out easy, but if Josh blind sides him with a knife that might as well be a small sword? *No, no, no.*

"Josh, please don't do anything stupid. I'll go with you, I'll do whatever you want, ok? Just don't hurt anyone else. Look, right now, you haven't done anything wrong." The words taste like ash on my tongue, but I force them out. I need him to think I'm on his side. He narrows his eyes at me, but there's a hint of interest there. I press my luck. "You came to get me, just like I wanted you to. I needed to see how much you loved me, remember? It was a test. If you cared enough to find me, then it would prove that we were meant to be together. And you *did*. You found me. We can leave and be together again." I see the hope light in his eyes, just a flicker, but it's enough. "*But*," I continue, "if you hurt anyone else, then they'll try to keep us apart again."

We both tense when we hear a car turn into the driveway, tires screeching. My mouth goes dry and my heart feels like it's going to beat right out of my chest, but I try to sound calm.

"Josh, you have to let me get rid of him. I'll tell him to go away and then I'll leave with you, alright? We can just go, I swear."

He looks like he's fighting some kind of inner argument, literally shaking his head like a dog trying to get rid of fleas. Is he honestly hearing voices in there telling him different things? Hell, maybe he is. I hear Connor's door slam shut and panic rises in my chest.

"Josh. Look at me. Cut the ties and let me get rid of him, ok? Please, baby. Let me get rid of him and then we can be together." My voice shakes and my bottom lip trembles, but I take a deep breath, trying to keep my shit together.

He stares at me for a heartbeat that feels like an eternity but finally nods. He rushes forward and yanks me up, turning me so he can slice through plastic ties. A painful rush of relief sears through my shoulders and I roll them trying to ease the ache. I glance down and barely stifle a gasp—my wrists are cut and bleeding, and pain flares, but I push it away. I don't have time to worry about my stupid wrists right now.

Josh throws an oversized hoodie at me from the back of the couch and I tug it on, pulling the sleeves down to hide my wrists just as the first pounding sounds at the door. Oh the irony that this is one of Connor's old hoodies, but Josh doesn't seem to be paying much attention to it other than to confirm that my injured wrists are hidden. I start for the door, but Josh grabs my arm—*hard*. I gasp as he tugs me towards him, leaning in so his face is inches from mine as he pulls my hair down to cover my cheek.

"If you try anything, Hattie, I'll gut your boyfriend like a trout while I make you watch. You don't want to know what will happen to you afterwards." His voice is calm and frighteningly cold, and I don't doubt him for a second. *Doting boyfriend has left the building, maybe permanently by the look in his eyes.* I nod just as Connor pounds on the door again, this time even more urgently.

"Hattie?! Hattie open up!"

Josh stows the knife in a sheath on his belt and reaches back behind him. My eyes widen and I instinctually shrink away when he pulls out a gun. A small pistol, maybe a .22. I had no idea he had it and things just got way, way more real. I don't know why, exactly. A knife is plenty scary and extremely capable of causing life-ending level damage, but a gun? I think I might be going into shock or something. I can barely breathe, but I will myself to remain in control for just a little bit longer.

"Nothing stupid," he whispers and walks with me to the door. He crouches down behind it and shoves the muzzle into my side. I don't know what the fuck to do, but things just turned way more serious. I take a heartbeat to come up with a plan, and can only pray to God that it's the right one. I take a deep breath to try to settle myself. It doesn't work for shit, but I open the door anyway, keeping half my body hidden behind it.

"Hattie," Connor breathes, relief clear on his face and making my chest clench. "Jesus." He runs a hand roughly through his hair. "Are you alright? I've been calling and texting!"

I try to sound and act normal so that Josh doesn't think I'm trying anything, but I need to somehow tip Connor off. I give him a small smile and lean my head against the door frame.

"Sorry, I fell asleep on the couch. I was wiped out."

Connor lets out a long exhale and glances around, eyes scanning the streets and looking like he's on high alert. "I was worried. Look, Rand called me and—"

I cut him off quickly. Between Rand's superior skills and connections and Connor's freaking out, I can do the math: they know about Josh.

"Oh, yeah, he called me earlier too. I think he found my purse at the arena, I left it last night." Connor's gaze narrows and I try desperately to have one of our weird, intuitive, silent conversations. *Please understand. Please, please, please.* I continue, "I'm sorry I worried you, but there was no reason to be. I'm fine. Just really sleepy." He studies me in that way of his, where his entire body seems to shift and get hyper focused on one particular thing. He moves forward but I give him a tight smile, not moving to let him inside like I normally would. Hell, I normally would have thrown my arms around him as soon as I opened the door, so he probably already knows something's up, but I just pray he doesn't make it obvious.

"So, can I come in, or...?"

"Um, you know what, I'm not really feeling all that great actually—I think that may be why I'm so tired—and I don't want to get you sick." He tilts his head and arches a brow in question, and I can tell it's clicking. His body tenses and my heart thuds in my chest. I shake my head imperceptibly, telling him he can't react, and I just hope he understands. Josh presses the gun further into my side, the threat clear: *get rid of him. NOW.*

"Aw, I'm sorry baby," Connor says, eyeing me critically.

Josh's hand is shaking with what I can only assume is rage, and I get the feeling that whatever thread of self-control he's hanging onto is about to snap at hearing another man call me *baby*. And if it snaps, I'm done for, and maybe Connor too. I can't let that happen.

"What's wrong?'"

I clear my throat, half to hide my terror, half to help my lie.

I make my voice light and flirty, "Now, I know that you're gonna say you can kiss it better, but you better just keep your butt right there on my porch, Connor Shepherd. I mean it, not one toe forward, mister." I hold his gaze, trying desperately to communicate and he's definitely on high alert now. He nods once, letting me know he understands what I'm saying: *stay there no matter what.*

"Yes ma'am," he says with a laugh that sounds shockingly carefree and real. Looking at him though, I can see the strain this is causing him. His every muscle is tensed and bulging, his hands balled into white-knuckled fists at his sides, the tattoos across his knuckles standing out starkly. "What's wrong?" he asks again.

I take a deep breath. *Here goes nothing. If it doesn't work, I'm just dead. No big deal.*

"My throat's just a little sore." I reach up with my left hand and run my fingers along my neck, leaving a small smear of blood from my wrist. I'd managed to get some on my finger tips without Josh noticing. At least, I hope he didn't notice...but since he hasn't shot me or stabbed me, I think the odds are in my favor that he didn't.

Connor's eyes fly wide and his nostrils flare, his jaw muscle standing out as he clenches his teeth so hard I wonder if he's going to crack his teeth.

He mouths "inside?"

I give a tiny nod of my head and cut my eyes to the right, right to where Josh is squatting just behind the door, practically vibrating with rage. I move the hand that spread the blood on my neck, momentarily using my thumb and forefinger to make the shape of a gun, like you do when you're a little kid running around the backyard playing Hatfields and McCoys. Connor swallows hard but nods in understanding.

"Ok babe, well why don't you get some sleep and I'll bring you some soup later on tonight?" He does a good job of keeping his tone even and I know that Josh won't be able to detect the anything off.

"That sounds perfect."

"Maybe around seven?" He puts an extra emphasis on the word "seven," and I *think* he's saying that he's going to give me seven seconds to get out of the way once the door closes.

"That sounds perfect," I say, trying to tell him that I understand. He nods and holds my gaze and I can tell that he's trying desperately to assure me that everything is going to be ok. I try desperately to believe him. His body has shifted from terror and strain to the game-time version of himself now: laser-focused; intense; scary.

"I'll talk to you later." I nod and close the door, hoping to God that he has a plan.

As soon as the door closes, I step back hastily and Josh straightens.

One.

He turns to stare at me, and the possessiveness and fury is so startling that my breath catches.

Two.

Hearing me with Connor pushed him over the edge. I hold my hands up in supplication as he stares.

Three.

"Josh," I whisper. "He's gone. Everything's ok."

Four.

He tilts his head, looking at me like he doesn't even really see me.

Five.

"If I can't have you, no one can," Josh says quietly.

Six.

His words send a cold sliver of fear down my spine. Just as he raises the gun, the door bursts open, knocking into Josh's back. I don't even have time to breathe out a sigh of relief that Connor was a second early. Josh stumbles and I scream, jumping back as Connor flies at Josh, quicker than I would have thought possible. He tackles him to the floor and I scramble out of the way. Connor is bigger and obviously knows how to handle himself, but Josh is fighting like a man with nothing left to lose—and he still has the gun. I don't know what to do. Would trying to help just make it worse?

They're rolling around, throwing punches and kicking out at each other, and it's all happening almost too fast to really track, but also somehow feels like it's in slow motion. Josh lands a punch across Connor's jaw, but he barely seems to feel it. Connor grabs Josh's wrist, trying desperately to keep him from pointing the gun. With his other hand, he punches Josh in the ribs in rapid succession, then lands one right across Josh's face, so hard that I think I can hear the bone crack. Josh grunts in pain, but doesn't let go of the gun. I don't know how, but he keeps fighting like a cornered animal: desperate and vicious.

"She's mine!" Josh roars before head-butting Connor in the nose. Connor rears back and loses his grip on Josh's wrists just enough that Josh can yank it free, pointing the gun. I watch in stupefied horror, with part of me not really believing any of this is real. The gun goes off with a deafening blow and Connor jerks back with a yell, his body tumbling backwards and landing with a thud on the wooden floor. My world goes black for a minute and everything sounds like I'm underwater, a dull ringing in my ears. Then a scream pierces the air, pierces the strange bubble I'm in. An agonized, desperate scream unlike anything I've ever heard in my life.

It takes me a minute to realize the scream is coming from me.

I scramble to Connor on my hands and knees, slipping once on the wood floors. Connor is on his back, blood soaking his chest and shoulder and the floor around him already. I can't tell where the wound actually is, the blood is too thick.

"Connor!" I shriek, my hands fluttering over him, not even really knowing what I'm trying to do. "Connor, stay with me! Oh God. Con—"

I scream in pain as Josh yanks my head back savagely by my hair. I reach back reflexively, gripping his wrist, desperate to stop the pain as he pulls me to my feet and back against his chest. My fingers, wet with Connor's blood, slip on his skin.

"You. Are. Mine," he growls at my ear. Sweat and blood from his face sticks to my own and I try to cringe away. *I want to be with Connor, I need to get to him!*

Instincts flare and my fight finally kicks in. I draw in all of my fear and anger, and with a cry of fury, I reach back and rake my nails across Josh's cheek at the same time I kick out against his ankle. He cries out, probably more from surprise than pain, I think, and loosens his grip enough that I can spin away from him. Without thinking, I reach down and grab the hilt of the knife, somehow still in the sheath at his hip after the tussle with Connor. I jerk it free and brandish it.

He grins, blood staining his teeth.

"You wouldn't da—"

I slash out at him, not giving myself time to really think about what I'm doing. His eyes go wide as I feel it tear through fabric and skin and Josh yells out—*definitely* in pain this time. There is absolute fury in his eyes as he stares at me, his hand flying to his side as he staggers backwards a step—right into Connor's chest. My mouth hangs open in shock. How had he gotten up after that?

Connor wraps his arms around Josh's neck, and for a minute, I'm terrified he's going to snap it, but he merely squeezes. He keeps squeezing, despite Josh's desperate clawing at his forearm, and eventually Josh's eyes slide closed and his body falls limp. Connor releases him and Josh's body falls to the floor with a thud, blood pouring from the wound in his side. I must have cut deeper than I thought, but my mind can't really even spare a second to focus on that.

"Connor!" I gasp, running towards him just as he goes down to one knee. His entire right side is soaked with blood, his shirt stained black. "Oh God, Connor!"

Someone else bursts into the house, but I can't tear my eyes off of Connor to see who it is or make myself even care.

"I'm...alright..."

But even as the lie leaves his lips, he collapses at my feet.

Chapter Twenty-Five

CONNOR

I blink my eyes open slowly, not really sure where I am or why. I feel pain, my body riddled with it, but I'm not sure of the reason, exactly...

"We've gotta stop meeting like this," a voice says from beside me, a bit hoarse and breaking at the end.

I turn my head, blinking hard a few times to finally focus my vision and see Hattie in the chair beside my bed. *Talk about déjà vu.* Her eyes immediately fill with tears and she throws herself at me. I grunt in pain, but squeeze her tight to my chest as everything comes flooding back: Hattie's blood; the fight; the gun.

I've never been anywhere close to as afraid as I was when I realized that the fucker was in her house. I squeeze my eyes closed as rage boils up inside me like an animal, some clawed thing ravaging my chest with venomous claws. I pull back and cradle her face.

"Are you ok?" I search her eyes and down her body, checking for injuries. There's a small bruise on her cheek and I swear to God I'll hunt that fucker down and finish the job if he hit her. "Hattie, tell me," I demand, my voice coming out harder than I mean it to.

"I'm alright," she breathes, leaning in to kiss me softly. "I'm ok, Con."

I let out a long, shaky breath, the relief flooding my chest almost painful.

"What the hell happened?"

"Josh found me," she says quietly. "Which I guess you already knew, but yeah, last night when I freaked out in the parking garage? I smelled his cologne by my car. I knew he was here, in Seattle."

"And you went to your place *alone* after that?" I ask, somewhere between incredulous and pissed the hell off.

"I wanted to check my old phone, to see if he'd left me any messages, so I had real proof to take to the police."

"And?" I grit out.

"He had. *Lots* of them. I'd just figured out that things were way worse than I imagined when he walked in behind me. Apparently, he'd been watching my place for weeks, watching *me*," she corrects with a shudder, swallowing hard. She goes quiet for a minute and I rub my hands over her arms, needing to touch her. Then I remember with a nauseating clarity, and my entire body tenses.

"The blood. The blood on your neck."

Reluctantly, she raises her hands and pulls her sleeves back. Bandages circle her wrists, but she quickly unwraps one, biting her lip and eyeing me warily. When the white cloth falls away, I suck in a harsh breath. A ring of angry red circles her wrist, deep cuts and slashes like...*Fuck*. Like she'd been tied up and she'd fought like hell to get out. *That motherfucker!* Fury courses through me in a way I've never felt before, like a river of fire raging through my veins. I reach out a run a finger gently over her cheek.

"And this?"

She looks away before whispering, "He slapped me."

I inhale sharply but try to force the rage away. I lean in and kiss her softly on the spot just over the bruise before I pull her wrist towards my lips and gently press a soft kiss to the damaged skin. I want to kill him for this, wish I fucking had when I'd had the chance. I want to tear him apart with my bare hands, limb from fucking limb. I've never been a particularly violent person, at least not off the ice, but if given the chance again, I would gladly murder Josh with a song in my fucking heart. I'm not positive what that says about me and quite frankly I don't give a shit.

Josh had bellowed that Hattie was his, that she belonged to him. But she's *mine*. Not in the same fucked-up, possessive way that he meant it, but in the way that she's a piece of me, a piece that every ounce of my being cries out for. She's mine just like I'm hers, and I fucking protect what's mine.

Except, I almost hadn't. I'd almost been too fucking late.

"Baby," I breathe, my voice choked and wavering, my eyes glassy and my throat thick with emotion. I think about what could have happened. She could have been taken from me today—forever. I barely keep the tears back, and her own eyes water as she looks at me. She reaches out to lay a hand on my cheek.

"I'm alright, Con. I promise. Thanks to you."

I meet her eyes and can't stop myself from leaning in to kiss her again, running my fingers along her cheeks and down her neck. We both exhale shaky breaths and eventually, I reluctantly pull away, resting my forehead against hers for a long moment.

"Tell me what happened...after."

"Rand got there just as you passed out and he secured Josh—none too gently, which I'm going to bake him some chocolate chip banana bread for, by the way—until the cops got there. Josh was arrested—"

"So the fucker is still alive then," I grumble.

"He is," she sighs, "I cut him up pretty good though. He's here under 24-hour guard and I heard a nurse saying that he had to have surgery. I don't know how I feel about what I did or the fact that I would have been happy if he died on that table." She takes a deep breath before continuing, "But, anyway, he's been charged with a whole host of things: breaking and entering, unlawful imprisonment, stalking, assault, attempted murder, a bunch more that I can't remember. And apparently he has warrants out for him back in Texas too—Rand said he already told you some of this. I guess Josh attacked someone at the post office and forced them to tell him what my forwarding address was—that's how he found me. It's a miracle the guy didn't die—Josh, uh, tried *very* hard not to leave any witnesses behind," she hedges.

Jesus. The guy really had gone off the deep end. I mean, she'd told me that he was getting there before she moved, but it hadn't seemed this serious. I guess once she was really gone he just...broke. He sure as fuck seemed completely broken and deranged when I'd been fighting him.

She clears her throat before continuing. "You lost a lot of blood and they had to do a transfusion during surgery, but the bullet thankfully didn't hit anything vital and they were able to remove it completely. You'll be totally fine. Full recovery and able to play again after some rehab."

And then she completely breaks apart. I blink in surprise, but hold her while she cries into my neck, letting her know without words that I'm here, that I'll never be anywhere else.

"I'm so sorry, Connor. God, you almost died because of me."

"Shhhh, none of that, Hattie. Look at me." She doesn't, so I push her back and force her chin up gently with the tip of a finger. "Eyes on me, baby." I curl my lips and that gets a choked half-sob, half-laugh out of her. I brush the hair from her temple, and cup her face, brushing my thumb across her cheekbone. Now I notice that there are smaller, round bruises too that look like they were made by...finger tips? *That fucker had gripped her face so hard he left bruises.* I bite back the rage that tries to claw free again, somehow keeping it caged.

"Hattie, none of this was your fault, do you understand me? *None* of it. The only person to blame here is Josh. He is the only one who can take responsibility for this. No one else, alright?"

She finally nods and her shoulders slump. "I just...I was so scared, Connor."

"I know," I say, pulling her against me again, ignoring the scream of pain from my shoulder. She rests her head on my chest and I rub the back of her head, smoothing her hair over and over. "I was too. You were so fucking smart and brave, do you know that? Tipping me off like that without letting him know. I wouldn't have had the balls to try that." She laughs shakily against my chest. "I mean it. I probably would have pissed my pants."

"Shut up," she says, but I can hear the smile in her voice. Small, but there, and I'll take it.

"We're alright, Hattie. We're both ok." She lets out a long, shuddering breath, as if she's finally letting go of all of the worry that's been trapped inside her since this all started. We stay like that for a while, just being together and letting each of us come to terms with what happened on our own. I'm not sure how much time passes, but eventually, she sits up, wiping her eyes and giving me a half smile.

"Well, you should be home before Christmas at least." I groan and she looks alarmed. "What? What's wrong?"

"I'm pretty sure that your psycho ex breaking in and trying to kidnap and possibly murder you and shooting me in the process probably squashes all my hard work of trying to make you love Christmas."

She laughs. Lightly at first, but then it builds and builds, and soon we're both in a fit, nearly unable to breathe, sides aching, tears flowing. I think it's a bit hysterical honestly, like all of the stress and fear from what happened is just coming out now in this insane laughter. We finally subside and she leans in to kiss me hard.

"The fact that you're still alive trumps everything else, baby." She kisses me again and pulls back, smirking. "Plus, you've still got three more days to *really* impress me."

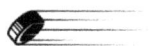

I get released, try to avoid the media frenzy—a professional athlete in the area getting shot in a home invasion and attempted kidnapping definitely makes the headlines—and do my best to just enjoy the next few days.

Hattie is staying with us, half because her house is still an actual fucking crime scene, and half because I honestly can't stand the thought of her being out of my sight right now. Rand was able to find out that Josh was moved from the hospital and is indeed in jail, locked up tight. The best news was that his rich father actually flipped the script: instead of bailing him out like he's done all his life, the bastard cut Josh off completely. No money, no fancy attorneys, nothing. He even froze all of Josh's accounts since they were all mostly under daddy's name anyway. Josh will waste away in jail until his trial and then most likely get the book thrown at him. I'm sure he'll try to use an insanity defense, but even still, he'll be locked away somewhere for a very, very long time. My heart absolutely *bleeds* for the fucker.

My shoulder is still pretty sore, but it honestly isn't the worst pain I've ever been in, so I can deal with it. I have to start physical therapy after Christmas and will be out of commission for games for a while, which I hate, but all things considered, I'm thankful. Beyond thankful. I can't even actually express how lucky and grateful and blessed I am.

Pretty much everyone in the entire organization ends up at my place at some point or another over the next few days. Rizzo hardly leaves, in fact, and I overhear him and Nat talking quietly at one point when they both think I'm asleep and Hattie's in the shower.

"It makes you think about how quickly things can change, doesn't it?" Nat whispers.

"It does," Rizz agrees, his voice tight. I crack my eyes just enough that I can see them at the kitchen table from the couch. Nat reaches over and places a hand on Rizz's forearm.

"Rizz, I...I mean, we..."

"Not right now, Nat. Please," Rizz adds quietly, pulling his arm away and running a hand through his hair. "I don't want a pity fuck and I don't want you making a decision based on this insane situation that's got everyone all keyed up."

Nat blinks several times in surprise or confusion or both, but then she looks at Rizz and it's like she's really seeing him, maybe for the first time. He looks up and holds her gaze for a long moment and whatever she sees there makes her nod. She doesn't look offended or upset that he rebuffed her, but instead with respect and...interest.

"Alright," she says, nodding.

Hattie comes back from the shower then, hair wrapped up in a towel and dressed in one of my old jerseys and leggings. The jersey is damn near a dress on her, but she looks adorable. And sexy. And beautiful. How does she manage to pull off all three at once? My lips curl upward and I almost forget I'm supposed to be asleep.

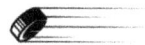

Christmas Eve finally arrives, and after leaving cookies, milk, and potato chips for Santa (Hattie questioned whether Santa would need something salty to go with all his sweets, barely keeping her face straight), watching *Elf,* and reading *The Night Before Christmas*, Ollie finally falls asleep.

"And now the little elves come out to play?" Hattie asks with a grin. We get everything set out and happily munch on Santa's goodies while we work. Well, Hattie honestly does most of the work, insisting that I take it easy and not move my arm too much. I usually hate being taken care of, but I'll admit, it's kind of nice watching Hattie fret over me so much. Plus, she'd gotten this ridiculous sexy nurse's outfit from the costume shop...

After that, Hattie and I stay up, sipping whiskey on the couch. The only light in the room glows from the fireplace and the tree, and it's just about the most perfect night I've ever had. Hattie's hair is pulled half up in a messy bun, the rest falling in soft curls, her sweater slouching off of one shoulder. I reach over and run my fingers lightly over her bare skin and she shivers. I grin, leaning in and planting a soft kiss there and she moans lightly.

A little breathless, she asks, "So, I'm not clear on all of the Christmas rules exactly, but are we allowed to exchange gifts tonight?"

I pull back, surprised by the question. She turns to face me, brow arched in question. I scrub my jaw and pretend to think it over. "Wellll, I *guess* I could allow that, since it's your first real Christmas and all." She swats my thigh and bounds to the tree, pulling out a medium-sized package wrapped in deep green and gold paper. "Grab the red one over on the other side," I tell her, nodding towards the side of the tree facing the windows. She smiles, bringing both packages over to the couch. Hattie had already given our little group a gift: custom made t-shirts with "Proud Member of the Vipers' Sin Bin" across the front. They'd gone over like gangbusters and Jules even vowed to wear his beneath his jersey to every game for the rest of the season.

So, I'm insanely curious as to what else she has up her sleeve in the gift-giving department.

"You go first," she says, handing me my gift. It's a big rectangle, obviously a box, and I shake it experimentally. One solid thump.

"Hmmm, not Legos then." She laughs and motions for me to go on. I take the bow off first and stick it on my shirt, and then tear into the package like a rabid squirrel, tossing bits of paper and ribbon all over the place. Hattie giggles.

"You are an overgrown child, you do know that right?"

"Of course. It's one of my best qualities, honestly."

Inside the wrapping is a plain white box and when I open it and part the tissue paper, my brows draw down in confusion. It's an old photograph in a beautiful mahogany frame. I study it for a moment, trying to figure out what it is and why Hattie would give it to me. There's a frozen pond, thick trees and mountains in the distance covered in white. A man and little boy stand on the ice, a little girl in the man's arms...

Then it hits me harder than that last dogpile in the goal, and my throat feels very, very thick. I run one finger gently over the glass.

"This was the Christmas I got my first pair of blades This is...this is my dad teaching me to skate for the first time. That's Hannah in his arms."

I look up from the picture and stare at Hattie, in awe and confusion. She bites her lip, looking nervous.

"How...?" I whisper.

It's all I can manage. Memories flood back in a rush and on their heels, that heavy feeling of grief that makes it hard to breathe. *God, I miss them. Dad, mom, Hannah—they're all gone now. I'm the only one left.*

"Sara found an old box of Chris's things—or what they *thought* were his things. Turns out, some of Hannah's stuff was in there too at the bottom, including some old family pictures. She told me about it when we went for drinks one night and I got the idea and asked her to keep it a secret." She stares at me as she fiddles with the package in her lap. "It was a smaller print and a bit faded, but I found a place that restores photos and had it printed bigger for you and...Do you like it?"

My nose burns and my eyes water as I stare at the photo. I've never even seen it before. Mom was always snapping pictures—

we found boxes and boxes full in the attic after she passed—so I guess it isn't surprising that I haven't seen this one, but it's like stepping back in time. I can remember the day so vividly: opening the box and being speechless; dad helping me lace up my skates for the first time; him helping me onto the ice and me being terrified and elated at the same time; me busting my ass repeatedly and mom fretting on the side while dad reassured her that I was fine. *He's gonna be a star, Vivi, just you wait and see*, he'd told her, smiling and winking and...and...*fuck I can't breathe*. I rub the heel of my hand in the center of my chest, trying to ease the beautiful ache there. A tear slips free and I quickly wipe it away with my good shoulder.

"Hattie, I..." I clear my throat. "God, this is amazing. You have no idea..." I close my eyes and shake my head. "You've given me something so incredibly special and irreplaceable and I can never ever thank you enough for it."

She smiles, her own eyes looking glassy.

"I made the frame myself you know," she says after a minute.

"What??" My eyebrows shoot upward. "You did?"

"Of course not, you idiot," she says giving me an *I can't believe you fell for that* look.

We both laugh, and I pull her towards me for a kiss that I hope somehow conveys everything I need to say to her, but don't quite have the words to vocalize it at the moment.

"Your turn," I whisper, kissing her once more before pulling away.

Chapter Twenty-Six

HATTIE

Seeing Connor's reaction to my gift is enough to make me love Christmas and forgive all of December's past indiscretions against me. I was honestly a bit nervous to give it to him, wondering if he would think it was stupid or be upset that I trespassed into his past like that, but I should have known better.

Now he smiles softly, waiting for me to open my gift, and though he seems relaxed I think he's the tiniest bit nervous too. I arch a brow at him, but he rolls his eyes and tells me to hurry up. I shrug and start unwrapping my gift. I add my bow to Connor's shirt beside his own, and pull the paper off—in a far more civilized manner than he did, I'd like to add. When I open it, I stare.

"It isn't..." I whisper.

"It is. Took me forever to track a decent one down."

I gingerly take out the old book and run my fingers along the worn cover. I open the front and my suspicions are confirmed: It's a first printing of Charlotte's Web—my favorite book when I was a kid. I'd told him about it after he helped me get the chair into my living room, when he'd noticed my built-ins full of books. And he *remembered*. He remembered how much I loved it, how I'd gotten lost in my memories and in all the feels of my mom reading it to me almost every single night before bed. Just a handful of pages a night, of course, but as soon as we'd finish, we'd start back over again. It was the first book I ever read on my own once I learned how—though to be fair, I think it was like ten percent *actual* reading, and ninety percent reciting it from memory.

He'd not only remembered, but he'd been thoughtful enough to find a way for it to become a gift. A treasured gift. One of the best I've ever been given.

And he said it took him forever to track it down, meaning he's been working on this since the day I told him, back when we were merely friends. He's...God, Connor Shepherd might just be the best man I've ever known. I mean, I was already fairly certain of that fact, but this just cements it. My eyes water—apparently it's the night for tears, but for once, they're happy ones in December.

"Do you like it?"

"Connor, I can't believe you did this for me."

He hikes his left shoulder, still having a hard time moving his right one easily. "It's nothing."

"It's *not* nothing. Con, this is—"

"I love you," he blurts, and then winces. I blink. Once. Twice. Did I hear that right? "Wow, that was...smooth." He laughs a little nervously. "But, there it is. I know it's fast and it's ok if you don't feel the same yet—or ever—but after everything that happened, I just...I was tired of not saying it, of having to fight to keep the words inside every time I saw you. I love everything about you, Hattie Jane McNamara. Even the things that drive me crazy, I love," he says with a grin, and my lips twitch. "I love that you have thirty-four different coffee mugs and add to that collection nearly every time we go anywhere, but you drink out of the same *Fox and the Hound* one every single day. I love that you are always thinking about other people, constantly doing little things that may not seem like much but mean the world. I love that you can cuss like a sailor and drink half the team under the table. I love how much you love Ollie," he whispers. "I love how strong and brave and determined and sexy you are. I love...I love *you*, Hattie. So fucking much."

I swallow hard and take a few deep breaths. The crackling of the fire sounds so very loud in the silence now.

"Hattie?" he asks, sounding worried that I haven't responded. I stare at him, gripping mamaw's diamond around my throat.

"You're like *The Order of the Phoenix*," I tell him. His brows draw down in utter confusion.

"Uhh...what?"

"*Harry Potter and the Order of the Phoenix* was the first book I remember staying up all night to read. I couldn't put it down, and after I finished, I thought 'wow, that was a good book.' I was drawn to it from the beginning, but it was just another book that I enjoyed, you know? But the more I thought about it, the more I couldn't *stop* thinking about it. It was constantly floating around in the back of my mind, even without me really realizing it. Then I went back and read it again. And again. And again. Each time, I would pick up on details I hadn't noticed before, appreciating the story for entirely new reasons, seeing it in new lights and finding new ways to connect to it. And then suddenly, it was my favorite book and I couldn't believe I thought it was *just* a good book at the beginning."

I meet his eyes, the firelight reflecting in the green and making them seem to glow from within.

"From the minute I met you, I couldn't get you out of my head. You were always there, always in the background, even before we became friends. Then we started hanging out and I knew you

were going to be a good friend, that we had a great connection—
and you were. You were an amazing friend, one of the best ones
I've ever had, but the more I got to know you, the more I'd find
all these new little details and facets of you, find new ways that
we connect, sometimes on levels I can't even really understand.
Half the time, it's like you can read my mind. And soon enough,
you went from one of my best friends to so, so much more."

He lets out a long, shuddering breath.

"So, what my weird book metaphor is trying to say," I murmur
as I place my beloved gift on the coffee table, placing his beside
it, and moving to straddle his lap and wrap my arms around his
neck, "is that I love you, Connor. A whole fucking lot."

He chuckles, low and deep as his lips crash to mine, his left
hand cupping my cheek before sliding to my nape. His right hand
settles on my hip, fingers clenching tightly. I know it still hurts
him to move his right arm much, but apparently the pain is far
from his mind at the moment since slides his hand up under my
sweater with no hesitation. I shiver at the touch, his rough palms
scorching my skin in the best possible way. He pushes the fabric
up and I pull back so that I can tug it over my head and quietly
scold him not to use his dang arm. He mutters a quiet *yes ma'am*,
but my bra quickly follows, being tossed somewhere across the
room. He groans, completely ignoring my chiding about his arm,
and palms my breasts as I kiss him again, unbuttoning his flannel
and sliding it gently off of his shoulders, careful of his bandage.

The kiss is deep, but languid, like we're both savoring this moment. I run my hands over his warm skin, over all of his tattoos,
all of the scars and marks that I've come to know like the back of
my hand. I grind my hips slowly over his lap as he leans forward
and kisses my throat, and soon we're both desperate for more,

though we keep things slow and steady. Things are always combustible between us, but this is a different kind of burn, slow and deep, but with enough heat to lay waste to everything in its path.

He lifts me up and maneuvers me out of my leggings and panties with an efficiency that I'll have to give him shit about later, and I undo his belt and pull his cock free. He hisses in a breath, but then his lips are on my breast, licking and twirling and sucking and I'm pressing up on my knees to position him beneath me. I'm already wet, already needing him so badly I can barely stand it. I slide downward in one long, slow glide, and we both moan at the feeling. His cock is so thick, filling me up so tightly it's the most amazing pressure. His piercings hit spots that I can't even understand, wasn't even sure existed honestly, and this angle is like heaven.

I pull back as I start to move, up and down in a tortuously slow rhythm that's agony and ecstasy all at once. His right hand rests on my hip, helping to glide me on top of him, and the other cups my face, forcing me to hold his gaze.

"Eyes on me, baby," he says quietly, but this time, it's different. It's not the sexy command by my sinfully sensual boyfriend that sends shivers down my spine. No, this time, it's something more. It's a plea. A promise. A connection that I can't explain.

So, I keep my eyes on him as I continue to slowly ride him. No dirty talk or games this time, just Connor and me and the feel of the two of us together in a way neither of us has ever felt before, will never feel again with anyone else if I have it my way.

"I love you," I whisper, my eyes still locked with his.

"God," he whispers, eyes sliding closed as if in pain for a moment. "Say it again."

"I love you, Connor."

His eyes snap back open and they're blazing with lust and love and I nearly whimper.

"I love you, Hattie. I fucking love you so much." He reaches down between us and slowly rubs my clit while I glide up and down, riding his cock long and hard. What could be minutes or hours later, I'm honestly not sure, he cuts off my scream with a kiss when I tip over the edge. He follows, moaning against my lips, and I collapse against his chest, tucking my face in the crook of his neck, still slowly rocking my hips as the little aftershocks of my orgasm shiver through me. He runs his fingers down my spine as we both find our breath again, and I don't think I've ever been so content in all my life.

We disentangle ourselves and clean up, and once we're dressed again, he lies down on the couch, pulling me down on top of him despite my half-hearted objections about his injury. He raises one of my wrists to his lips, gently kissing my still-healing cuts, something that he does at least once a day. I don't know if it's more for me or for him, but every time he does it, it makes me fall a little bit more in love with him.

I rest my head on his chest as he pets my hair and my lids grow heavy. I stare at the tree, the lights making the glittery ornaments sparkle like diamonds; at the stockings all hanging along the mantle—at the one Ollie had made for me with puff paint; at the snow gently falling outside the windows in the background.

"Merry Christmas, Hattie," Connor whispers.

"Merry Christmas, Connor."

I fall asleep with a smile on my lips, excited for what tomorrow holds, for what the rest of forever holds.

So, maybe Christmas isn't so bad after all.

Southernisms Glossary

Created by Hattie McNamara at the request of the
ridiculous (but loveable) members of the
Vipers' Sin Bin.

- ❖ Y'all – a group of people
- ❖ Bless your heart – could be meant as a sweet endearment ("aw, bless your heart for bringing me that tea") or as a way to show sympathy ("Oh bless his heart, his daddy just passed"), but more often than not, it's a nice way of saying you're an idiot.
- ❖ If the creek don't rise – saying I'll be there or a certain thing will happen as long as circumstances beyond our control don't stop it; if you wanna get *real* southern, go with "Good Lord willin' and the creek don't rise."
- ❖ Cattywampus – something is crooked or out-of-whack
- ❖ Gimme some sugar – give me a kiss
- ❖ Yes sir/Yes ma'am; No sir/No ma'am – an absolute must. It doesn't mean the person speaking thinks you're old. It's a respect thing.
- ❖ It'll all come out in the wash – don't worry, everything will work out; a southerner's version of *Hakuna Matata*
- ❖ Bein' ugly – behaving badly or not minding your manners; being rude or catty
- ❖ That dog won't hunt – that idea or plan isn't going to work
- ❖ Highfalutin' – someone who's trying to act fancy or better than others, when they really aren't

- ❖ Too big for your britches – you got a big head/are full of yourself
- ❖ Slicker than pig snot on a radiator – a person who is sneaky, conniving, or knows how to get away with things. Don't trust anyone who is slicker than pig snot on a radiator!
- ❖ Cold as a witch's titty – really cold (which, in the South, is anything below 70 degrees)
- ❖ Sweatin' like a hooker in church – you're sweating A LOT
- ❖ How's your moma an' 'em? – a greeting
- ❖ Rode hard and put up wet – you look like hell
- ❖ Over cookin' my grits – something is getting on your nerves or trying your patience
- ❖ Nervous as a cat in a room fulla rockers – you're nervous
- ❖ Full as a tick – you ate too much
- ❖ Fixin' to – you're getting ready to do something
- ❖ Let me let you go – a nice way of ending a conversation
- ❖ Cute as a bug's ear – adorable
- ❖ Hush your mouth – be quiet
- ❖ I tell you what – an exclamation or used for emphasis. Don't expect anything to come next.
- ❖ Well butter my backside and call me a biscuit – shows surprise

Hockey Slang for Dummies*

Rizzo added the "dummies" part. ignore him.

- Apple – an assist
- Barn – rink in an arena
- Barnburner – a high-scoring game
- Beauty – a good guy; funny; good personality; gets along well with everyone
- Beaver Tap – when a player taps his stick on the ice to signal to the player who has the puck
- Biscuit – puck
- Bucket – a helmet
- Celly – celebration
- Chicklets – teeth; might just see them flying across the ice during a fight
- Chirp – trash talking
- Deke – a quick move to get around another player where you psych them out and use misdirection; think of it like a juke in football
- Dirty – actually a good thing: it means an awesome deke (can also say "filthy" here)
- Duster – someone who doesn't get a lot of playing time; they collect dust on the bench
- Face Wash – shoving your glove into another player's face
- Five-Hole – between the goalie's legs
- Gino – a goal scored

- Gongshow – a really rowdy game; lots of fights and sometimes also lots of goals
- Hat Trick – scoring three goals in a game
- Hoser – loser; Anthony Rizzo* (*note added by Shep*)
  - Haha good try, fucker. More like Connor Shepherd** (*note added by Rizzo*)
    - Both of you stop messing up the list! It means loser. The end.*** (*note added by Mac. I apologize for these guys...*)
- Light the Lamp – triggering the red light behind the goal to go off by scoring
- Lip Lettuce – a mustache
- Office – the area directly behind the net
- Pigeon – unskilled player; usually used as a good-natured insult
- Pillows – goalie's pads
- Puck Bunny – usually refers to good-looking girls who try to score with players; also the thing Rizzo likes to put his dick in* (*note added by Mac*)
  - .....Fair** (*note added by Rizzo*)
- Stripes – the referee
- Sin Bin – penalty box
- Snow Shower – intentionally spraying ice shavings in the goalie's face; usually done when you're pissed off they made save
- Tarps off – shirts off
- Turtle – when a player ducks down and covers up to avoid a fight
- Yard Sale – when you get hit so hard your equipment flies off and scatters across the ice

ACKNOWLEDGMENTS:

- To husband for always snoring beside me while I write. Kidding...sort of. Thank you for always supporting me. I love you and I like you.
- To my family and friends: thank you for always supporting this strange little hobby.
- To my awesome PA, Laura, who rocks my socks on a daily basis and helps keep me (relatively) sane.
- To my fantastic ARC team for always being up for reading and reviewing my nonsense, especially when I can't seem to pick a lane with respect to genres...
- To Lexie, Kayleigh, and Kala (ha) for always hyping me up, for always supporting me, for helping me make decisions because I am incapable of making them myself, and for the endless hilarious Book Babes chats. I love y'all so hard.
- To Google, for teaching me ALL about, uh...*piercings...*
- To the NSA agent monitoring my Google searches – I swear it was for book research purposes!

More books by K.D. Miller:
(ALL available on Amazon and included for FREE with Kindle Unlimited subscriptions!)

New Adult Sci-Fi:
Titan Rising

Titan Unleashed

Titan Reckoning

New Adult Fantasy:
Evansfire

Adult Paranormal Romance:
Dark Burning (Veracity of the Gods, Book 1)

Sweet Tempest (Veracity of the Gods, Book 2)

Red

Adult Contemporary Romance:
Carpe F*cking Diem

www.kdmillerbooks.com